BRIDE OF A HU$TLA 3

Destiny

Lock Down Publications & Ca$h
Presents
Bride of a Hustla 3
A Novel by *Destiny Skai*

Destiny

Lock Down Publications
P.O. Box 870494
Mesquite, Tx 75187

Visit our website at **www.lockdownpublications.com**

Cover design and layout by: Dynasty's Cover Me
Book interior design by: Shawn Walker
Edited by: Lauren Burton

Stay Connected with Us!

Text **LOCKDOWN** to 22828 to stay up-to-date with new releases, sneak peaks, contests and more…
Or CLICK HERE to sign up.
Thank you.

Like our pages on Facebook:

Lock Down Publications: Facebook

Ca$h Presents: Facebook

Follow us on Instagram:
Ca$h Presents: Instagram
Lock Down Publications: Instagram

Email Us**: We want to hear from you!**

Submission Guideline.

Submit the first three chapters of your completed manuscript to ldpsubmissions@gmail.com, subject line: Your book's title. The manuscript must be in a .doc file and sent as an attachment. Document should be in Times New Roman, double spaced and in size 12 font. Also, provide your synopsis and full contact information. If sending multiple submissions, they must each be in a separate email.

Have a story but no way to send it electronically? You can still submit to LDP/Ca$h Presents. Send in the first three chapters, written or typed, of your completed manuscript to:

LDP: Submissions Dept
Po Box 870494
Mesquite, Tx 75187

DO NOT send original manuscript. Must be a duplicate.

Provide your synopsis and a cover letter containing your full contact information.

Thanks for considering LDP and Ca$h Presents.

DEDICATION

In loving memory of Bernice "Quick" Jefferson. You were a true fan of my Bride of Hustla series and movie. R.I.P Beautiful. I will never forget you ~Destiny

Destiny

Preface

Down at the station, Sasha was placed in the holding cell with another female. She was rocking designer gear, so she figured maybe she was in for fraud and not prostitution, or maybe she just took a drug charge for her boyfriend.

She walked over to the phone mounted to the wall and frowned before picking up the receiver.

"That phone don't work. You gotta use the other one."

"Oh, thanks." She went to the other phone and picked it up. The smell coming from the mouthpiece was like ass and sweat. "Ew!" She scrunched up her face, rubbed the receiver against her pants leg, and called Blue. The first time she dialed his number, he didn't pick up, so she called back.

"Hello?" he answered with a little hesitation in his voice.

"Bae, come get me."

He recognized her voice immediately. "Where you at? And whose phone you calling me from?"

"I'm calling from the free phone at the jail."

"What?" he shouted.

"I'm in the Broward County Jail."

"For what?" He was lost because he left her in the hotel room on the beach.

"Fighting Carmen."

"How the fuck did you end up in Broward?"

"I went to her house and we fought."

"What the fuck you went to her house for? I left you in Miami, and that's where you s'posed to be."

Sasha was not in the mood for the lecture or 21 questions. "Blue," she shouted. "Can you please just post my bail and pick me up? We can fuss about this later."

"I'm coming, damn!" He didn't wait for a response. He simply bammed it on her ass.

In her mind she already knew it was about to be a very long and noisy night. He was gon' preach to her and say how wrong she was for going there in the first place. Sitting down on the cold, steel bench, she leaned up against the wall and pulled her knees to her chest in order to rest her head.

As soon as she closed her eyes, she was being interrupted.

"Excuse me."

When she looked up, it was the girl sitting on the opposite side of the cell. "What?"

"I don't mean to get all in your business, but –"

Sasha cut her off quick. "Well, don't."

"All I was gon' ask you was," she paused and smirked, "if that was Darian on the phone."

Sasha heard his name and looked up. Now she had her attention, and she needed to know how she knew her man. Clearly she knew him because she addressed him by his government name. "Yes, it was. And who are you?"

The chick smiled. "I'm not important, so don't worry about me. I just want to give you a warning."

"About?"

"You having energy when he pick you up, 'cause he gon' whoop yo' ass when you get home." She smiled and pointed in her direction. "You Sasha, right?"

"You asking a lot of questions for someone that don't know me." Sasha sat up in her seat just in case she needed to beat this bitch ass.

"I know your man, though, and that's all that matters."

"And how the fuck do you know him?"

"I used to be in your shoes, once upon a time, and he has a very bad temper. When he was that mad with me, he would come home and fight me all the time."

"Well, guess what? You and me are not one and the same, and he has never put his hands on me."

"Well, tonight is your lucky night, 'cause he gon' beat that ass, whether you believe me or not."

"Bitch, please. You got me fucked up 'cause he ain't gon' do shit to me."

She ignored the fact Sasha had just called her out her name. "I would've been his babymama, but he beat me so bad I lost the baby. And you know he never apologized for taking my child's life."

Sasha tried ignoring her, but she wouldn't shut up to save her life. The only thing she could do was hope and pray Blue had posted her bail already.

A few hours later, the door buzzed and in walked a female officer. "Banks, let's go. You just made bail."

"Damn, he got you out quick. Good luck, girl, and remember what I said."

Sasha ignored the irrelevant comments and kept it moving.

"Tell our man Red said he can come through tonight and punish this pussy again when he drop you off."

Sasha stopped in her tracks and gave her a homicidal stare. That was the bitch Blue cheated with.

Red smiled and blew her a kiss.

Destiny

Chapter 1

Quamae was relieved as he cruised through traffic easily. He was finally free from the deceitful grips of Gigi. She played him good, but he played her better. Laughing out loud, he was amused at what he had done.

***

12 Hours Earlier

Quamae and Chauncey had just executed Dirty, but he had one more body to drop. However, he had to keep his hands clean with this one. It was one thing to kill a drug dealer or murderer. No one would care. To kill a mother? The press would eat that shit up and raise money to catch the killer. For this special murder, it was going to take precision.

After driving home, he came up with the perfect plan to get rid of his little problem. He walked into his bedroom and closed the door behind him. Once he pulled Dirty's phone from his pocket, he scrolled through his call log until he found Blue's number. Quamae shot him a text message.

Dirty: Slide thru tomorrow and grab the bitch while he gon'
Blue: Ima have them boys in place so don't fuck this up
Dirty: I got this
Blue: U better

The following morning Quamae made sure he was nowhere near his house and in a place where he would have a solid alibi. That place happened to be on his favorite couch with his therapist. Sitting with her guaranteed him an airtight alibi.

Once they had her in their possession, it would only be a matter of time before they called about the ransom money. As soon as that call came through and he denied their request, he already knew they would kill her just to hurt him. But little did they know they had just been set up.

Blue was a street nigga, so Quamae wasn't worried about him

snitching. Niggas like that would rather die before being known as a snitch, snake, or rat. In other words, his secret was safe with Blue.

***

Present

Quamae hit the corner heading up the street to his house, and it was swarming with police. That could only mean one thing: they were aware of the kidnapping. The closest he could get was two houses down, and he was bumper-to-bumper with an unmarked car. Taking quick steps, he approached the house in a matter of seconds and was intercepted by a detective.

"This is a crime scene, sir. You can't come up here."

"This is my house, and I need to get in there and check on my fiancée."

"Your fiancée?" he repeated as if he wasn't hearing him correctly.

"That's what I said." Quamae brushed past him and jogged up the driveway, where he was stopped by another detective.

"Are you the homeowner, Quamae Banks?"

"Yes, I am. Now, what's going on?"

"I'm Detective Miller, and we are responding to a call from your neighbor witnessing a kidnapping." He glanced back at the house. "Who lives here with you?"

"My fiancée and her kids."

"They're not your kids?" his eyebrows rose in utter shock.

"No."

"Okay, and where are you just coming from?" He pulled out a notepad to take a few notes.

"My therapist."

Detective Miller looked up and focused on Quamae's eyes. "Exactly what are you seeing a therapist for?"

"I don't think that's any of your business." He rubbed his chin hair. "I do believe there is something called doctor-patient confidentiality."

"I understand your frustration, sir, but we're just trying to figure out what happened here."

Quamae cut him off. "Well, I don't see how my business has anything to do with what happened here."

"In most cases like this the spouse is always the prime suspect until they are cleared. As long as your alibi checks out, you're good to go."

"I know it will."

"All I need is the name and address of your therapist."

Quamae reached into his back pocket for his wallet to look for the business card. When he pulled it out, he handed it to the detective. "Her name is Christine Lowry."

Detective Miller glanced at the card and placed it in his shirt pocket. "Can you think of anyone that would want to harm her? Any known enemies?"

"Not that I know of."

"Mr. Banks, let me ask you a question. Are you involved in any drugs or illegal activities?"

Quamae smirked. "Let me guess, it's my nice home in a nice neighborhood, car, clothes, and jewelry that made you assume I sell drugs, huh?"

Detective Miller's face began to flush. "No, that's not what I'm implying. We have to check all possibilities."

"Detective Miller, let me ask you a question. How much do you make a year?"

That question was a slap in the face because, unlike Quamae, Detective Miller lived in a mediocre neighborhood in a two-bedroom apartment, and he drove a Dodge Charger. The 40K he made wasn't nearly enough to live so lavish.

Quamae saw that was a difficult question for him to answer, so he continued. "Okay, I see that's a tough question for you, so don't worry about it. I know you make a measly 35K, no more than 40K, and you are about to be very upset to learn I make that in a week. Sometimes less time than that."

Detective Miller was new to the team, and he was still wet

around the ears. Quamae was able to detect that about him. Using his right hand, he adjusted his collar, then wiped the sweat that leaked from the pores of his flushed skin. "That will be all for now. If you have any questions or hear anything, just give me a call." He handed Quamae his card and left the driveway.

Once Quamae was able to get inside the house, he saw a woman standing by the twins. She greeted him immediately.

"Hello, I'm Miss Jenkins with CPS."

"CPS?" he questioned.

"Child Protective Services."

"Oh, okay. And what do you need help with?"

"Since the kids were in here alone, I was called in. My job is to ensure the safety of the kids."

"They're safe. Now what?"

"I can leave them here with you."

Quamae scratched his head. "Nah, they can't stay here."

The case worker cut her eyes. "Why not?"

"'Cause those are not my kids."

"Don't they live here?" she questioned.

"They did, but those are not my kids," he repeated.

Ms. Jenkins challenged him. "Oh, really? You sure about that?"

"Yes, I am. Do you need to see the proof?"

"Yes. I would definitely need to see that."

"Hold on one second."

Quamae walked away and headed to the bedroom to retrieve the results to the paternity test. He stood in front of the mirror and took a deep breath. Pulling the drawer open, he removed the results and clutched them in his hands tightly before going back downstairs. The caseworker was waiting patiently for his return. He handed the papers to her and watched her facial expression as her eyes roamed from side to side.

Miss Jenkins finally looked up. "Okay, Mr. Banks, this is all the confirmation I need. Does she have any family members that would take them into their home?"

"She has a mother, and I can give you her number."

"Yes, that would be good." She scratched her head. "I'm curious to know why they can't stay if you are with their mother."

Quamae was becoming agitated by the worker and her questions. "If you must know, we are not together anymore. She was moving out today."

"You don't seem too concerned about her safe return."

"I don't believe she was kidnapped. Gianni has mental issues, so she probably staged her kidnapping to keep me from leaving her."

She nodded her head. "Because you found out the kids were not yours."

"Correct."

"I'm ready for that number now."

Quamae stepped away and made his way back to the nursery while she made the call. Grabbing Gigi's suitcase, he removed the twins' clothing from the dressers and tossed them inside. He made sure to send diapers, wipes, and formula as well. There was no need to keep any of that shit because her mother was definitely gon' need it.

After pausing for a brief second, he looked around the room and noticed she had none of her things packed up for her big move. "This ho must've thought I was gon' change my mind." He laughed wickedly. "Ho, you had a nigga like me fucked up."

Minutes later he was placing their belongings at the front door when Freeman walked in. He stood close to Quamae and whispered in his ear, "You gon' have to find you a new house since the department can't stay away from this address." He laughed.

"Fuck you laughing at?" Quamae didn't see the humor in what he said.

"The fact this house always comes across my radio." Freeman looked around to make sure no one could hear him. "On a serious note, sell this house and get out of dodge. This kidnapping has your name all over it."

Quamae stepped closer to his worker. "I don't pay you to think about my actions. I pay you to keep my face clean, and it's your job to make sure there's no evidence. Now, unless you ready to disappear, I advise you to go and do your fuckin' job."

Freeman took heed of what his boss said and walked away in silence.

***

Sasha was fuming as she stood at the counter, waiting on them to give her back her keys. All she could think of was how true the accusations about Blue were. As long as she'd been with him, he had never physically abused her.

The deputy handed her the keys and she stormed outside. Jogging down the long flight of stairs, Sasha couldn't wait to give him a piece of her mind. It was bad enough he cheated with the bitch, but she had the nerve to brag about the fact they were still fucking.

Once she hit the sidewalk, she recognized his truck parked in the front. From the looks of things he was talking on his phone. Sasha walked up to him and snatched the phone from his hand and pressed end.

"What the fuck you did that for?"

"You still fucking Red?"

Blue shook his head. "Man, look, I'm not about to keep going down that same road with you. I told you what happened between us, and you steady asking the same fuckin' question." He snatched his phone back. "Don't try to switch this shit up on me because you got locked up. You can't beat me getting mad."

"Well, I am." She pointed at the jail. "Do you know that ho's in there? I was in the holding cell with her and she gave me an earful about yo' ass."

"And you listened to that ho?" Blue smirked and shook his head. "You just as silly as that broad."

"I don't find shit funny."

"I do."

"You lied to me," she screamed. Blue reached for her, but she pulled away. "Don't touch me! You just like him."

18

"Calm yo' ass down and get in the fuckin' truck. You causing a scene. You trying to get a nigga locked up or some shit?"

Sasha did as she was told and got into the passenger seat. As soon as Blue closed his door, he looked at her with a cold stare and raised his hand to her, causing her to flinch. "What the fuck you jumping for? I'm not about to hit you."

"That's not what Red said."

"And again, you listening to that ho? For real?"

"She said you used to come home and beat her ass, and you made her lose a baby." Sasha had tears in her eyes. "Then she said you can come punish her pussy again tonight after you drop me off at home."

Blue wanted to slap her silly for being so gullible and listening to the lies of a bitch that wanted the dick. "Let's get one thing straight: I have not been to that girl's house since that night. Me and her never lived together, she was never pregnant, and I never put my hands on her."

Sasha didn't reply. She just sat there and cried.

"Why are you crying? I'm telling you she lying, and yo' ass believe her?" He paused. "Damn, you'll take the word of a bitch I used to fuck over me, huh?" Blue started the truck and pulled out of the parking lot. "I see you don't know me at all after all this time." He glanced over at her. "And don't ever compare me to that nigga again. We ain't shit alike."

Sasha opened the glove box and pulled out a napkin so she could wipe her face. Deep down inside she wanted to believe him, but her trust issues from her marriage were ruining it. She knew it was unhealthy to bring her issues to another relationship and it was unfair to Blue as well. Although he received head from Red, she respected the fact he came home and told her about it when he could've lied about it.

Sasha took a deep breath before she responded. "I'm sorry I didn't believe you, but you have to understand where I'm coming from. You cheated with her recently, then I run into her and she tells me all this bullshit."

"That's what she wants to do, ruin what we have because I

told her coming to her house was a mistake. A bitch will tell you anything to cause problems. If you leave me right now, she accomplished what she set out to do." Blue stopped at a red light, then looked over at his lady before grabbing her hand. "Listen to me. I know I fucked up, but I can't take it back. All I can do is make sure that never happens again. I promise you I haven't touched that girl, and I put that on my old girl. Do you believe me?"

Sasha nodded her head.

"Don't respond like that. I want you to mean it. I'll do anything to make sure I never see that pain in your eyes again. I love you, and another bitch can't take your place."

"I love you, too, and I don't want you to hurt me again."

"You gotta trust me."

The light changed and Blue focused on the road ahead. His thoughts went to Red, and he couldn't wait to pay that ho a visit. She was really trying to sabotage his relationship, and he wasn't having that. Nobody was going to take her away from him, not even her punk-ass, soon-to-be-ex-husband. The way Quamae was moving, Blue was ready to make Sasha a widow instead. All he kept thinking about was how the nigga was able to outsmart him and have his boys kill his bitch to keep his hands clean. The damage was already done, but he wanted to know what the motive behind the killing was. That answer would probably never surface. He also couldn't help but wonder why he killed Dirty. Blue was certain he found out about the plot.

Sasha interrupted Blue's thoughts. "I need to get my car from Carmen's house."

Blue nodded his head. "When we get there, get in the car and pull off. I'm not on that part-two shit to a girl fight."

"If that ho come outside, we fighting again."

"For what? You already went to jail, and she didn't get the dick. I handled it already."

"Yeah, but I need her to know I don't play about my man."

Blue finally saw the humor in it and laughed. "Man, you crazy. Just let that shit go."

"It's the principle. She already know how I get down."

Her feistiness was amusing. "Bae, you gotta chill out. You can't be going to jail and shit unless you trying to find you an ol' lady in there. And if that's the case, you can find one out here so we can have a threesome."

Sasha cut her eyes. "I am not sharing you with nobody. I can't watch you fuck another bitch in my face. That would be a fight if you got into it too much."

"Damn, that's fucked up. You just ruined my dream."

Minutes later they were pulling up to Carmen's place. Sasha grabbed her keys and exited the truck. As soon as she opened her car door and sat down, her ex-best friend walked outside.

"Sasha, wait. Can we talk for a minute? Please?"

Sasha looked up and became angry all over again. "Ho, you want these hands again?" She jumped out of the car and ran toward the door, but was snatched up in the air by Blue.

"Man, what did I just tell yo' ass? Get in the car and let's go. I'm not playing with you." Blue pushed her into the car and closed the door. "Pull off, now," he shouted, "and I'm not playing with you."

Sasha put the key in the ignition and started the car. Before she pulled off, she mugged Carmen hard.

***

A few days later Blue sat back in Sasha's car in the parking lot of King of Diamonds. It was dark and the club had just closed. The back of the club didn't have too many lights, so he was able to sit with no detection. The car was foggy from the weed smoke, and he was a little buzzed from the Remy he consumed. A female silhouette could be seen gliding through the darkness, catching his attention. He recognized her right away. Blue was parked directly next to her, so he waited until she put her bags in the backseat before he slid out of the driver's seat with his cellphone in his hand. Just as she was about to close the door, he grabbed it and snatched it open, causing her to scream.

"Shut the fuck up," he spoke through gritted teeth. "Why the fuck you told my lady that bullshit?"

"Fuck you and that bitch. You think you about to live happily ever after with that ho?" Red spat angrily.

Blue placed his hand over her mouth and squeezed. "Watch yo' muthafuckin' mouth before I break yo' jaw and have you eating from a straw."

Tears were building up in her eyes. "Blue, stop," she mumbled.

"Answer my fuckin' question." She mumbled once again, but he couldn't understand her, so he let her mouth go. "Speak."

Tears streamed down her cheeks as she watched the man she once loved treat her like shit. "She needs to know who she's dealing with, so I told her what you did to me."

"And did you tell her why?"

"No."

"So, when were you pregnant? 'Cause you already know I strapped up with you every time."

"Okay, I lied about the baby, but you still beat my ass."

"I had a good reason to."

"Because I flattened your tires and hit you for talking to another bitch?" she confessed.

"We wasn't in a relationship, so you didn't have a right to get mad. I met her in the same place I met you, a fuckin' strip club."

"That was foul, and you know it."

"Fuck all that." He looked into her eyes so she would know he meant business. "I don't give a fuck where you see the mother of my child at, don't say shit to her to make her think we still fuckin'. I'm telling you right now that I will fuck yo' world up about that one."

Red was shocked. "Baby mama?"

"That's what I said."

"So, you had a baby with her?"

"You can't hear?"

"Damn, that's fucked up," she cried.

"Listen, you heard what I said. I don't wanna come back here, 'cause if I do, it won't be good for you." Blue walked away and got back into the car without a second look at Red.

Destiny

Chapter 2

"You what?" NJ had to make sure he heard her correctly.

"I'm pregnant," she repeated.

"How you know?"

"I took a test."

"Nah, that can't be right."

That was not the reaction she was looking for. "What do you mean by that? NJ, we don't always use condoms, and you know it."

"I'm not ready to be nobody daddy."

Jazz folded her arms across her chest. "Well, you should've thought about that before you ran up in me raw."

"You gotta get an abortion, man. Find out how much it is and I'll pay for it."

"Are you serious right now?" she cried. "I'm good enough to fuck, but not carry your child?"

"We're not ready for no baby, and you know this."

Jazz lay back down on the bed and buried her head in a pillow. She couldn't believe NJ wanted her to have an abortion. Deep down she thought he would be happy about the surprise, or at least be more supportive about the situation. She at least thought the baby would bring them back together, but NJ showed her just how wrong she was. Now she didn't know what to do because she wanted to keep the baby. The thought of telling his parents came to mind, but she was unsure about their reaction. True enough, she was cool with his dad, but this pregnancy could change everything altogether.

"Bruh, stop all that crying, 'cause I don't wanna hear that shit. I'm not changing my mind." He was standing firmly on his decision. All he could think of was how a baby could ruin his life. Having a baby by Jazz meant he would be tied to her forever, and he wasn't trying to think that far into the future. The only thing on his mind was making it to live another 24. The way Lauderdale was set up, he could be here today and gon' tomorrow. A nigga will bust another's head if he thought he was getting stupid cash.

"You can't take care of yourself, so how you expect to take care of a baby?" He was harsh with his words, trying to make a point and hoping to change her mind in the process. "All that shit gonna fall on me, and I'm trying to get myself together right now. All that baby gon' do is hinder me from what I'm trying to do."

Jazz finally lifted her head, exposing her red, puffy eyes. "You are being selfish right now, and that's not fair. You act like I can't get a job when I turn sixteen."

NJ shook his head, then laughed. "Do you hear how stupid you sound right now? You would rather work than go to school? That's exactly why you getting an abortion, dummy."

"You can't make me have one," she screamed.

"You can either have the abortion or you can get the fuck out and raise it on your own."

"Wow, NJ, you would really do that to me?"

"You sound like you trying to trap me or some shit. I'm telling you I'm not ready, and you steady pushing me to change my mind."

Jazz heard enough of his disrespectful mouth, so she got up and got dressed. There was no way she could sit there and endure the pain he was subjecting her to. He acted as if she planned to get pregnant or made the baby on her own. After gathering her things, she opened the bedroom door without another word. There was no point in arguing with him because he made it very clear he wasn't interested in being a father. As she walked through the living room, she could hear footsteps behind her. She placed her hand on the doorknob and paused, awaiting an apology from him.

After standing there for a few seconds, NJ finally said something. "Are you leaving, or what? Or you just gon' stand there?"

Jazz turned to face him. "I hate you, and I wish I never met you." She opened the door and slammed it behind her.

NJ walked back into his room and lay down as if nothing happened. After a while he decided to call his mom.

"Hello?" Sasha picked up.

"How you doing?" he asked.

"I'm good, and yourself?"

"I'm good," he lied. The news he just received from Jazz had him feeling some type of way, but he wasn't about to say anything about it just yet. Hopefully she would come to her senses and get rid of the baby.

"That's good. So, what's going on?" She was skeptical about the call because they hadn't spoken since the dinner. Nonetheless, she was happy he called.

"I was thinking we should hang out this weekend. I think that would help us build a bond."

Sasha was happy to hear he wanted to spend time with her. "Of course we can do that. What did you have in mind?"

"It doesn't matter to me." All he wanted was quality time with his mother. He had some issues, and only she could help him get through them. NJ had feelings for Jazz, but he didn't know how to express them or treat her. Growing up without Sasha played a huge role in his behavior toward females. There were times he cared about Jazz, but then there were times where he didn't give a fuck about her. Today just so happened to be one of those days.

"Okay, I'll plan us something for the weekend. I'm happy you called me."

NJ paused for a long period of time.

"NJ, you still there?"

"Yeah, I'm here." He paused. "I want to apologize to you about the dinner and for taking so long to reach out to you."

"That's okay, NJ, I understand. You don't have to apologize," she pleaded with him.

"Nah, it's not okay, and yes I do. I should've came at you differently since I wanted to see you. It's just that I had a rough life, and I feel like if you were around things would've been different. I know what you went through, and I guess it made sense for you to give me up. You're here now, and I want us to have a relationship."

Hearing her son admit he wanted a relationship brought tears to her eyes because she wanted the same thing. Being a mother for the first time officially gave her a new outlook on family and life. Although she gave birth to him, she was never a mother to him, and now she had a second chance at it. "That really means a lot to me, and I want the same thing from you. I know I have a lot of catching up to do, but I'm ready to take that next step." She thought for a moment. "Okay, so let's grab lunch and go to the mall."

"That's cool. Are you sure you're up to walking with that big belly of yours?"

Sasha laughed. "I had the baby already."

"Word?" he shouted.

"Yeah."

"What did you have?" he asked, sounding interested.

"A little girl. Her name is Dream."

"Dang, I got a little sister?"

"Yes. She's so adorable, too."

"You have to bring her so I can meet her."

"Of course I'll bring her."

"Good. I can't wait."

"Okay, so I'll see you Saturday. Text me your address and I'll be there to pick you up around eleven. That's not too early, is it?"

"Of course not," he confirmed.

"Okay, good."

"Alright, I'll see y'all on Saturday," NJ smiled. He always wanted a little sister, someone he could protect and go hard for.

"Okay."

"Talk to you later."

"Alright, bye-bye."

"Bye."

NJ hung up the phone and felt a little relieved. Maybe this new bond would be just what the doctor ordered. Placing his phone on vibrate, he threw it on the floor and closed his eyes so he could take a nap.

***

Chauncey was off his rocker, and in order to cope with what he did, he turned to drugs. Popping pills was his drug of choice, but when that didn't suffice, he added coke to the list, which was stronger. Tossing and turning, Chauncey was fighting and sweating.

"Get the fuck off me, Monica, and stop playing," he shouted.

"No, I'm going to kill you. Look what you did to me!" she screamed.

"It was an accident."

"No, it wasn't. And I guess you fucking that bitch in your apartment was an accident, too?" Monica wrapped her hands around his throat and squeezed tightly, stopping his breathing.

Right before he was out of breath, Chauncey jumped up in a cold sweat, his heart beating fast. He looked around the room and no one was there. This was the fourth nightmare he'd had in one week about her. The guilt behind Monica's death was driving him insane. It didn't matter what time of the day it was. Whenever he closed his eyes she was there, waiting to haunt him, and there was nothing he could do to stop it.

"This bitch won't let me sleep in peace," he shouted.

Quickly jumping from the bed, he looked around for the liquor he was drinking earlier. "Where the fuck is it?" He was growing impatient looking for it. His apartment wasn't the tidiest anymore because he neglected to keep his place up. Between getting drunk and high, he couldn't focus long enough to go through a day of being sober.

Finally stumbling onto the bottle of Remy, he took the top off and took a few gulps. Checking his pockets, he found the pills he had been consuming. He popped two flakka pills and washed those down with alcohol. Dripping some from his chin, he used the back of his hand to wipe it off.

Chauncey knew he had to get out of the house, so he decided to slide up on Dirty. In a hurry, as if he was running for his life, he threw on a shirt and some jeans and headed for the door. Halfway down the stairs he stumbled and missed the next few steps. Chauncey landed on his back, hitting his head against the concrete wall. "Fuck!" he shouted. Rubbing the back of his head, he could feel moisture. Chauncey brought his hand forward slowly and panicked when he saw the blood. Drawing his gun, he aimed it forward. "Bitch, you gon' trip me?" He wiped his nose. "That's how you get down, ho?"

There was no one in front of him.

He rose quickly to his feet and ran to the car. Unlocking the door, he jumped inside the car and locked the doors. "This bitch trying to kill me. I gotta get the fuck outta here."

Chauncey made it to the trap house in no time and got out of the car. He took slow strides to the door and jiggled the knob only to see it was locked. "Why the fuck this nigga got the door locked and shit? Ol' scary-ass nigga." Using the key, he unlocked the door and stepped inside, closing the door behind him. "Dirty, where the fuck you at, nigga?" he shouted. Chauncey walked from room to room yelling Dirty's name, but he didn't get an answer. He then walked into the kitchen and paused when he stood in front of the refrigerator. The image before him took the wind from his body, causing him to do the mannequin challenge. It took a minute for it to register.

He stepped closer and grabbed the obituary. "Damn." He scratched his head. "Dirty dead."

Chauncey walked out of the kitchen and went to take a seat on the sofa. Lying back, he closed his eyes, and the incident was clear as day in his head. Dirty betrayed him and Quamae in the worst way, and they had to end his life. It was funny how the drugs made him forget he had a part in the killing.

Once again he found himself in a slump, popping more pills and drinking more alcohol. One hour turned into two, and he was still in the trap house getting lit. That had become his temporary safe haven since there were no memories of Monica there. Suddenly, that lonely feeling kicked in and he called Ayesha. He called her back-to-back to no avail and tossed the phone on the floor.

"Why the fuck this bitch not answering her phone? She better not be in the club giving my pussy away," he snapped. "I'ma have to slide up on this bitch." He sat up in his seat and rubbed his hands together. "As a matter of fact, I am."

***

Ayesha sat in the car looking at the missed calls from Chauncey. "He keeps calling me. What am I supposed to do?" she asked.

Quamae looked in her direction. "Tell him it's over and then block his number."

Ayesha broke their eye contact and looked down at the floor. "Okay," she said softly.

"What's wrong? Don't tell me you fell for that nigga?" He could tell she had developed feelings for Chauncey, but that wasn't in her job description.

"Believe it or not, he treats me good." She shrugged her shoulders. "I haven't had that in a long time, but to answer your question," she thought about her answer for a few seconds, "I did."

"That's not what I paid you for, Ayesha. You wasn't supposed to fall for this nigga." Quamae was furious with her. "Y'all females let niggas fuck and fall in love. I don't understand."

"It's not like that."

"You know he killed his last bitch?" he added, trying to sway her.

"Who?" she raised her head.

"Monica."

Hearing that name sent her into shock and back to the night they were caught. "Oh my God, he killed her?"

"Yeah, and that's why you need to leave him alone. If he finds out about what you did to him, he'll try to kill yo' ass, too, but I ain't gon' let that happen."

Quamae watched her demeanor change in a matter of seconds. He never had any intentions on telling her, but he needed her to leave him alone right away. Ayesha was a down-ass chick in his eyes, and he couldn't let anything happen to her. Chauncey was down bad, and his actions were unpredictable. He would never forgive himself if she fell victim to his wrath.

He placed his hand on her shoulder. "I'm only trying to protect you. This nigga is spiraling out of control, and there's no telling what he would do if he found out."

Ayesha was full of disappointment. "Okay," she whispered.

"I would have to kill that nigga if something happened to you."

She opened the car door and placed one foot out. "My shift is about to start, so I have to get inside."

"Be careful, and remember what I told you."

"I will." Ayesha stepped out of the car, and just as she was about to close it Quamae stopped her.

"Hold up." She paused, hoping he was not about to issue another lecture. "Take this, just in case." He passed her a .380 caliber pistol.

"What's this for?" she asked.

"Chauncey."

"I can't take this, Quamae." Ayesha passed it back, but he wouldn't take it.

"You rather be safe than sorry. The nigga is off his rocker." He could see the uncertainty in her face. "Use it if you feel like you in danger."

Ayesha thought about it, then smiled. "Okay, I will. Goodnight."

"Be easy, ma." Quamae watched Ayesha walk into the club before he pulled off.

After going straight home, Quamae pulled into the driveway and parked his car. Grabbing his heat, he stepped from the car and checked his surroundings. The beef between him and Blue was crazy, and there was no telling what he had in store for him. One thing he wasn't having was being ambushed at his own home, and he had Sasha to thank for that. Quamae walked toward the door, but slowed down when he saw a package on the step. He turned around and made sure no one was behind him. Once the coast was clear, he grabbed the package and went inside the house.

Anxious to see what was in the box, he sat his gun down on

the floor and knelt down beside it. Quamae snatched the loose piece of tape off and opened the box. The contents caught him off guard. Staring up at him was Gigi's head, and her eyes were wide open. It took a minute to come to the conclusion they did the unthinkable with her body. He was expecting a gunshot wound, not a dismemberment of her body from an episode of Criminal Minds. He shook his head, then rose to his feet while heading into the kitchen. Rummaging through the drawer, he located a Tracfone and placed a call.

"Who is this?" Blue answered.

"Nigga, you think I'm supposed to be fazed by you sending me that bitch head in a box?" Quamae spat.

"Gotta be since you hittin' my line." Blue was expecting a call, especially since he knew who he was dealing with. "I was waiting on your call, though. I knew you would hit me up after seeing yo' bitch without a body."

"Nigga, I don't give a fuck about that ho, but get ready to see me soon 'bout my wife and baby."

"Nigga, you had your turn. That ass belong to me now, and you can stop claiming my daughter." Blue knew that would set him off, and that was the plan.

"Just know that when I catch you, I'm gon' kill you," Quamae snapped.

"Well, until you catch me, I'll be nutting all up in that wet, tight pussy and getting my dick sucked like a boss," Blue teased. "I know you miss that shit," he laughed. "She a beast with the head, bruh."

Quamae was so mad he hung the phone up and tossed it back into the drawer. There was no need in tongue wrestling. Blue would be seeing him sooner than he thought. Just the thought of Sasha performing in bed the way she did with him made every vein pop in his neck and forehead. It didn't matter that he wanted a divorce. The point was he wanted her back, and he wasn't going to stop until he got her. People made mistakes every day, and leaving her for Gigi was his biggest regret in life. She played him, but she lost tremendously in the end. Now it was time to make things right with Sasha.

He needed to get himself together before he called the police, so he rolled a blunt and went out back to smoke. Afterward he was stuck and ready for action. He dialed 911 from his cellphone and waited in the front yard for them to come. The sound of sirens could be heard from a distance. Quamae smiled. "Showtime."

He shifted his thoughts to Sasha and his baby and sadness filled his heart, building tears in his eyes. He tilted his head back until the cops pulled up. As they got closer, he dropped his head and the tears began to flow freely down his face. He was approached by two cops, one male and one female.

"Good evening, sir. Did you call the police about receiving a head in a box?" the male officer asked.

"Yes. It's my fiancée," Quamae sobbed.

He introduced them. "I'm Officer Stephens, and this is my partner, Officer Douglas."

Officer Douglas stepped in closer. "Can you tell us what happened?"

Quamae sniffled. "When I came home there was a box on my front porch. I took it in the house and," he paused and sobbed loudly, "her head was in the box."

"Where is the box now?" Officer Douglas asked.

He nodded toward the house. "It's in there."

Officer Stephens looked at his partner. "I'm going inside to check it out. Continue taking his statement, and I'll be right back." There were other officers by the road, along with the crime scene van. He shouted toward the road, "Get crime scene up here."

Chapter 3

Chauncey took a pull off the blunt he laced with flakka and blew the smoke through his nose as he sat in the car outside the club where Ayesha worked. It was almost closing time, so he knew she would be walking out soon. The smoke had him choking hard, but that didn't deter him from getting higher than a kite. This was the only thing that helped him cope with his demons and nightmares. Ayesha was an exception, and she helped in more ways than one, but she wasn't answering his calls.

"Now, where the fuck you at, girl?" He peeped out the window like he was on a stakeout. "I see everybody but yo' ass." He took another pull and hunted for his prey.

Ten minutes later the parking lot had become deserted and Ayesha was nowhere in sight, so he figured she was gone for the night or hadn't shown up to begin with. Chauncey picked up his phone and tried calling her again, but she didn't answer. He growled into the phone, "Yo' ass better be home." Tossing his phone into the passenger seat, he ate up the highway, trying to get to Ayesha's apartment to see what was up with his girl. "I know you better not be wit' no nigga or it's gon' be some real fuckin' problems tonight."

Chauncey ran damn near every light, and he was lucky it was late 'cause with his level of intoxication he was going straight to jail. Making a sharp turn into her complex, his tires screeched as he hit the speed bump hard, but he ignored it. The only thing he was worried about was getting inside that apartment. Tossing the car into park, he bolted from the car and through the parking lot.

The inside of her apartment was dim, so he knocked on the door. One thing he knew was she kept a light on when she slept in there alone.

Knock! Knock! Knock!

He repeated his knocks for about two minutes, and he became furious. "Open this muthafuckin' door before I kick this bitch in." Turning his back to the door, he used his foot to get her attention.

Boom! Boom! Boom!

Ayesha still didn't come to the door. "Bitch, I'ma kill you when I get in there." He was furious, and sweat beads were present on his forehead.

Suddenly he remembered he kept a pocket knife in his car, so he jogged back to his car to get it. Once he had it in his possession, he went back to the door to break his way in. Sliding the tip of the knife into the top lock, he wiggled it around until he got it open. The bottom knob didn't have a lock, so he got in with no problem.

Chauncey walked through the apartment expecting the worst, so he pulled out his ratchet. Based upon the silence, he was certain she was sprawled out naked wit' another nigga, so he walked light to keep from waking them up. Prepared to catch two bodies, he walked into the bedroom slowly and took aim at the bed. Using his left hand, he flicked on the light, ready to blast.

Bringing his gun down to his side, he chuckled. "This bitch ain't even home."

Placing his gun on the dresser, he kicked off his shoes and got comfortable. Whenever she made it in, she was in for a rude awakening. To pass the time, he decided to get just a little bit higher than he was. Inside his wallet was a small bag of powder. He pulled it out and thumped the bottom of the bag. "Oh yeah. This 'bouta get a nigga right."

Placing the baggie on the dresser, he pulled his money out of his pocket, took off a hundred dollar bill, and stuffed the rest back into his pocket. Once he had it rolled neatly, he dumped the powder onto the dresser and pulled out his driver's license and made two lines. Picking up the perfectly-rolled bill, he leaned in and took a long sniff.

"Ah, shit." Chauncey shook his head, tossed it back, and swallowed hard. "Woo! That shit strong."

Making his way to the kitchen, he fumbled around in the cabinet looking for her stash of liquor. There was a bottle of Ciroc. It wasn't what he wanted, but it would have to do. Snatching the top off, he tossed it onto the counter and took a huge gulp, then walked back into the room.

The thought of calling Ayesha crossed his mind a few times,

but he wanted to catch her in the act just in case she was bringing home another nigga. While he continued to wait on her, he rolled up a blunt and finished the rest of the bottle. By the time she did make it home, he would be good and fucked up.

Chauncey was out his mind when he heard the front door open and close, so he picked up his gun and sat quietly on the bed in nothing but his boxers. The sound of her locking the door and the jingling of her keys could be heard. Seconds later Ayesha walked into the room and was taken by surprise when she saw him sitting there. Instantly she jumped back and placed her hand over her chest.

"Chauncey, what the hell you doin' in here? You scared the shit out of me."

He was up on his feet rapidly with his gun clutched in his hand tightly. "Don't question me. Why the fuck you just getting here?"

"I do work late nights, in case you forgot." Ayesha walked into the room and hung her keys on the key hook that hung from the wall. When she turned, he was standing in her face, breathing like a goddamn dragon.

"Sounds like you tryin' to fuck some other nigga tonight."

"Why the fuck you trippin'?" Ayesha walked past him, bumping his shoulder in the process. He turned to face her.

"'Cause I was at the muthafuckin' club and you wasn't there."

"I was there. I didn't stay until closing, and afterward we went out to eat." Ayesha sat her purse down on the bed. "Listen, I'm tired. I had a long-ass night, and I just want to take a hot shower and get some rest."

Chauncey grabbed the back of her neck and pushed her onto the bed.

"Chauncey, stop!" She tried to remain calm since it was late and she didn't want to wake the neighbors.

"You stop with the lies." Separating her legs, he stood in between them and lifted her dress. "I know you was out fuckin' some nigga after the club. Unless you gave him a private show in that bitch." The sight of her bare ass made his dick hard like a rock. The pressure alone made it ache.

"Baby, you drunk. Let's just go to bed and talk about this in the morning. I haven't fucked anybody, I swear." Everything Quamae told her earlier was playing in her head, and she was afraid of what he would do to her under the influence. It was in her best interest to get him to calm down, and she knew fighting with him wasn't the answer.

"After I see if you been fuckin', then we can go to bed." Chauncey was aggressive, and it showed when he ripped her thong off so easily. Stepping from his boxers, he kicked them to the side and stroked his dick before forcing it into her roughly.

Ayesha's scream was faint because her mouth was pressed against the mattress.

Plunging deep, he let out a loud grunt from the depth of his soul and grabbed her hair. "Yeah, my shit better be tight."

Ayesha closed her eyes. No matter what the circumstances were at that moment, she couldn't deny the fact she loved rough sex with him. The way he was beating the box had her going wild, and she couldn't help but throw it back at him.

"Yeah, that's my girl. Throw that pussy on daddy just like that."

Constant moaning filled his ears, giving him the motivation to show her who was in control and who owned the prize between her legs. The grip he had on her hair was as tight as her pussy on his dick. Her muscles squeezed it tight like she had that bitch in a chokehold. Pressure really did burst pipes, and he was that much closer to climaxing. A few more thrusts and grunts and a million of his little soldiers were spewing from the tip of his piece, making their way through her tunnel.

Chauncey slowed down the pace damn near to a halt until his body allowed him to move from behind her. Wiggling his body a bit, he pulled out of her and stretched.

"Now you can take a shower and tell me where the fuck you been at and why you haven't been answering my calls all night."

Ayesha's heart started to pound because she knew she couldn't tell him the truth, and he was already drunk and high. That would only lead to another argument and possibly a fight or deadlier. The fact he murdered his ex said a lot, and now she felt like she was in danger. Even with the gun in her purse, she didn't feel safe because she had never fired one before.

After she left the room, she went into the shower and took her time in there. Her mind was boggled up with so much emotion due to the fact she cared deeply for him. In her heart she really didn't see him as a threat, but truthfully *how well do you really know a person*?

When she stepped from the shower, she draped her body in a towel and went back into the bedroom. To her surprise Chauncey was snoring like a grizzly bear, and she felt a sense of relief. He needed to sleep whatever the fuck he was on off and snap back to reality. Quietly she picked up her purse and removed the gun Quamae gave her and placed it inside of the nightstand for safe keeping.

Ayesha opened another drawer in search of some pajamas. Once she found them, she slipped into them quickly before tip-toeing to the bed. The reality of having to sneak into her own bed didn't sit well with her, but the man she lay beside had her heart. Climbing into bed, she slipped underneath the covers and cuddled up closely to him. She didn't understand how a person with such a good heart could carry so many demons. If she could change his ways, he'd be the perfect man for her. The snoring didn't bother her one bit, so she closed her eyes and fell asleep instantly.

"Get the fuck off me, bitch, before I kill yo' ass!"

Ayesha's eyes were barely closed when she awakened from her sleep. Squinting at the clock, she realized it was five in the morning and Chauncey was straight trippin'.

"Ho, you trying to kill me."

Sitting up in the bed, she placed her hand on his shoulder. "Calm down, baby, it's just a dream."

"Get the fuck off me, Monica, before I kill you again." Grabbing her arm, he twisted and she yelped in pain.

"Baby, let go of my arm. You're hurting me."

"Shut the fuck up!" he yelled and slapped her repeatedly in the face. Forcing her down on the bed by her shoulders, he straddled her, applying all of his weight on her 145-pound frame.

"Chauncey, please stop," she whimpered.

Ignoring her cries, he punched her over and over in the face. Ayesha wiggled and squirmed as she tried to roll over and protect her face. "Fuck you, Monica, you no-good, dirty bitch."

At that moment she knew he was out of it because he didn't know who she was. Tears were streaming down the sides of her face and her head was pounding in pain. "I'm not Monica. I'm Ayesha."

"Bitch, don't lie to me." Using both hands, he squeezed her neck tightly like he was trying to snap it like a popsicle stick. For the first time she was in fear for her life, so she tried reaching for the nightstand, but her arms were too short. Quamae warned her he was dangerous, but she didn't take heed to what he told her, and now she was about to pay for it.

Suddenly he snapped out of it and started to sob loudly right before he collapsed onto the bed. Burying his head in his hands, he cried harder like he knew he had done wrong. Ayesha was grateful to be free and breathing on her own once again, but now she feared him. Creeping slowly from the bed, careful not to startle him, she grabbed the gun from the nightstand and put it back in her purse. There was no way she was sleeping there tonight when she could save herself. A friend of hers lived in the same complex, and it was best she slept there.

Chauncey stayed in that position for ten minutes, and she was hoping he would fall asleep soon, but her dream was shattered when he got up from the bed. Fear pumped through her veins as she watched closely and prayed he didn't come her way. Realizing he was headed to the bathroom, she prepared to haul ass. The sound of his piss hitting the water was her cue to get ghost since he didn't close the door.

Standing to her feet with her purse clutched tightly in her hand, she tiptoed from the room and stopped by the door to see which direction he was looking in. His head was down, so she darted past the door.

Ayesha turned the lock, but froze when she heard him coming

behind her.

"Ayesha, baby, where you going?" he asked in a gentle voice. She just stood there without a word with her hand on the knob and the other inside her purse.

"Um. Um," she stuttered.

"You tryna leave me?" He took a step forward and bumped the end table, causing her to jump and turn around quickly.

"Chauncey, please leave me alone," she cried.

The marks on her face were visible to him with the little bit of light in the apartment. "Ayesha, I'm sorry. I didn't mean to hurt you." Chauncey had become emotional and wiped the tears from his eyes. "I have a problem, and I need help. You can't leave me like this."

"Chauncey, I can't help you, and I can't let you beat on me like this. We need to end this now."

"No, baby, don't do this to me. You keep me grounded."

"Obviously I don't if you getting high on God knows what."

Chauncey frowned and tilted his head. "You judging me now?"

Ayesha sniffled. "I'm not, but I can't be with you. I'm going to leave, and when I come back I want you gone."

"You ain't goin' nowhere, and I ain't either, so get back here."

"No." She stood firm on her word. It wasn't like they could be together anyway. After it was all said and done, she would have to leave him. The mission wasn't to fall in love, but things got a little more difficult along the way.

"I'm sorry," he pleaded. Chauncey started taking steps in her direction and she knew she was in danger.

Ayesha fumbled with her purse and pulled out her li'l pea-shooter. "Chauncey, stay right there, please." Her lip quivered and her hand trembled as she tried to keep the gun steady.

"Put that thang away before you hurt yourself." She wasn't the violent type, and he knew she didn't have a violent bone in her body.

"Proceed with caution," she warned.

"I'm not gon' hit you again." His eyes had sincerity in them, and she wanted to believe him so desperately, but she didn't trust him. On her shoulders the angel and devil were debating, and she didn't know who to believe.

Spreading his arms apart, he approached her slowly, but she took a step back until she bumped against the door and fired the gun.

Pow!

Chauncey fell to the floor and grabbed his leg. "What the fuck you shot me for?"

Ayesha couldn't believe she shot him in the leg, so she dropped the gun on the floor like it was hot in her hand. Easing down on the floor across from him, she cried, "I'm sorry, baby. I don't know what I was thinking."

Crawling over to him, she looked down at the bullet hole and grabbed his hand. "I'm going to call the police and tell them what happened."

"No. I'm good. I'll have my man come stitch me up." He applied pressure to the hole. "Go and get me a towel and my cellphone." Chauncey had been shot before, so it was nothing to panic about.

Ayesha got up and dashed to the bathroom to get what he needed and rushed back to his aide. "Baby, I'm sorry. I swear I am," she pleaded truthfully. Chauncey had her heart, and sometimes a person couldn't control who that muthafucka loved.

Fifteen minutes later there was loud banging on the door. "It's the police. Open up."

"Shit!" she panicked. "What we gon' do?"

"Just be quiet and let them go away," he whispered. "One of your neighbors musta called them."

The banging continued. "I know someone is in there, and if you don't open up I'm breaking it down in three seconds. Your choice," he barked.

"I'm just gon' open it, Chauncey. I can't have them kicking in my door and getting me evicted."

"One, two."

Ayesha jumped up off the floor and snatched the door open. "How can I help you, officer?"

"We received a call that a shot was fired from this apartment."

"No, that was from my television. I had it up too loud. Thanks for stopping by." She attempted to close the door, but he pushed the door with his hand.

"What happened to your face?" He peeped around Ayesha to see if anyone was in the living room with her.

"I got into a fight with some girls," she lied easily.

"Who's in there with you?"

"Nobody. I'm here alone." She assumed Chauncey had gone into the room since they didn't see him sitting on the floor.

"Do you mind if we come in and check?"

"Yes, I do mind, 'cause I just told you no one was here and I would like to go back to bed."

The officer was disgusted, but there was nothing he could do to make her let him in without a warrant. "Okay, ma'am, keep it down and have a good night."

"Same to you."

Ayesha hurried up and closed the door so she could go and check on Chauncey. When she got into the room, he was sitting on the floor with the liquor bottle turned to his lips.

"They're gone."

He swallowed what he had in his mouth and looked up at her with sleepy eyes. His focus was on her black eye and the bloody bruises on her face. The guilt of what he did to her was a tough pill to swallow. The last time he beat a woman like that she ended up dead, and it wasn't right at all.

Chauncey motioned for her to sit down on the floor next to him. Raising his hand to her caused her to flinch and cover her face. "Relax. We good, and I'm sorry for doing this to your face. I just snapped, and I don't know why."

Ayesha held her head down because she couldn't look in his eyes with her face beaten and battered. "What's gotten into you? And why were you calling me Monica?"

This was the one thing he didn't want to discuss, but he owed her an explanation after the way he beat her. "A few weeks back I had a fight with Monica 'cause she tried to call the police on me, and in the process she stabbed me. I chased her into the bathroom, and she slipped and hit her head on the tub." Chauncey's breathing was more rapid and short the more emotional he became. "I killed her, but I didn't mean to."

Ayesha forgot about the pain he had just caused her and tended to his needs. Seeing him remorseful and full of regret pulled on her heart, and she instantly felt sorry for him. Easing closer to him, she draped her arms around him, giving him a shoulder to lean on. Dealing with dope dealers was the norm for her. They killed people all the time, but never had she witnessed this type of behavior.

***

Later on that night, after his wound was cleaned and stitched up by his friend Doc, he was drowsy from the medication. With his lady by his side, he was able to lay down comfortably and get some rest. A few hours later Chauncey woke up in a little pain, but it wasn't unbearable. Sitting up in the bed, he watched Ayesha as she slept peacefully for a few minutes. Her face was puffy from the attack and he saw her lip was busted up pretty badly. The words his mother taught him kept repeating in his head: *if you have to beat her, then you need to leave her.* Those words stuck like glue, and he knew what he had to do.

Pulling open the dresser drawer, he looked for a piece of paper and a pen to scribble up a quick note for her. Once he found it, he wrote her a message.

I'm sorry, and I'll never hit you again. I promise you that. I'm leaving 'cause I need to get myself together and I'm not healthy for you. I wish you the best in life, shawty. I love you.

Love always,

Chauncey

Placing the note on the dresser, he tossed a stack of one hundred dollar bills next to it and walked away from her for good.

He needed rehabilitation, and he needed it fast before more blood splattered on his hands.

Destiny

Chapter 4

Quamae woke up feeling like the man of the year. The star player that *was* on his team violated and had been eliminated permanently. Loyalty meant everything to him, and that bitch didn't deserve the air she was breathing. He couldn't count how many times he quoted that saying. On his way out of the door, he set the alarm and locked up the house.

For it being the month of March, the weather was pretty fair. The sun was out, but it wasn't blazing. A cool breeze kissed the back of Quamae's neck. "I see you workin', God. You know a nigga hate to sweat," he laughed and got into his truck, switching on the engine. Adjusting the volume on his stereo, he connected to the Bluetooth, pressed play, and backed out of the driveway humming. The song was talking to his spirit.

"I can't see you being with no one else but me. Baby, I can't stand thinking 'bout you touching another man." Quamae sang along thinking about Sasha, and he missed her terribly. Admitting he fucked up was a no-brainer, but he made a promise to himself he would get her back. He also made Dream a promise. It didn't matter the price or the body he had to drop. Going toe-to-toe with Blue was something he was willing to do.

Thirty minutes later he was pulling up to his lounge. Quamae leaned up in his seat and smiled at the sign. Previously it was called Gianni's Palace, but that changed quickly once he dismissed the bitch. The new sign meant everything to him and more. The name was absolutely breathtaking, putting a sparkle in his eye. The words *Dream's Palace* sparkled in front of the building. Dream's paternity hadn't been established, but something in his gut told him she was his daughter. During Sasha's pregnancy he could count the amount of times he fed her. Until the test told him otherwise, Dream was his daughter and rocking another nigga's last name. That was the first thing he was changing when he got back his results.

Quamae finally turned the truck's engine off and got out to go inside the lounge. No one was there except for his assistant, Terri.

It looked like she was doing inventory before the doors opened.

"Good morning, Terri." Quamae walked up and placed his elbows on the countertop.

"Hey, boss. How you doing today?" Terri smiled and set down the clipboard she had clutched tightly in her hand.

"Better than ever."

"That's good to hear. Do you want a drink?"

"Nah, I'm good." Quamae's body went erect. "I have a lot of work to do, so I'll be in my office if you need me."

"Okay."

When he made it inside his office, he sat at his desk and thumbed through his phone's gallery. The precious memory that plastered a permanent smile on his face was only a month old, and she captured his heart at first sight. The fact he couldn't stop thinking about her was confirmation he needed to handle his business and get the answer he so desperately wanted and needed. That would be the day he rubbed those results all over Blue's face. To gloat was his mission, but if it didn't come back in his favor, his entire world would be meaningless.

Those thoughts were quickly pushed away when he realized he had so much work to do. Quamae picked up the office phone to make a call.

"What's up, brother?" Jon asked.

"Hey, I need you to do something for me."

"What's going on?"

"I need you to switch that property back into my name and pull that 25K from her account."

Jon sighed heavily into the receiver. "I don't know why you did some dumbass shit like that in the first place."

That was one thing he didn't want to hear: a damn lecture. "Bruh, can you just do what I asked you to do without taking this shit to the third degree? I fucked up, I get it. But damn, we all did shit we regret."

"The power of the pussy," Jon joked.

"Nah, I was just trying to make sure my seeds were straight."

"Yeah, and that ho played you like a fiddle, bruh."

"Well, karma's a bitch, and you live and learn from that shit."

"I hear that." Jon spun around in his chair before taking a stand at his desk. "Anyway, I leave the office today at five, so I'll stop by and give you an update."

"Cool. I'll be here."

"Don't make anymore bad decisions without me." He couldn't miss an opportunity to clown his boy.

"Fuck ya."

***

Time was moving at an unusual rate of speed, and it was close to five in the afternoon. Nevertheless, he was able to get everything done for the grand opening thanks to Terri. She was a Godsend about her business, and he admired that about her. Putting in the extra hours for them to be up and running was nothing. Terri was a dedicated female who was about her money and treated his business as if it was hers. That was who he needed on his team.

He placed another call. "Hey, Jerry, it's Quamae."

"Hey, my man, how's it going?"

"Everything on my end is A1. Just calling to see if you handled your end of the deal."

"Of course I did. My guys Claude and Jake will be there on Friday."

"Good. Make sure they arrive early." Quamae jotted a few notes on his calendar.

"Come on, Q. Have I ever let you down?"

"Not yet."

"Don't speak that shit into existence. The tongue is a powerful sword." Jerry's chuckle was loud and hearty, booming through the speaker.

"Yeah, man, I hear ya. I'll see if your word is as solid as you say come Friday."

"You'll see. I'll check up on you then."

Quamae sat the phone back down on the base and there was a

tapping on the door. *Knock, knock!*

"It's open."

Terri opened the door and peeked in. "Jon is here to see you." She stepped to the side and let him in.

"Thanks, beautiful."

"You're welcome." She blushed and closed the door to give them some privacy. Jon looked at his brother from another mother and smiled. "Shorty fine, dawg."

Quamae held his hand up in the air, trying to kill the direction of the conversation. "Stop it right there and keep your eyes off the merchandise."

"Damn, bro, you smashin' that?" Jon didn't try to hide the disappointment in his voice.

"Nah, she's my assistant."

"And what the fuck does that mean? Do you know how many guys fuck their assistants and secretaries?"

"Just 'cause you fuck yours don't mean I'll do the same," Quamae couldn't help but laugh at him because it was downright hilarious. No matter what Jon did, that would never change their bond. "And you better stop all that shit before you get sued. All these bitches looking for is a quick and easy come-up. You see what's goin' on with Tyrese?"

Jon played with his beard and sat down across from his boy. "I ain't that nigga, and I'm not leaving no sperm laying around. And I didn't smash all of them. Nigga, I done seen *Being Mary Jane* too many times wit' Tisha ass."

"Almost, my nigga, and that's why you can't keep a secretary longer than ninety days."

"Temptation is a muthafucka, and they know what they be doing wearing them li'l-ass dresses. They know damn well they ain't supposed to come to work like that." Quamae observed Jon grabbing his crotch. "On the real, though, once they get ahold of this white chocolate and I hit 'em with that thug passion, they asses fall in love."

The laughter in the office bounced off every wall. Jon was showing every tooth in his mouth and his eyes were barely open.

His laughter was so contagious Quamae couldn't help but join in. Both of their eyes had begun to water.

"I ain't fuckin' with you." Quamae was trying to calm himself down.

"You my nigga, so you ain't got no choice."

"You already know."

The playing had come to an end and it was back to business. Jon dried his eyes with his hands and took a deep breath. "So, I was able to handle the names on the property, but we ran into a little issue."

Quamae sat up with his hands underneath his chin. "And what's that?"

"That psychotic bitch never cashed or deposited that check."

Quamae was surprised because after that ass-whooping he put on her, there wasn't a shadow of a doubt she didn't get rid of it. "Damn, I gotta find that shit."

"Or just put a stop payment on the shit and pay that fee."

"Yeah, I'm not worried about that. My main concern is protecting my account number."

"Get a new one."

Every dilemma he could come up with, Jon had a solution for it. "That would be nice, but I have pending checks I can't have bouncing around like a ball."

Jon sighed. "Well, go home and search for that bitch high and low. It has to be in there somewhere."

"Yeah, I'm on it as soon as I get outta here."

Jon stood up and stretched. "Can I go down and have a drink on the house now?"

Quamae gave him that look and shook his head, knowing damn well his boy was full of shit. "I don't think a drink is what you want, but the drink's on me." Then he rolled his chair backward, stood up, and placed his phone into his pocket.

"Don't give me that look. I'm just trying to make her my Woman Crush Wednesday."

He walked over to where Jon was standing patiently and patted his chest. "My sis better be the only one you crushing on."

"She's my W.C.E., and I own that pussy. I just need a chick to hold down Wednesdays."

"Man, sis gon' kill yo' ass. Just keep on." They started to walk off, but Quamae paused and looked back at Jon, who was still smirking. "Why Wednesday, though? What's so special 'bout that day?"

"That's Tisha's late day to work, and she ain't givin' a nigga no ass when she get off. Always saying she tired and shit. Fuck my needs, huh? So, I just need a li'l baby who wanna Netflix and fuck, that's it."

"Man, let's go out here and get you a drink so you can get home to Tisha, 'cause I ain't yo' alibi, nigga."

"That's foul, dawg, and you know that shit. I was about to hit her up and say I'm chillin' with you at the lounge until later on."

Quamae pushed him toward the door. "Getcho ass out my office 'cause I ain't fuckin' with you."

When the men approached the bar, Terri was on the phone, but she quickly dismissed the caller when they took a seat.

"Ready for a drink now, boss?"

Her voice was the sweetest, and Jon was smiling harder than a muthafucka. "You supposed to ask me first." He licked his lips, then reached out and grabbed her hand.

Terri was intrigued by his swag and handsome face. The way his suit fit on his muscular shoulders was a complete turn-on. There was nothing sexier than a man that could rock business attire and get you aroused at the same damn time. However, that was a line she wasn't willing to cross.

She gently took her hand back. "Well, when you start signing my paychecks, you will have that luxury."

Jon stroked his chin, amused by her comeback. "I like you. Where ya man at?"

"If you must know," she picked up a glass and rinsed it out. Her attention was back on Jon, batting those long beautiful lashes at him. "I'm single. What are you having?"

"Surprise me," he winked.

"I can do that."

As soon as Terri walked away, Jon leaned over and whispered to Quamae, "I'll fuck the lining out her pussy."

"I bet you will."

The hunger in his eyes said he wasn't gonna stop until he had her feet to the ceiling, and he never lost focus while she was fixing their drinks. She stood at 5'5" with a small waist and little perky titties that sat up in her tank top with no bra. Her ass wasn't the biggest, but it fit in those tight-ass jeans like a glove in all the right places. After fixing their drinks and walking back over to them, Jon noticed the extra swish in her hips.

Setting the drinks in front of them, she smiled and said, "This is my specialty drink."

Jon sniffed his glass. "What's in it?"

"If I tell you, then I have to kill you."

"As long as you wearing those jeans, you can slip me a date rape drug anytime and have your way with me."

"You crazy."

"About you."

Quamae sipped his drink and watched his boy cut the fool.

If her skin was a little lighter, her cheeks would be rosy from all the blushing. She flipped the bangs from her eyes. "You don't even know me."

"I'm trying to change all that. I'm a good nigga. Ask my brother right here."

He nodded his head towards Quamae, but he shook his head no. "Don't put me in that shit. I already said no from the jump."

Jon took a swig from his glass and sat it back down. "You a hater, bruh, but I need to holla at you about some business real quick before I forget."

Quamae signaled Terri over.

"What's up, boss?"

"Give us about ten minutes."

"No problem." When she walked away, he laid it all out on the table.

Destiny

Chapter 5

Sasha pulled into the Somerset apartment complex and placed a call.

"What's up, ma? You here?" There was so much excitement in NJ's voice.

"Yeah."

"Okay, I'll be down in a second."

"Okay."

Setting her phone in the cup holder, she looked in the back seat to check on Dream. Giving birth to her had been one of her proudest moments, and all she wanted was the chance to prove she could be a great mother. But first she had to start from the beginning, where it all started.

When she finally looked up, her new beginning was walking down the sidewalk in her direction. NJ was the spitting image of his father. He had his smooth brown skin and eyes, and their walk was even identical. Pulling the car door open, he was cheesing hard, and that made everything she was doing worth it.

"How you doing?" he sat down and closed the door.

"I'm good, can't complain. How about you?"

"I'm good." NJ leaned toward the backseat to get a look at the baby. "Aw, look at my sister. She cute."

That made Sasha smile. "Thank you, and you're handsome, so I guess those are my genes showing up and showing out."

"That's funny, 'cause Pops said the same thing."

"Yeah, I bet he did say that."

They ended up going to the Sawgrass Mall in Sunrise. He insisted because they had, like, a million stores, including designer. There were no restrictions for her only son, so she let him pick up whatever his heart desired. They went from store to store until he ended up with a plethora of shopping bags.

"This is more than enough. I can't carry anything else cause my arms are numb."

"Are you sure?"

"Positive." He looked over at his mother. "We splurged

enough for one day."

"Okay, well, let's go to the food court. I'm starving."

"My stomach touching my back."

They both shared a laugh and headed to find some food. The gifts would never make up for the lost time, but it was a great gesture. After all the years of not knowing his mother, NJ was finally getting everything he deserved and more.

When they finally made it back to his living quarters, Dream was bawling her eyes out, and that meant one of two things: she was wet or she was hungry. "I need to come upstairs and change her diaper."

"You know you don't have to ask that." NJ opened up the back door and pulled out the baby seat. "I got her, just get her bag and I'll come back down and get my stuff."

"You sure you want to leave your clothes and shoes out here? I don't want anyone to break in my car and steal your stuff." Sasha was serious as a heart attack, and he could tell by the way she was canvassing the area.

"Nah, it's good out here. They ain't crazy."

Sasha followed NJ up the stairs to the second floor and hooked a left by the post. Stopping by the second door, he pulled out his key, unlocked the door, and stood to the side to let her in.

When she crossed the threshold, she was surprised at how immaculate the place was. It was fully furnished with two nice, black leather couches, a recliner, a big-ass flat screen TV and a PlayStation. Typical man accessories.

She found her way to the kitchen and fixed her a bottle. NJ carried Dream and sat her down in front of the sofa.

"DJ, you too pretty to cry. Stop all that." Unbuckling her straps, he picked her up and cradled her in his arms so she was close to his chest. The crying stopped immediately. "Big brother gotchu, don't worry."

Sasha watched him in action catering to the needs of his baby sister, and her heart warmed up instantly. "I think she likes you." She smiled while measuring the powdered formula and dumping it into the bottle.

"She know big bruh got her."

"Where is your father?" The house was extremely quiet for him to be home. If he was in his room, she was certain he would've come out by now after hearing voices in the living room.

"I don't know, but he should've been here." He looked over at her. "You want me to call him?"

"No, that's okay. I was just wondering if he was here."

Sasha mixed up the ingredients by shaking the bottle and walked over to where he was standing. "Come on, sugar, let Mommy feed you."

NJ handed Dream to their mother. "I'm about to go outside and get my stuff."

"The keys are on the kitchen counter."

NJ walked out the door and closed it behind him while Sasha took a seat on the sofa and started feeding the baby. A few minutes passed and the door opened. "NJ," Sasha shouted, "can you see if I left my phone in the car?"

There was no response, but when she looked up, it wasn't her son at all.

"What's up, babymama?" Nate walked in shirtless, glistening in sweat as if he had just been dipped in milk chocolate. His six pack alone would make a bitch snatch her own panties off. She eyed him from his head all the way down to the bulge in his sweats. And they had the nerve to be gray. He definitely belonged in that group *Gray Sweats Matter* on Facebook.

"Um." Sasha cleared her throat and made eye contact with him. "Hey, how you doin'?"

"I'm good. Just finished working out." He walked over and sat down in the recliner. "That's your newest addition, huh?" he smiled.

"Yes. This is my princess, Dream." She tried her best to keep her eyes above his neck to keep from drooling all over the place. Those fifteen years in the penitentiary did his body damn good.

"She's a beauty, just like her mama."

His comment made her blush hard. "Thank you."

Nate couldn't take his eyes off of her, either. When he went away she was shaped, but now she was all grown up with a woman's body.

"If you was single when I got home, I could've put one of those up in you, but I see somebody beat me to it."

When he licked his lips, Sasha looked away. That was just too much sexy to look at without wanting to cheat on her man. "Yeah, I bet." That was all she could say. What she really wanted to do was let him get a sample of it for old times' sake. There was no doubt in her mind the dick was still good.

"I'm serious. I mean, we can practice if you want to." Nate wasn't slow by a long shot, and he knew she was checking him out from the time he walked through that door.

NJ finally made it back and she was relieved, but instead of coming into the living room he made his way into his room and closed the door.

"You still a mess, I see," she said while removing the empty bottle from the baby's mouth. Sitting her upright, she patted her on the back until she burped a few times. "Good job, mama." Sasha smiled and sat her back in the seat. Preparing to change her diaper, she spread out a blanket and sat out her diaper and wipes.

"Change her, and I'll be right back so we can talk." Nate winked at her. "Don't bail out on me again."

As soon as she heard the door close, she started to fan herself. "Lord, please help me keep my legs closed, 'cause this man is too damn fine."

After she changed the baby, she sat her down in her seat and she fell asleep right away. As she sat and waited for Nate, she tried to keep herself busy on Facebook and Instagram, but that didn't last very long. Looking around the room, she spotted the remote, so she got up to get it. There was something on TV that was sure to hold her attention until he returned. After flipping through the channels for a few minutes, she stopped on the ID channel to see what the crazies were doing.

Just as she got all into it, she heard a door open, and it was NJ. "You good, ma?"

"Yeah, I'm fine."

"Okay. I'm about to head out for a few, and I'll be back."

"Okay. If I'm not here when you get back, just text me and let me know you made it back safe."

"Okay, I will." NJ caught Sasha by surprise when he walked over and gave her a hug. He was really making an effort on building their relationship, and she loved that. When she let him go, he made his way to the front door and walked out.

"Oh Lord, I said help me keep my legs closed, not send away the one person that can help me stay at a distance."

"Who you talking to?"

Nate scared the shit outta her 'cause she never seen or heard him coming. "Oh. Um. I'm talking to the people on this show," she lied, trying hard not to stare at him in his towel.

Nate smiled and walked away. "I'll be right back. Let me go and put on some pants."

Sasha waited until he walked away. "Thank you."

Temptation was so strong in the air, and if she stayed there any longer they would be doing more than talking. Making a promise to herself, she decided she was leaving right after they had their *talk*.

Nate finally came back to the living room and sat down. And this time he was wearing black joggers.

"So, what do you want to talk about?" She asked, trying to rush things.

"Anything. I just wanna catch up on lost time. Fifteen years is a long time to be away from the person you claim to love."

That was shade at its finest, but she didn't take it personal because she knew what she did was wrong. "I did love you, Nate, and you know that."

"You sure it wasn't 'cause I saved you from your situation at home?" His tone was low, yet firm, and he wanted her to be straightforward with him. No bullshit.

The instant reminder of her childhood brought her back to that dreadful day she lost her virginity against her will. A lump big as an orange formed in her throat. She had a hard time getting her words together, but she knew he needed confirmation. In the back of her mind she always knew one day he would bring it up. Today was that day.

"Nate, I fell in love with you because you were the only person that was interested in me and not what I had between my legs. You saved me, yes. That's true, and that made me love you even more."

"Then why did you leave me for dead in there and give up our son? That ain't love, baby girl."

Sasha's eyes filled with water, ready to fall at any minute. "How was I supposed to take care of a baby when I couldn't take care of myself? They took you away for 15 years. I didn't know how to handle losing the only person I loved." The tears finally begin to flow, and Nate could see that 15-year-old girl all over again.

Nate stood up because the conversation took him back to his sentencing day when he lost everything. "My niggas woulda helped you." He clapped his hands a few times out of anger. "Slim woulda did everything to make sure my son and woman was taken care of, but you were only thinkin' about ya'self."

By this time Nate was yelling, but Dream didn't move at all. She was tired.

"Sasha, I did 15 years for you. I didn't get out early, I didn't snitch on nobody. I took that shit to the chin and accepted my fate as a G 'cause that's what a real man would do. A real man wouldn't let his woman do prison time." The veins in his head were protruding, demonstrating his anger as he paced the floor, expressing his feelings. The more he talked, the more emotional he became. "You coulda did ya' thang while I was gone. I wasn't gon' trip, try to keep the pussy on lock or stop you from living ya' life."

Sasha interrupted. "Nate, I'm sorry. I swear I am, and I should've told you, but all that was gon' do is make your time that much harder, placing the weight of my problems on your shoulders when you had your own shit to deal with."

"You didn't let me make that choice. You made it for me, and that's fucked up."

Sasha dried her face with the bottom of her maxi dress. "Nate, I'm sorry, but I have to go. This is too much for me right now." The only thing on her mind was getting out of his sight because he had opened up the wound she thought was stitched up and healed years ago.

Once he noticed she was trying to leave, he stopped her. "Sasha, don't go, please. I just want answers after all these years." He stepped closer to her, but she ignored him and picked up the baby seat. "I deserve that much."

"I can't do this right now." Sasha turned on her heels to try to walk away, but Nate stopped her.

"The least you can do is converse with the man who allowed you to live ya' life free from a cell. The whole time I was there I thought about you and wondered if you were okay. Wondering if I even crossed ya' mind." He was standing so close to her he could hear her heart beating. "Do you know how I feel, going in at 21 and gettin' out at 36? I missed everything."

Sasha just stood there crying, looking at the floor. She couldn't stand to look in his eyes. Just the thought of her going down for those 15 years should've been reason enough for her to stick by his side regardless if she moved on or not. "I'm sorry," she whispered.

Nate lifted her chin so he could look into her eyes. The emotion was there, and he knew she was remorseful for what she did. His feelings for her were clearly still present. Leaning in, he placed his mouth on hers and kissed her lips gently. To his surprise, she didn't resist, and he was good with that. From the first time he saw her he imagined this day, and it came quicker than he thought.

Exploring her body, his hands roamed freely over her breasts, all the way down to her ass. When he squeezed it, it felt so soft in his hands and his dick rocked up. Being away from a woman for 15 years will make that shit rock up from any type of physical contact.

Sasha could feel his dick pressing up against her. The stickiness between her thighs indicated she was ready for penetration. The kiss became more intense, and she was ready to fuck him right where they stood. Her only concern was getting caught in the act by her son. Shit was shaky at the house with Blue, so she wasn't worried about him calling and checking on her.

Sasha broke their kiss. "Wait."

"Wait?" Nate repeated, looking down at his stiff soldier. "He ready."

"I don't want NJ to catch us." She wiped her bottom lip.

"Shit, we grown," Nate chuckled. "He gettin' mo' pussy than me right now."

"No, let's go in the room," she said while picking up the baby bag and her purse.

"I got the baby, go 'head." Nate picked up the car seat and walked behind her. His eyes were stuck on the way her ass jiggled in that dress. A panty line was nowhere in sight. "My room on the left."

Walking inside, she placed her belongings on the dresser and sat down on the bed, kicking off her sandals. Nate locked the door and sat the baby's seat on the side of the bed, facing her toward the closet just in case she woke up. Then he walked over to where his old love sat patiently and stood in front of her.

Springing to her feet, she bent down and slowly rose while lifting up her dress. It had been a very long time since she gave him a strip tease. That was another thing he taught her. Pulling her dress over her head, she tossed it onto the floor and placed her hands on his face. She needed to feel his soft lips again. Kissing him hard, she sucked on his bottom lip and closed her eyes.

Grabbing a handful of her breast, he pinched her nipples gently. Nate had so many dreams during his incarceration about fucking her again, and it was finally about to go down. The trail he made from her nipples, down to her opening made her body shiver. Parting her lips, he rubbed her clit and stuck one finger inside.

"Mm," she moaned as he dipped his finger in and out.

"I used to dream about this pussy and jack my dick like

crazy." Removing his finger, he brought it to his mouth and licked the juices from it. "Get on the bed," he instructed while slipping from his joggers.

"Do you have condoms?" she asked out of curiosity. The last thing she needed was to go home pregnant and unaware of who the father was. Been there, done that, it ain't fun.

"I trust you would keep it a bill with me if something was wrong, and I'm clean. I haven't fucked a woman in 15 years. Shit, you the first one," he smirked.

Sasha dismissed the idea and crawled to the middle of the bed and opened her legs, not wanting to ruin the mood. Sliding between them, Nate rubbed his dick up and down her opening before pushing his way inside. It was tight, so he pulled out and put it back in. The man was hung like a horse, so he had to force his way in.

Sasha wiggled her hips, trying to help him get access to her throbbing center. "Ah!" Biting down on her lip, she closed her eyes when she felt his thick dick stretch her opening and make its way through her tunnel, filling her up. "Shit," she sighed. It hurt, but it felt good, too.

With every stroke Nate grunted. It was so warm and tight. Being inside some pussy was the best feeling in the world right now, and that was something he never thought he would get to experience again in life. A tingling sensation made itself known. He knew what that meant, so he tried to keep his pace down to keep from bustin' too fast. That wasn't working, so he pulled out and shook his meat.

Sasha stopped moaning. "Why you stop?"

Nate chuckled. "Shit, a nigga 'bouta bust quick as fuck."

Bending her legs and pushing them down at her sides, he slid back in and pumped in and out slowly, taking deep strokes. The bottom of her stomach moved up and down from the pressure he applied.

Sasha was panting constantly. "Nate. Nate. Ooh." He was digging all up in them guts, the same way he did when they were younger.

The same feeling returned minutes later, and there was no fighting it this time. Picking up the pace, he pounded in and out until he busted a nut up in her.

"Damn!" he said, pulling out his limp nigga. "That pussy still good."

His comment made her giggle. "Yeah, I know."

Nate lay down beside her and kissed her face. "I swear I dreamed 'bout catchin' that nut."

Sasha slapped his arm. "You didn't pull out, either."

"I know. I'm tryin' to put another baby in there." Laughter followed, but he was serious as a heart attack. All he wanted was a chance for them to be a family, something that was taken away from him without his knowledge.

"Oh, really?" she smiled.

"Yes, really." Nate reached for her hand and held it for a few seconds before he kissed it. "You know I never stopped loving you."

"I didn't know that. It didn't seem that way the first time I saw you." Breaking their eye contact, she looked down at their hands.

"I was still adjusting to everything around me, and when I saw you were pregnant from that young nigga, I figured there was no chance of us getting back together since you seemed so happy." Nate brought her hand up to his mouth slowly and kissed it. "But now you here with me."

That was a subject she wasn't ready to touch on. Her life was already a mess, and she needed to get it together. Dream had two daddies. Quamae wanted her back. And now Nate wanted to come back into her life as well.

Sasha sighed. "Honestly, Nate, I have so much going on, and I don't know if I'm coming or going. I don't know where my life is headed right now."

"Here's some food for thought. I waited 15 years to be with you and rekindle what we had. I don't have anymore time to waste. I'll wait on you to figure it out, but I won't wait too much longer. I wanna give NJ what he didn't have growing up, and that's a mother and a father."

"Okay," she responded truthfully and thought maybe she should give him another a chance. "What time is it?" she asked, looking around for a clock.

He figured she had to go, but he wasn't trying to hear that just yet. "Can I get a round two before you go?"

Sasha leaned forward and stuck her tongue in his mouth, engaging him in another passionate kiss. "Of course you can."

Destiny

Chapter 6

It was a little after nine when Sasha made it home after fuckin' Nate for hours. Blue's truck wasn't in the driveway, so that was a good sign. Her strides were slow due to the pain between her legs. Nate had really put it on her after he got that first nut out of the way and punished the box. Even after she said she was sore, he was still trying to dig in it. Prison had his stamina through the roof 'cause he wasn't tired, but shit she was tapped out.

Turning the locks on the door, she made her way inside and down the hallway to their bedroom. If Blue was out getting drunk, nine times out of ten he wanted sex when he got home, but tonight that wasn't happening. She was wore out and ready to fall asleep with her baby. A shower wasn't necessary since she had taken one at Nate's spot. Dream was still asleep, so she placed her gently inside her bassinet. Opening up the dresser drawer, she pulled out her special pajamas and crawled into bed herself before shooting Nate a text that she made it home safe. NJ hadn't texted her yet, so she assumed he wasn't at home yet.

Sleep didn't come easy as all the thoughts in her head attacked her all at once. The three men in her life wanted her, and now she was confused by them all.

Nate was the love of her life before he left the streets, and he was the one who kept her sane and protected her. Not once did he lay a hand on her when they were together, but there was some doubt they would work out because they had been apart for so many years.

Quamae was her stability, and he took care of her one hundred percent, but he would beat the brakes off her at any given moment. Their relationship was fucked up when she left, and who's to say he really changed? At the end of the day he was still her husband, and she took a vow to love him until death did them part.

Blue, on the other hand, was everything she wanted and needed in a man. He provided for her, but it was different only because of their living arrangements. The age difference wasn't an issue in her eyes, and she really wanted to be with him. There was so much to think about with little time.

The room door opened, and she instantly thought about that old saying, *speak of the devil and they will appear.* Blue wasn't a bad person, but there was a part of him she didn't know.

The room was dark, so he cut on the light. "Bae, you 'sleep?" he asked while tossing his keys onto the dresser.

Sasha didn't answer, hoping he would just lie down and go to sleep.

Blue took off his clothes, tossed them onto the chair, and walked over to Sasha, pulling the covers back. She was wearing her special pajamas, so he covered her back up and hit the light. Snuggling up behind her, he played with her ears.

"Sasha," he whispered.

"Hmm." Playing sleep was her motto when she didn't want to be bothered.

"Why you wearing these?" he tugged on her bottoms.

"My stomach was hurting bad, so I took a pain pill. That's why I'm lying down."

"Well it ain't time for your period to come on yet, so what's wrong with you?"

That was one thing she hated about him. Blue always paid attention to detail by trying to clock her period. Quamae didn't pay attention to none of that shit, and that's how he got caught up with stupid-ass Gigi.

"I know that. I think it was something I ate at the mall. It's probably food poisoning or something," she lied.

"Oh yeah? How did that go?" he asked, referring to NJ. He knew he could be stubborn, and if he needed to step on his neck for disrespecting Sasha, then it was done.

"We had a good time," she replied.

"Did his daddy go with y'all?" Blue didn't hold back nothing he felt was a pertinent detail.

Sasha rolled her eyes in the dark, knowing what he was getting at. "No, he didn't go with us, and no, I didn't see him. When I got there I called NJ and had him meet me downstairs."

Blue could sense the attitude in her voice, but he didn't give a damn. If he wanted to twenty-question her ass to death, she better respond.

Instead of cuddling underneath her, he rolled over onto his side and dozed off.

***

Gigi's viewing had finally come up, and Quamae was ready to close this final chapter in his life. All he needed to move on was to see her dead body in a coffin, and he could go on with life. He still hadn't found the missing check, but he was certain it would show up eventually. All throughout the week he had been packing up the twins' belongings. They were not his children, so there was no need in keeping anything that reminded him of the treachery.

After he finished loading up his backseat, he got into his whip and hauled ass to the church. On the way there he rode in silence. He needed time to think and figure out where the fuck was that check. See, the bitch was so clever that he didn't have a clue, but he wasn't gon' stop until he had it back in his hand.

The parking lot wasn't crowded yet, and that's what he was banking on. It would be distasteful to do what he needed to do in front of a jam-packed church. Bad enough he was doing it in front of the pastor.

Quamae killed the engine, got out of the car, and removed the two suitcases. As he approached the church, there were a few people standing outside talking, but he kept it moving without looking in their direction. Making his way into the chapel, he spotted Gigi's mom sitting on the first pew right up front, rocking back and forth. The sound of someone wailing from the pit of their stomach could be heard, but he couldn't tell if it was her or not as he stepped forward. The closer he got, the louder it became, and that's when he knew who the painful cries belonged to.

"Oh, Lord, not my baby. Why did you take her away from me and these babies?" her mother screamed out, as she continued to rock back and forth uncontrollably.

Quamae stopped alongside the pew where she sat and placed

his hand on her shoulder. "I'm so sorry for your loss, Ms. Pam."

She looked up with saddened, puffy red eyes, but she didn't say a word. It looked as if her eyes were bleeding. Her face was swollen as well. Gigi's death had really taken a toll on her, and she was barely making it through the days and nights. Eating wasn't an option. If she didn't have to care for those babies, there was no telling what she would've done.

Despite the fact she was grieving, he didn't waste any time placing the two suitcases beside her. Looking down at the suitcases, he said, "These are clothes for the kids. I know you can use them, and if you give me your address, I can have the rest of their things delivered to your home."

Ms. Pam's teeth chattered as she tried to speak. "Quamae, I'm confused. I spoke with Gigi and she told me you are the father of the babies. Why won't you keep them?"

Just the idea of telling her the truth made him feel a little bad for her because her daughter told her a bald-faced lie. He knew that bitch couldn't tell the truth if it slapped her in that lying-ass mouth of hers. "I hate to be the bearer of bad news, but those aren't my kids. She cheated on me, and we were broken up before all of this happened."

Her eyes stretched wide as he explained to her the situation at hand. It was like she didn't want to believe Gigi would lie to her. Tilting her head to the side, she asked, "Why would she lie to me?"

"You know, that's a very good question. But to be honest, I can't answer that for you. I don't know how she could do the things she did when all I did was take care of her."

Pam cut her eyes right before she rolled them hard enough for them to fall out of the sockets. "Let's not forget you were still a married man while y'all were together." Now was not the time to discuss her daughter's indiscretions, but he took it there. "So, you weren't faithful to either woman in your life."

"The difference between the both of us is she knew the truth about me. I didn't lie to her, and that's one thing I can't stand is a liar. All she had to do was tell the truth, but I can see where she

70

gets her way of thinking from."

"Excuse you, and what is that supposed to mean?"

"Nothing. I've said my piece. Now, call me when you are ready for the remainder of their things, and again I'm sorry for your loss." Quamae stepped away, leaving her mouth hanging to the floor without taking a second look back. Not once in the history of their relationship had he displayed cold feelings toward her mom, but her conniving daughter changed all of that. All that nice shit was out the window.

Gigi's casket was all white with purple flowers painted on it. There were dozens of flower arrangements that suggested she was loved by many, but not from him. He couldn't fathom the idea of wasting another dollar on that triflin'-ass bitch. Dead or alive.

Quamae stood there for a few seconds with his hands in his pockets to take in the view of her lifeless body. Once upon a time he was happy with her and really thought their marriage would turn out better than he and Sasha's, but that was far from the truth. As he took one more baby step, he was close enough to climb inside. Raising one hand, he placed it on her forehead, and she was cool to the touch. Then he leaned in and placed his lips next to her ear.

"I see they stitched yo' ass back together," he giggled, surprised they were able to put her back together again after her body had been dismembered. "This what I do to bitches and niggas that cross me. I send them through the gates before they ready. You ungrateful, disloyal, lying, conniving-ass ho. You thought you could take a nigga's kindness and love for a weakness. Bitch, you had me fucked up. I should've never left my wife for you, ol' mutt-ass ho. You made yo' bed, bitch, so sleep in it forever and just know I will never help yo' mammie with those kids. You should've found they real daddy. Now I got the last laugh, and I hope ya' ass burning right now."

Quamae rose up and adjusted his jacket, then walked away gracefully. The final chapter was finally closed, and he could move on with his life. When he stepped outside the church it was like a breath of fresh air, and he was ready to focus on his next mission. Pulling his cellphone from his breast pocket of his coat, he unlocked his phone and pressed number one for speed dial.

***

Sasha was sitting on the bed talking to Blue when her phone vibrated and sang *You Needed Me* by Rihanna. Both of them looked down at the screen at the unsaved number. She refused to answer the call, so she silenced it.

Blue was suspicious because of her past and the pajama incident the other night. The first person who came to mind was Nate. In his mind he wasn't convinced she didn't see that nigga or let him fuck her. "Who the fuck is that?" he snapped.

She took a deep breath as if she was irritated by the caller. "It's Quamae."

"What the fuck he callin' you for?" The name alone rubbed him the wrong way 'cause he hated that nigga with a passion, and all he wanted was to send him to hell on a one-way flight.

Sasha shrugged her shoulders and sucked her teeth. "I don't know."

"Well, answer it." At first she hesitated, and he sensed that. "Pick up the fuckin' phone now, and I ain't gon' repeat myself. Unless you started back fuckin' the nigga and that's why you don't wanna answer his call all of a sudden."

"You know damn well I'm not fuckin' him, so stop. We don't have a reason to talk, that's it." Her voice softened. "I don't know why he's callin'. I swear." She shrugged her shoulders.

"You heard what the fuck I said." In his mind he wondered what the real problem was, 'cause right now she was on that fuck-shit, and he wasn't buying that shit for one second.

Sasha was very apprehensive about picking up the phone, knowing he was only calling to make her foundation with Blue a shaky one. The last thing she wanted was a confrontation with her man. When she finally decided to pick it up, the ringing stopped. That relief was short-lived 'cause he called right back. This time she picked up without Blue having to be verbal about it. His cold stare was enough to make her obedient.

"Put it on speaker." Blue needed to hear everything he had to say. That way it would be out in the open.

Sasha did as she was told and sat Indian-style with the phone on her leg. "Hello." There was a slight tremble in her voice.

"What's up?" Quamae was still sitting in his truck outside of the church.

"Nothing." Her response was dry.

"I need to talk to you, and it's important. Can you meet me somewhere?"

"Huh?" Sasha's heart rate picked up speed and she became tense, praying he wasn't about to make any sexual advances or mention the fact she met him a while back.

"You heard what I said." He paused for a split second and thought to himself. "Oh, that nigga must be around you since you can't talk."

Blue nodded his head to assist her in answering his question. "No, he's not here." She had a bad feeling about the conversation on the way.

"Well, just listen to me. I want to apologize for everything I said and did to you. It wasn't okay that I cheated on you, and I should've never let Gigi come in between us." Quamae exhaled deeply. "It's gon' kill me to say this, but I forgive you for sleeping with Chauncey. My therapist shed light on your situation as a child and made me realize you were a product of your environment. And because you didn't get counseling, that assisted with your behavior as an adult."

Blue sat quietly and nodded his head in amusement. If he didn't know about Chauncey at that moment, she would've gotten her ass beat. As bad as he wanted to say something, he knew it was best he remained silent if he wanted answers. The only question now was what happened in her childhood that he knew nothing about?

"Is that right?"

"Yeah." Quamae cleared his throat. "I also wanna see Dream. Ever since I saw her I can't stop thinking about her. All I do is stare at her picture. I know she's mine, and that's why I want us to go and take a test together."

Sasha's eyes stretched as wide as Florida. That was the last thing she needed him to say, knowing how he felt about her husband.

Blue rose to his feet slowly and mugged her hard. He rubbed his hands together and bit down on his bottom lip.

She reached for his hand and attempted to speak. "Please –"

Before she could apologize for what he heard, Blue cocked back and knocked the words back down her throat.

Whap!

Then he snatched her phone up quick. Sasha covered her mouth to keep from making any noise and catching the blood from her split lip.

"Sasha!" Quamae shouted into the phone.

"Nah, nigga, it's me. Now, let's make one thing crystal muthafuckin' clear. Dream is my daughter, so you can get that shit out yo' head. Y'all won't be takin' no muthafuckin' test, either, so make this yo' last time callin' her phone."

Blue ended the call and threw her phone into the wall, causing her to jump. "What the fuck wrong wit' you?" He stepped closer to Sasha and mushed her in the face. "You took my baby to see that nigga? 'Cause he real muthafuckin' comfortable askin' you to meet him."

"I'm sorry," she cried. Words couldn't express the way she was feeling because he had never laid a hand on her until now. Suddenly he wasn't that sweet, innocent Blue she once knew.

"That's why you pretended to be sick last night, so I wouldn't touch you?" Tilting his head to the side, he asked the million-dollar question. "You back fuckin' this nigga?"

"No!" she cried. "I swear I'm not."

Snatching her up by the collar of her shirt, he pulled her close to his face so she could feel the words he was about to spit. "I'ma say this one time, and one time only. Keep my muthafuckin' daughter away from that nigga, and I'm not playin' wit' cho ass. 'Cause if you do, I'm fuckin' both of y'all up, and I promise you that."

Blue pushed her backward, releasing the grip he had on her. "Go clean yo' fuckin' face."

Sasha was trying hard to keep her cries silent as she eased off the bed and onto her feet. Over the time they had been together he was slowly revealing his true colors. All before he was against abuse, but to her his actions flowed so naturally.

When Sasha left the room, he sat down on the bed. Being a woman beater was something that wasn't embedded in his bloodline, but somehow she managed to bring it out of him with the slick shit she was trying to pull. Maybe this wasn't the relationship for him after all.

Destiny

Chapter 7

Chauncey walked back into his room and lay across the bed, thinking about the actions he took that landed him behind the brick wall. After he left the note for Ayesha, he turned himself in to the authorities. The guilt for murdering Monica and then the assault on Ayesha was too much to deal with. If he stayed out any longer there would be harsher repercussions. After confessing what he did to his attorney, he ushered him to the police station in an effort to get a deal for his confession.

His bunkmate, Juan, walked into the room carrying a newspaper. "You straight, homie? Everything cool at home?" he asked.

"Nah, but it is what it is." Chauncey was thinking about Ayesha and how she just up and disappeared. Granted, he jumped on her and left her, but he didn't expect her to get ghost like that. "I expect to ride this bid solo. These hos only want a nigga when he up, and when he get knocked, they on them knees for the next nigga."

"These hos ain't loyal," Juan sang while tossing the paper onto the top bunk. "Let's get outta here and snatch up some commissary."

Chauncey stood up on his feet. "Yeah, I'm with that. Go out there and round them niggas up while I take a piss."

On the spades table Chauncey was killing their opponents, Dee and Pablo. "Man, y'all some sorry-ass niggas." Juan felt comfortable using that word since he considered himself black. He was born and raised in the projects, right off of 10th terrace in the city. "I know y'all tired of losing."

"Shut the fuck up, you lame-ass Mexican," Dee replied.

"Bitch, I'm black and Latino, so you shut the fuck up and deal the cards," Juan argued.

Chauncey looked at his hand and said, "Game over, niggas. It's cleanup time. Come on, Juan, what you got over there?"

He looked at his hand and said, "I can get you three books,

homie."

"Oh yeah," Chauncey nodded his head up and down. "It's a wrap. Let's run this ten and get these busta-ass niggas up. Jump out yo' ride, nigga."

Dee led out with the ace of diamond, and all game faces were on. Dee and Pablo racked up two books off the bat. "That's all y'all getting, 'cause the rest is mine." Chauncey stood up, slapping his cards on the table. "Big joker, nigga."

Dee was talking shit with him. "That's all, nigga?"

Chauncey grinned, slapping down another card. "Li'l joker, nigga. Deuce, nigga. Get muthafuckin' naked, nigga."

Dee was pissed off when the game was over. Not only did he lose his commissary, he lost it three times back-to-back.

During all the commotion, no one heard the door pop when the officer walked in. "Thomas," he yelled. No one heard him, so he blew the whistle. That got everyone's attention. "Alright, little girls, can y'all hear me now?"

Chauncey responded first. "I got your 'little girl,' you faggot."

A voice behind him yelled, "That's not what your wife called me last night."

Officer Walker laughed. "I'm sure she called you a short-stabber." All the men laughed at his humor. He was actually a pretty cool officer. "Okay, Thomas, you have a visitor."

Chauncey jumped off the table, surprised because he wasn't expecting a visit. Then he figured it was his attorney coming to give him some info about a plea deal.

When he walked up to the window, to his surprise it was Ayesha, and she looked sexier than ever. Chauncey smiled because he was happy to see her. He picked up the phone. "Damn, baby, you looking good."

She smiled back. "So do you in your li'l orange suit." They shared a laugh.

"Damn, I thought you left a nigga for dead in this bitch."

"No, I've just been going through a lot, you know." Ayesha missed being with him, and now that he was going away for a long time, that would make it easier to leave him alone. But what hurt the most was the secret she kept from him. "I was in the hospital for a few days, but I'm good now."

"It's because of what I did to you, ain't it? Baby, I'm so sorry. I was fucked up out there, getting high and shit."

"No, that's not it, and I forgive you," she replied honestly. How could she be upset when her dirt was worse than what he did to her?

"You sure you okay?" Chauncey sat up in his seat and looked her in the eyes. "You pregnant?"

"No, I'm not pregnant, baby." Ayesha was feeling her emotions come on, so she decided to lighten their conversation. "I do miss us practicing."

"Shit, I miss it already." Chauncey took a deep breath. "And it's gon' be a long time before I nut up in that again."

"You haven't went to court yet? Did they say anything about giving you a bond?"

"That's not gon' happen just yet. My lawyer has a murder trial in front of the same judge on Monday, so I might have to wait until it's over before I can even see the judge."

She shifted in her seat. "So, when was the last time you spoke to him?"

"A few days ago."

"Oh," she replied with a puzzled look on her face. He could tell she had something on her mind and was holding something back from him. He just didn't know what it was.

"What's wrong? Did something happen?" he asked curiously.

Ayesha opened her mouth to answer his question, but she was taken aback, by the inmate standing behind Chauncey. Her pupils suddenly became dilated and her wind pipe was closing in on her. Ayesha gasped for air, but felt herself suffocating. Chauncey watched as she held her hand over her chest.

"Ayesha, baby, you okay?" Chauncey stood up and placed his hand on the glass. He never noticed anyone standing behind him.

Ayesha dropped the phone and her body collapsed to the floor.

"Help!" Chauncey shouted from the top of his lungs. Moments later two officers went to her aide while another escorted him back to his dorm.

Over the next few days Chauncey hadn't heard a word from Ayesha. Every call he attempted to make to her went unanswered. All he could think of was what caused her to pass out like that and if she was okay. Chauncey lost plenty of sleep thinking about the wellbeing of his girl.

The walk to medical was a long one. It was Chauncey and a few other inmates walking in a single file line through the corridors. Once they came up to the clinic, they were seated in the hallway on some hard, blue plastic chairs.

"They sho want a nigga uncomfortable in these hard-ass seats," Chauncey laughed. "Damn, the state cheap as fuck."

Juan laughed at his celly. "Uncle Sam trying to pocket all the cash for his li'l private vacays."

"Inmate Thomas." The nurse was standing at the door smacking hard on a piece of gum, holding a clipboard in her hand.

Chauncey got up out of his seat and looked down at Juan. "And they damn sho don't want you to forget that a nigga locked up." He walked toward the nurse with a smile. "I'm Thomas."

"Well, let's go. I ain't got all day."

"Coulda fooled me," Chauncey smirked.

Once they made it inside the room, he sat down on the stool.

"That's my seat, you get up on the table." After he moved, she continued. "I have read over your test results, and I want you to do the same. I will answer any questions you may have."

Chauncey went from line to line until he saw something he didn't want to see. "Nah, this wrong. Ain't no fuckin' way this is right. You better retest me and get this together."

"Mr. Thomas, calm down. I am here to help you."

"Fuck that!" he yelled. Chauncey jumped up and became belligerent, storming out of the room, cursing at everyone in his path. Two officers were standing by the door, and when they heard him they rushed over and tackled him to the ground with excessive force, knocking him out cold.

***

It was Monday morning, and Blue was up early getting dressed. Sasha was sitting on the edge of the bed feeding the baby, watching him in silence. They hadn't really been talking since he slapped the shit out of her and roughed her up a bit for being disrespectful. In her mind she was curious as to where he was going so early, but decided it was best not to question him on where he was going. If they were on better terms she would've said something and twenty-questioned his ass to death, but something told her to leave it alone in case he was on his Ike Turner shit today. The last thing she wanted was to be hit again. Too many ass-whoopings would humble a female and keep her mouth shut. That was a lesson she learned at the hands of Quamae.

After Blue finished getting himself together, he glanced over at her and kept his eyes on her for a moment. He was really trying to see where her head was at. Slapping her up wasn't his intention, but she had him fucked up if she thought he was gon' let that shit fly between her and that nigga. He had already warned her he would beat a bitch's ass if he was provoked. Deep down he really loved her, but now he was starting not to trust her. Ain't no telling what or who she been doing, and that hurt his heart, being oblivious to whatever it was.

Sitting down beside her, he kissed his daughter and looked Sasha in the eyes. "I'll be back in a couple of hours." She nodded her head. "I'm goin' to register for school, and I don't know how long it's gon' take, but when I get back we need to have a serious talk."

Sasha was nervous now because she didn't know what to expect from him when he returned. "Okay," she responded softly. Blue was everything to her, and she wanted it to work, so she was hoping he was gonna apologize for jumping on her.

Blue got into his truck and crunk up his sound system. Young Jeezy's *Let 'Em Know* was blazing through the speakers as he peeled out of the driveway, boppin' and rappin' to the beat. This shit had him lit, and he wasn't even on the liquor yet. Zippin' through the traffic, he was mad hype, and he made it to US-1 in no time and headed south.

I'ma show you how to kill 'em when they hate, dog.
Sometime ya gotta let a nigga know, dog.
Sometime ya gotta fuck a nigga ho, dog.
You nigga gonna learn who to fuck with.
Y'all hos gon' miss me with the fuck-shit.

The University of Miami wasn't too far from his house, so with his speed and the short distance he got there quick and parked on campus. When he stepped out of the truck, he peeped a flock of groupies checking him out. He already knew they was sweating his designer belt that held up his designer jeans, flashy truck, and icy jewelry. Blue walked past them without so much as a nod of his head, and he could hear them giggling and hissing at him, but he wasn't on that li'l girl behavior. He liked women who knew what they wanted and wasn't afraid to approach him, although he wasn't looking for another chick.

The campus was packed and students were everywhere. A few baddies caught his eye, but all he did was nod and keep it moving. He wasn't no friendly-ass nigga. "Damn these hos gon' make a nigga cheat," he mumbled while checking out their asses.

Continuing his journey, he walked to the front of the school and through the doors to the admissions office. That muthafucka was even packed. "Damn, a nigga gon' be in this bitch all day," he complained while he signed in so he could be seen by an advisor.

When he was done, he found a seat and checked his surroundings. It ain't like he was paranoid or nothing like that, he was simply checking out the merchandise that walked in and out of those doors. One female in particular caught his attention when she walked in. The way she strutted across the floor displayed her confidence, and he was hooked.

Shorty was cute and definitely a brown-skinned bombshell, just how he liked them. What he liked the most is the fact she looked like a lame. Those were the best ones, but sometimes them hos ended up being crazy in the end.

He watched her as she stood at the counter talking to another student. Apparently she was already enrolled 'cause he didn't see her sign in and she seemed so comfortable. His eyes stretched wide as quarters when she leaned over the counter on her tippy-toes to grab something. The gap between her legs showed her pussy print from the back, and he could imagine bending her over and fuckin' the shit outta her.

Blue grinned and shook his head. "Goddamn, li'l mama." The throbbing between his legs let him know he had gone too long without sliding in some twat.

Wild thoughts were in his head, and that wasn't what he needed right now, but he couldn't help it. There were too many unresolved issues with Sasha, and he needed to get that in order.

Not even ten seconds later her sexy ass twirled around and walked in his direction. The seat next to him had just become available, and that's exactly where she was headed. Stopping in front of him, she smiled and asked, "Is someone sitting here?"

"Yeah, you," he smiled back.

"Thank you." She was blushing hard. There were a lot of boys on campus, but no one was as fine as the one sitting in front of her. Right after she walked into the admissions office she peeped him and was determined to get him. Her girl was working the counter, so she did the most while she stood there, bending over, reaching for a piece of paper and a pen. She knew he was watching her, so she wanted him to enjoy the view until she joined him. And if they hit it off, he would get to sample the goodies.

As soon as she sat down, he caught a whiff of her scent. The fruity flavor tickled his nose, arousing him immediately. Before he could compliment her on the perfume she was wearing, she was engaging him in small talk.

"I've never saw you on campus before. Are you new here?"

He couldn't resist looking into her pretty brown eyes with the twinkle in them. "I'm new this semester, but that's only because I took a hiatus for a while."

The smile on her face never left. "Well, it's nice to have you back."

"You say that like you know me." Blue ran his hand across his neatly-shaved beard and licked his lips. He knew females were crazy about bearded niggas.

"No, but I wouldn't mind getting to know you." She played with the keys in her hand. Being shy wasn't her forte, but that was the role she needed to portray to get what she wanted. The last thing she needed was to show her other side. It was too early for that.

"Oh, that can definitely be arranged."

What started out as harmless flirting was quickly turning into something else when she pulled out a piece of paper from her pants pocket.

"Darian Joyner," a woman shouted loudly across the room, interrupting their conversation.

Blue looked up and saw it was the advisor calling, so he stood up and acknowledged her. "Right here." Before he walked off, he turned his attention back to shorty. "I'll be right back."

Rising to her feet, she handed him the paper she was holding. "Call me."

He looked down at the number, but there was no name attached. "So, who am I asking for when I call?"

She extended her hand to him. "I'm Emani."

Blue kissed her hand. "It was nice meeting you, Miss Emani. You'll be hearing from me soon."

"I hope so," she winked.

Chapter 8

NJ was sprawled out across his bed watching ESPN. The constant flashing from his cellphone caught his attention. When he finally looked down, he saw he had seven missed calls from Jazz. She was determined to speak with him, but he wasn't ready for that just yet. The idea of him becoming a father at 16 wasn't sitting well with him. NJ was already a product of the same situation, and look at how that turned out for him. Standing on the outside looking in, it seemed bad, but he was doing what was best for the both of them because he knew his temper.

The point he was trying to make was to simply show her how it would feel to be alone in hopes he could sway her decision. Hopefully his actions would teach her a baby would not keep him at all, 'cause he was certain that's what it was, and at any given moment he could get up and walk away whenever he felt like it. Jazz didn't understand the consequences of her actions. The life he lived could force her to become a single mother at any given time, leaving her to struggle with trying to go to school, work, and trying to make ends meet.

It wasn't long before he got tired of seeing her name pop up on his screen. Powering off his phone, he tossed it to the side of him and went back to watching sports. Not even five minutes later there was a knock on the door.

Knock! Knock!

"What now?" he mumbled. Nobody wanted him to kick back and relax, and he was ready to snap.

"NJ," his father yelled.

"It's open," he yelled back.

Nate opened the door, taking a quick peek to make sure he was alone. "What you doin'?"

"Watchin' sports."

"You got a visitor," he responded, rolling to his side.

NJ's eyes stretched wide when he saw Jazz step from behind his father. Now he wished maybe he had answered her calls after all. The one thing he was certain about was the fact she loved to make a scene. But pregnant or not, he'd slap fire from her ass if she stepped him wrong.

Jazz paused in front of Nate and turned to face him with a half-smile. "Thank you."

"I'll just leave the two of you alone so you can talk in private," he said, then backed up and closed the door behind him.

NJ's body language gave the impression he didn't want to be fucked with, but he couldn't help but notice her stomach was poking out slightly. Since she had a small frame it was barely noticeable, but he knew her body well, and her stomach had always been flat. That disturbed his soul badly. Shaking his head, he turned back to continue what he was watching.

Jazz was a nervous wreck, but that didn't stop her from walking over to the bed and taking a seat next to him. The rejection and treatment she was receiving from her baby's father was not something she expected. Yeah, he had a bad temper, but he never displayed any ill feelings toward her until she turned up pregnant. She wouldn't wish this on her worst enemy.

Utilizing the silence between them, she played with her fingers and got her thoughts together. A long five minutes passed, and he still hadn't acknowledged the fact she was present, but she had to find the strength to speak up.

"NJ," she spoke softly. "So, you just gon' sit there and pretend like you don't see me right here?"

NJ didn't bother to take his eyes off the television, not even for a second. "I ain't blind. Who the fuck you think I am, Ray Charles or some shit?"

"But you not talking to me, though," she whined, trying to get his attention.

"Ain't nothin' to talk about."

"No, we have a lot to talk about."

"Oh, you finally changed your mind?" NJ finally looked over at her, and if she said what he wanted to hear, then things could go back to the way they were.

Jazz hung her head low. All the while she had been gone, he still hadn't changed at all. "I don't understand why you don't want me to have our baby."

NJ took a deep breath and exhaled loudly just to be rude. The fact she was oblivious to the situation is what was blowing him. "For the last time, we are not ready to be parents. Shit, you damn near a child ya'self," he snapped, trying to get his point to sink into that thick-ass skull of hers.

That was an insult to her, so she had to clap back. "Now I'm a child?" Rolling her neck, she got up in his face. They were close enough to kiss. "But I was old enough to suck and fuck you, though. Now that yo' li'l pull-out method didn't work, I'm a child. You have a lot of fuckin' nerve."

NJ stared at her long and hard. She was skating on thin fuckin' ice, yelling in his face like she lost her goddamn mind. "And this is why I been ignoring yo' calls. You always on that dumb shit." Tuning her out completely, NJ rolled over and faced the opposite direction.

Everything about the visit had gone terribly wrong. That was not the outcome she had hoped for. She hopelessly thought if he saw her in the flesh carrying their child, he would have a change of heart, but she had been sadly mistaken.

Silence was bestowed upon them for the next 15 minutes, and she could've sworn she heard him snoring as if he was asleep. Just like before, she had to initiate the conversation. "NJ, please talk to me," she begged as the tears began to well up in her eyes and cascade down her brown cheeks slowly. Her skin was radiant with that pregnancy glow.

Her sniffles were loud, but he pretended not to hear them. Comforting her wasn't what he wanted to do unless it was under one particular circumstance. "If the convo ain't 'bout that abortion, then I have nothin' to say."

His vicious words spewed from his tongue like venom, poisoning every good memory she shared with him. Jazz had the hardest time digesting the fact she could love someone who didn't give a fuck about her. There was no regard to her feelings, yet she sat there allowing him to hurt her feelings and make her feel like shit. The words of her aunt played in her head like a broken record: *You young girls are young, dumb, and full of cum. Don't care nothing about school 'cause you too busy thinking about dick.*

With him being so adamant about not having this baby, her family would never let her live that down. She would be called every name in the book from slut, tramp, and loose to jezebel. Every name except for a child of God. There was only one person who would never switch up on her, and that was her favorite cousin who treated her more like a sister, Blue. Passing judgment wasn't his thing, and he would stand by her side through all of her trials and tribulations.

The longer she sat there, the more her sadness was rapidly turning into hate, and she was ready for any repercussions that were about to come her way. "NJ, you acting like I made this baby by myself, and that's not fair. You had the opportunity to prevent this from happening just as much as I did. This baby is coming whether you want it to or not," she folded her arms across her chest and sucked her teeth, "so you might as well get ready to be a daddy."

"I ain't getting' ready for shit, so miss me with all that bullshit. You steady talkin' 'bout having a baby, but you don't have no fuckin' money." NJ jumped out of the bed quick and stood to his feet. "You so fuckin' stupid, bruh." And he walked out of the room.

Jazz sat there thinking of a comeback for his ass. She was a lot of things, but stupid wasn't something she wanted to claim.

A few minutes later NJ returned drinking a soda. He climbed back into the bed and went back to what he was doing.

By this time Jazz was ready to pick a fight. Being pregnant, she figured she was safe, so it was time to get the ball rolling. Rising to her feet, she stood over him and waited until he put the soda can to his mouth. As soon as it touched his lips, she slapped it from his hands. The soda slashed all over his face, shirt, and bed.

"What the fuck is your problem?" he yelled.

Placing her hands on her hips, she mean-mugged him. "Do I have your fuckin' attention now?"

NJ jumped up and snatched the wet shirt off his body and threw it in her face. "You want me to beat yo' ass?"

"And you wanna go to jail?" she clapped back.

"Fuck jail. Fuck you and that baby, crazy-ass bitch," he spat, standing directly in her face.

She could feel specks of spit hit her face, and before she knew it she cocked back with her fist balled up and hit him dead in the face. That was the last straw. He had disrespected her for the last time.

NJ was definitely caught off guard by the impact of the punch as he stumbled just a little. Catching his balance, he leaned forward with his arm in the air and backhanded her in the eye. A loud scream escaped her lips. Being slapped wasn't what she expected at all, but that didn't stop her from fighting back. Jazz ignored the fact she was pregnant, put it to the back of her mind, and charged at him with her arms flying full-force.

NJ grabbed her by the arms and pushed her backward until her body crashed against the wall, causing it to vibrate. "Bitch, keep yo' muthafuckin' hands off of me befo' I fuck yo' ass up."

"Let go of my arms." She tried to pull away, but his grip was too strong.

"Ain't lettin' go of shit," he yelled in her face.

"I'm not playing with you. Let go of my fuckin' arms."

"You a stupid-ass bitch."

"Fuck you. Yo' mammie that abandoned you is a bitch, fuck-nigga," Jazz coughed and spit in his face, hittin' him where it hurt.

At that moment he let go of her arms and wiped his face. He was in disbelief she could be so disrespectful and try him like that. NJ bit down on his lip and rubbed his face. Moving swift like lightening, he smacked her twice in the face and stepped in close. Placing both his hands around her throat, he squeezed her tight and slammed her against the wall repeatedly.

"NJ, stop before I lose the baby," she screamed. Her cries fell on deaf ears, but suddenly the Lord answered her prayers because his room door flung open and hit the wall.

"NJ, what the fuck you doing to that girl? Let her go," Nate shouted while taking long strides toward them.

As soon as he was close enough, he snatched NJ up by the collar. He immediately released her from his grip. "You don't put your hands on no female, nigga. What the fuck wrong with you?"

He looked his daddy in the face. "Fuck her. She deserved that shit for spitting on me."

Nate shook his head and turned his attention to Jazz. She was on the floor with one hand on her neck, gasping for air. He squatted down to her level and placed his hand on her shoulder. "You okay?"

She looked up with tears in her eyes and shook her head no. "You wanna know why I did it?" Her voice cracked with each syllable spoken.

"What happened?" He grabbed her by the arm and helped her get on her feet.

"I'm pregnant." She was still trying to catch her breath. "And he wants me to get an abortion, but I don't want to."

Nate turned back to face NJ, trying to find the words to say to him, but before he could get a word in NJ was explaining himself.

"I tried to tell her we ain't ready to be parents."

Nate cleared his throat. "Jazz, step out the room for a few so I can talk to him." It was time he kicked some knowledge to his inexperienced son.

Jazz honored his wishes and grabbed her phone on the way out to go to the bathroom. Inside, she sat down on the toilet to relieve herself. After she was done, she pulled some tissue from the roll, wiped herself, and looked at it. On the paper were specks on blood. She panicked and jumped up to find blood in the toilet.

"Help!" she screamed.

Chapter 9

"So, you really thinking about getting' out the game for real?" Zoe said while taking a pull from the blunt he rolled just minutes ago.

"Nah, bruh. I'm gettin' out the game. Ain't no thinkin' 'bout it." Blue nodded his head back and forth, confirming his next moves. "I have a daughter to think about, and my ol' girl keep reminding me I promised her I would finished medical school. So, you already know how that go."

"Yeah, I know, bruh. And I ain't mad at cha." Zoe passed the weed and chuckled. "Goddam school boy, Blue. The streets gon' miss ya."

"How I'm feelin' right now, fuck the streets. They ain't do shit but take my uncle, Quint, and TJ out too muthafuckin' early. The streets don't love a nigga." Blue took a long pull and filled his lungs before he exhaled the smoke.

"You can say that shit again. Lauderdale done got crazy as fuck. These niggas hate to see the next man chasing that bag. The minute you do," Zoe demonstrated a gun with his fingers. "*Pow*! They takin' a nigga away from they family and have the nerve to show up at ya funeral, rockin' ya t-shirt and shit like they ain't have nothin' to do with it."

"Facts, bruh. You already know." Blue passed the weed back to his homie. "I'ma stack this paper for another month and it's over. Ya feel me?"

"G-shit, my nigga."

Blue's phone rang, but he ignored it since he was already in the middle of a conversation and vibing with his boy. A few seconds later it started up again. This time he picked the phone up and looked at the screen. It was Jazz, but she would have to wait until he was free. Placing the phone face down on the counter, he went back to the subject at hand.

"Shorty wanna talk bad as fuck," Zoe laughed.

"Nah, it ain't nothin' like that. I'm faithful," he answered truthfully.

"Bullshit, my nigga. I know you."

"That's my li'l cousin Jazz calling me," Blue laughed. "You wit' the shits, dawg."

"Nah, I just know how my nigga get down, that's all." Zoe had been friends with Blue long enough to know he loved females and kept them on heavy rotation.

"I'm a changed man. A family man. I cut off all my hos. Maybe you should try that."

"These hos just like Lay's potato chips to you. You can't have just one," Zoe burst out in laughter.

"And that right there just got your black card revoked," Blue couldn't help but laugh at his humor.

"Damn, dawg, that was a bad joke?" Zoe laughed like that was the best one yet.

"Hell yeah, it was. Fuck you thought?"

Blue received a text notification, so he picked up his phone and stared down at the screen for a few moments. Zoe sat and watched his eyes move from side to side rapidly. Whatever he was reading was long and apparently juicy, 'cause he hadn't looked up yet.

Of course that made him curious. "You good?"

"Nah." Blue put his foot down and got up from the bar stool with a scowl on his face.

"What it is? We need to run down on a nigga or some shit?" He was ready to smash on any nigga his homie had a problem with.

"It's cool, man. I gotta hit it, though."

Blue walked out of the kitchen and made his way to the living room where Lelah and Sasha were sitting and talking. They were so caught up in a deep conversation they didn't see him approaching them.

"Sasha, let's go," he frowned.

She looked up smiling, but that quickly changed when she saw that look on his face. "What's wrong, baby? Is everything okay?"

"Let's go."

Sasha didn't hesitate getting up out the seat and grabbing her purse. "See you later, girl. We'll finish this another time."

Lelah stood up to give her a hug. "Yeah, call me tomorrow."

"I will," she replied.

Blue and Sasha walked outside. His strides were short and quick. In order to keep up with him, she had to move just as fast. She was tempted to ask him again, but used her better judgment to wait until they got in the truck. He clicked the locks, got into the driver's seat, and fired up the engine.

"What's going on?" she asked again. "Did something happen?"

Without saying a word to her, he opened up his messages and handed the phone over. Sasha took it from his hand and began to read the message in its entirety. After she was done, she handed it back to him.

"I'm gon' fuck yo' son up," he barked and pointed his finger in her direction. "Since he wanna hit on a female, he better hope his hands up to date."

"And what is that gon' solve?" Sasha turned to face him so she could look him in the eyes.

"The same thing it solved when he put his hands on my cousin." Blue hit the gas, peeling out of the parking lot in a hurry.

"Blue, I love you, but I can't let you hurt my son. I'll talk to him and we can get to the bottom of what happened together, but there are two sides to every story."

"And what you think a talk gon' solve? This li'l nigga is out of order, and he needs to be put in his place 'cause he fuckin' wit' the wrong one."

"You need to calm down, because we don't know what happened over there. We –"

Sasha was interrupted by the song playing from her phone. When she took the phone out of her purse, she saw it was Nate.

"This his daddy right here." Swiping the green button to the right, she put the phone to her ear. "Hello."

"Hey, Sasha, we have a problem," Nate said.

"And what's that?" She chose her words carefully to keep the coo-coo next to her from coming out of his cage.

"NJ got Jazz pregnant and he don't want the baby, so they was over here fighting and shit."

Sasha needed a few moments to gather her thoughts. The bomb he just dropped on her was entirely too much to take in. "Hold up." she held her finger in the air to stop him from talking like he was standing in front of her. "NJ got who what?" She could barely talk.

"The girl he dating is pregnant," he reiterated.

"She's pregnant?" she repeated as if she didn't hear him clear as day the first time he said it.

"Apparently so."

Blue took his eyes off the road to make sure he heard that correctly. "I know my cousin ain't pregnant." He was trying his best to stay focused on the cars in front of him and listen to the conversation at the same time.

Sasha pointed her finger at him, signaling him to wait. "Where are they now?"

"He in the room, and she in the living room lying on the couch, talking to the 911 operator."

"For what?" Sasha's voice elevated up at the sound of the police being involved. "Don't let them do nothing to my son. I'm on my way." She could feel herself becoming teary-eyed, and the rate of her heart increased. Just thinking about all of the recent violence against black men had her on edge.

"You know I ain't lettin' shit happen to our son. I got him, so try and calm down." Nate was a protector, and he meant every word he said. It didn't matter that he had just gotten out of prison. The only thing he cared about was protecting the ones he loved.

"So, why is she on the phone with them?"

"When she went to the bathroom she was spotting, so she wanna go to the hospital and check on the baby." He hoped that would keep her sane for a while.

"I'm still on my way." There wasn't a snowball's chance in hell she'd abandon him again.

"We'll be here," he replied.

"Okay."

Sasha put her phone away and grunted loudly. "I am so not in the mood for this bullshit."

"What happened?" Blue asked. The hostility in his voice faded a tad bit, but he was still pissed.

"Apparently your cousin pregnant, and NJ wants her to have an abortion, but she doesn't want to."

Blue needed something to take his frustrations out on, so he threw a right hook into the steering wheel. "This that fuck-shit I be talkin' 'bout." The whole situation had him on ten, and he was ready to bash a muthafucka's head in, on God.

"You need to relax and find out what happened while you over here losing your mind and shit," Sasha snapped back, tired of his ranting and raving.

"This ain't the first time he put his hands on her, but it will be the last, and I promise you that."

"Oh, you mean like the way you slapped me up the other day? You can put your hands on me, but when it happens to a female in your family, it's a problem?" Sasha shook her head. "You funny."

"Don't start that shit, 'cause you know why I did that. It ain't like I slapped you for nothing." He looked at her out of the corner of his eye. "You tried me wit' that nigga."

"You can't prove shit 'cause I ain't did shit." Brushing him off, she turned to the side and gazed out the window. "I'm not about to argue with you about this 'cause clearly something is wrong with you. I haven't fucked that man since I left him."

When they finally arrived in the complex and pulled in front of the building, Nate could be seen outside, talking with one of the paramedics. They had Jazz on a stretcher and NJ was off to the side, staring off into space. Blue parked directly behind them, put the truck in park, and jumped out with Sasha on his tail. He was on a mission and dared anyone to get in the way.

"Jazz, you okay?" he asked while staring at the red mark on her face. Since he knew where it came from, there was no need in asking her about it.

"I think so," she replied.

"Why the fuck you didn't tell me you was pregnant? Does

your mama know?"

The paramedic tending to her looked back at Blue like he was crazy. "Sir, you need to calm down."

"Do ya job and don't worry about me." He could catch a fade, too, coming at him sideways.

"No." She had been keeping the pregnancy a secret out of fear of her mother making her get an abortion.

"How the fuck yo mama don't know and y'all live under the same roof?" He knew her mother was an alcoholic, but damn. How could she not know her own daughter was carrying a child?

Jazz took a deep breath. "You know she doesn't pay me any attention." And that was the main reason she wanted to go through with the pregnancy. Having someone to love her unconditionally was all she ever wanted, and having the baby would fill that empty void.

"Go to the hospital. I'll be up there soon." Blue kissed her on the forehead and went in the direction of where Sasha was standing with her son and baby daddy. He could hear the sound of the paramedic pulling off.

"Aye, what I told you about puttin' yo' hands on my cousin?" He mugged NJ hard as hell as he approached him.

Nate wasn't going for that shit, though. He stepped in front of Blue, blocking his path with his hand out and placed it on his chest. "Aye, don't roll up on my son like that when you don't know what the fuck goin' on." He was a few inches taller than Blue, so they weren't eye-to-eye.

"Fuck that! He shouldn't be hittin' on no muthafuckin' female." Blue puffed his chest out to let him know he couldn't intimidate him.

Sasha grabbed his arm. "Calm down and listen," she pleaded.

NJ stepped from behind his dad and mugged Blue back. He knew he was safe in his daddy's presence. "She started the shit, and she spit on me. I bet she didn't tell you that."

Blue wasn't trying to hear none of that shit. "I don't care. You need to learn how to keep your hands to yo'self." He knew she was wrong, but he needed to make a point.

"Listen, nigga, I ain't gon' say it no' mo' 'cause I swear you don't want these problems. You need to go and talk to ya family 'bout being disrespectful." He looked over at Sasha. "Take yo' nigga home, 'cause I ain't knock a nigga out since I been free, but he can be the first."

"So, what you wanna do?"

Blue was ready to catch that fade, but she knew no good would come from the two of them fighting. Stepping between them, she placed both hands on his chest. "Blue, let's go."

Blue was so pissed all he could see was red, so he pushed Sasha out of the way. "I ain't leavin' this muthafucka! Fuck outta here. If this nigga didn't spend most of his life locked up, he could've raised this nigga right."

As soon as his last word left his lips, Nate hauled off and punched Blue dead in his shit, but he shook that shit off quick and squared up with Nate. "That was a sucka-ass move, nigga."

"I'ma beat ya like ya daddy should've did a long time ago." Nate pulled his shirt over his head and tossed it on the ground.

"Beat that nigga ass, daddy," NJ shouted from the sideline.

"Stop, please!" Sasha screamed.

From there it was gloves-off, and Blue swung first, but Nate dodged the hit and snuffed him with an uppercut. To Blue's advantage, his opponent was taller than him, and he was able to deliver a body shot. After a few swings, they locked up.

"Break it up! Break that shit up right now." The voice blaring through the intercom got everyone's attention.

Sasha stepped in, grabbing Blue's shirt in an effort to pull them apart. "The police is here, so stop before y'all go to jail." She looked over at NJ. "Grab your daddy."

NJ did as he was told before the police finally made it to where they were. Both men were breathing hard, but no one resisted. The last thing Nate needed was to go to jail again after spending more than a decade in there.

There were two officers who emerged from the patrol car with their hands on their holsters. The first officer was a husky, older cat, and the other was a little bit younger. It was easy to determine he was a rookie. "What's the problem here?" he asked.

"They just had a little misunderstanding, but it's all good now," Sasha tried to explain.

"Thanks, baby doll," he winked at her with a creepy smirk, "but I was talking to the muscle-bound nigga that just got out."

Nate eyeballed that nigga hard as fuck. He was ready to spaz on his ass. "Bruh, who you talkin' to like that?"

The officer stepped a little closer so he could get closer to Nate. "Tighten up, soft-ass git, before I take off my belt and whoop ya ass."

Sasha was confused because she thought he was talking to her son, and apparently so did NJ. Looking over at his mother, he had this mean snarl on his face. "Who the fuck this nigga talkin' to?"

Not wanting any confrontation between her son and the officer, Sasha elbowed NJ in his side. "Hush, 'cause I don't need them fuckin' with you." She cut her eyes and looked over at Nate. Blue was at her side, looking like he was ready to body the father-son duo, rocking side-to-side.

Meanwhile, Nate was sizing up the chump-ass officer who was slowly approaching him. It was dark outside, so that impaired his vision just a little, but once he was close enough his memory came back. "You couldn't whoop me when I was a jitty-bug, nigga, so you know ain't shit change."

Nate and the officer stepped close to one another, slapped hands, and G-hugged. "When the hell did you come home? I thought yo' ass wasn't gon' make it back to the free world."

Nate rubbed his chin. "Don't ever count a nigga out, ya' dig?"

Officer Brooks looked back at his partner. "Stand down, it's all good." Then he quickly turned his attention back to the old neighborhood's wild child. Growing up, he would always catch Nate doing shit he had no business doing as a child. Back in the day he had sticky fingers, and he would always steal from the convenience stores.

***

One day Nate decided to steal a car when he was 13, and Brooks caught him. He tossed his scrawny ass in the back of the police car. Nate didn't know what the hell was going on, but he kept it cool.

Brooks drove him around for 30 minutes before he pulled over at the park. Nate was confused as hell 'cause he wasn't sure what to expect. "What we doing here? I thought I was going to jail."

Looking over his shoulder, he growled, "Hush yo' damn mouth until I tell you to talk."

For the first time in his life Nate did as he was told. All he wanted to do was go home and forget about what he did to lead him up to this point. In his heart he knew the officer was going to do something to him. The streets were dark as fuck, and there wasn't a single soul hanging at the park that night.

Brooks finally opened up the door and stepped out with something in his hand. Nate never took his eyes off him as he walked around to the passenger's side. Opening up the door, Nate leaned back just a little.

"Man what you doing?" his voice cracked.

"Shut up and get out." He then snatched Nate out by his collar and threw him against the car. Breathing down in his face, he spoke through gritted teeth. "You think it's cool to be out stealing cars and shit? Yo' black ass must wanna go to prison, 'cause these crackas will lock yo' ass up and throw away the key."

Nate just stood there without a thought or rebuttal, trying to figure out what the hell was going on for a few moments. And that was when it dawned on him. "You about to kill me?"

"Nah, but I'm about to do something yo' daddy should've did a long time ago." Brooks stepped back, raised his hand at Nate, and struck him with a hard-ass leather belt.

Nate screeched and tried to move, but he couldn't get away. The grip he had on him was too tight. His ass-whooping lasted for all of five minutes, but not once did Nate cry. He did everything he could to hold it in. Brooks knew he wasn't making any progress, so he continued for five more minutes.

After the last time, Nate finally broke down and cried. "I

won't steal again. I'm sorry."

"You better not, 'cause if you do, it's gon' be a lot worse than before."

***

"I see some shit ain't change in the chain gang," he smirked, referring to the fight.

"You know how it is when young niggas think they got something on a real muthafuckin' G." He looked over at Blue and nodded his head. In return, he mugged him back.

The radio on Officer Brooks' waist said something about gunshots in the area, catching everyone's attention. "I'm in the area. Copy that."

"Can we leave now?" Sasha was already agitated, so she was dying to get out of dodge.

Brooks heard Sasha, but he didn't reply. Instead, he continued talking to Nate. "I feel ya', but I gotta slide up outta here. I'ma fuck witcha later. This where you live?"

"Yeah," Nate replied.

"Here, take my card. Give me a holla and stay outta trouble."

"No doubt." They shook hands one last time and he walked off, heading back to his patrol car. When he opened up the car door, he realized they were still standing in the same spots. "Everybody who don't live here, go home before I take you in for trespassing."

That was all they needed to hear before they went their separate directions. Blue was still heated as he walked to his truck.

"This shit ain't over. I got something for that ass," he smirked and jiggled his keys in his hand.

Chapter 10

Since the fight between Nate and Blue, things had been really rough for Sasha at home. She and Blue barely spoke, but when they did it was only in reference to the baby. Other than that all they did was argue about any and everything they could think of, especially the situation between NJ and Jazz. In her eyes it was childish, but she couldn't tell him shit when it came down to his hot-in-the-ass cousin.

"So, how long we gon' keep doing this?" Curiosity was killing the cat, but Sasha had another feline that was dying to be killed, and if he didn't tighten up soon, she'd be back in Somerset riding Nate's dick.

"I'm good. What you talkin' 'bout?" Right then he was taking playing dumb to another level.

"You know exactly what I'm talking about, so stop playing games."

Blue's phone buzzed, notifying him he had a text message. Before he opened it, he looked up at Sasha. "I'm good." He smiled, then opened up the message. It was Emani. Changing her name was mandatory.

Admissions: Hey sexy. How r u?
Darian: Lol…. You the sexy one
Admissions: I'm glad you noticed ☺ Wyd
Darian: Making moves
Admissions: I wanna see you
Darian: I think I can arrange that
Admission: Please do
Darian: A'ight I'll hit you in a few

Sasha was sitting on the bed with her arms folded across her chest with a major attitude. "Are you finished now?"

"Why you trippin'?" Blue tucked his phone away in his pocket.

"Nah, it ain't me. It's you," she pouted.

"I wasn't aware silence was an issue." Blue stretched out across the bed and laid his head on the pillow.

"Yeah, silence speaks volumes, in case you didn't know." Sasha patted the top of her head to stop her weave from itching. "I just don't get you. You hard-down pissed off with my son because he hit your cousin, but at the same time you okay with that fact she spit in his face, and that shit don't make sense to me. Then you had the nerve to push me."

"Now, you know that wasn't intentional. Yo' punk-ass baby daddy caught me off guard."

On the defense, she snapped, "You started that shit. I told you to calm down, but no, you wanna try and attack my son. You thought his daddy was just gonna sit there and not do nothing."

Blue had to sit up from the hostility in her voice. "So you defending this nigga?"

"Just stop," placing her palm toward his face, she told him to talk to the hand, "'cause now you being ridiculous. That fight should've never took place to begin with. All you had to do was listen to me."

"Okay, you win," he surrendered. "I'm over it."

"I'm not trying to win anything. I'm only stating the facts. Both NJ and Jazz are to blame, and you jumping in when we both know they'll be back together."

"Not if I can help it."

"And what the hell is that supposed to mean?" It was clear to her their conversation was going nowhere. "They're having a baby together, and I'm pretty sure it's not over between them."

"Yeah, okay."

Fed up with the back-and-forth, Sasha got up and put on her shoes. "I'm done arguing with you about this. The shit is stupid, and there's no talking to you, so fuck it."

Blue watched as she packed a bag for Dream. When she was done, she grabbed her things and snatched her baby from her bed. "I'll be back later."

"Where you going?" Now she had him curious.

"I need a break from you," she replied.

"You must be going to ya' baby daddy house."

"If you must know, I am not going over there, thank you very much." Sasha rolled her eyes and stormed out of the room, leaving him in his thoughts.

Blue grabbed his cellphone and sent out two text messages.

Joker: I need you to handle something for me

Admissions: I'm free what's up

***

Sasha pulled up to the address she was given and disabled the GPS. Although she was familiar with the area, checking her surroundings was mandatory. After being with Quamae for so long, she knew what to look for. Living the high life always had its perks and downsides, so she was aware she needed to be cautious at all times.

When things looked okay from the outside, she opened up her call log and pressed the green icon. "Hello," he answered.

"I'm outside," she replied.

"I'm coming out. Sit tight."

"Okay." She hung up the phone and placed it inside her purse. Looking into the mirror, she applied some lipstick to her lips and pressed them together, making sure she covered every inch. Upon closing the visor, she glanced over to her right and saw who she was waiting for stepping out of the door. When he was within a few feet from the vehicle, she opened up the door and pushed it out with her foot.

"What's up, wifey?" Quamae smiled.

Sasha giggled. "Uh, don't you mean ex-wife? In case you forgot, I signed the divorce papers you sent to me."

She would be lying if she said signing those papers wasn't hard for her. Despite all the drama and pain she caused him and herself, she still loved Quamae. When she took those vows, she knew they would be together forever. Maybe if she had received

103

help when she was younger her life would've played out differently. See, if the shoe was on the other foot and he was the only one doing all the cheating, she would've never left him, but men and women were different. A woman could never cheat on a man and be taken back. His ego and pride wouldn't allow it, and that was the reason the two of them were no longer together. Society definitely had a way of fucking people up.

"The papers were never finalized. Besides, we're forever, and don't you forget it." His cockiness was on one thousand, but it was a complete turn-on.

"Says who?" she smiled.

Nodding his head toward the backseat, he replied, "My little princess behind you." The more he saw Dream, the more he fell in love with her. There were no results confirmed to say the truth, but in his heart he already knew the answer. "So, you came by to honor my request and get a DNA test done?"

"Can we go inside and talk about this?" She removed the keys from the ignition and clutched them in her hand, all while staring into his brown eyes.

"Sure. Let's go." Quamae grabbed her hand and helped her out of the car. It was evident something was still there by the way he held her hand, as if he didn't wanna let go.

"I see the old you is slowly coming back." It was nice to see the good in him for a change. Both of them stood there for a few seconds, just looking into one another's eyes. "That's a good thing." It was funny how she hated him a while back, and now that she was standing in his presence, he had her with butterflies in her stomach. It was either that or gas. She wasn't too sure, but seeing his sexiness all dressed up in a suit made her juices flow. She would definitely need to concentrate on keeping her panties on.

"Yeah, I'm a changed man." He adjusted his tie and licked his juicy lips, making them extra wet and succulent. "I'm a distinguished gentlemen, but a work in progress, though." The therapist was responsible for his sudden change. Reflecting back on his past, he realized he and his wife had more in common than he ever cared to admit.

"Good for you. I'm happy to hear that." She meant that genuinely. "Get the baby out of the car before it gets hot and we both end up in jail."

Quamae finally let go of her hand. "Take a look around. What do you see?"

Sasha's eyes roamed around at the things she had already taken a look at just moments ago. "I checked my surroundings before you came out here."

Heading to the passenger's side, he said, "Nah, look at the building." Opening up the door, he smiled when he saw her face. "Hey, gorgeous. Look at daddy's girl."

"Oh my gosh! When did you do this?" Clearly she was in utter shock because she could remember when he denied being the father, but all of a sudden he had a change of heart.

"After I saw her for the first time." Quamae was holding the baby seat when he closed the car door. "I know she's mine, and that's why this test is important to me. I want to make sure there isn't a shadow of a doubt so I can set her up for life."

"That's fair." Sasha walked behind Quamae inside the building, but they stopped abruptly at the bar.

Terri was in her usual spot, smiling. "Aw, who is this cutie?"

"This is my daughter, Dream, and my wife, Sasha." Nothing made him happier than to acknowledge the fact he had a family, something he always wanted from the beginning.

"She look just like you, too." She then turned her attention to Sasha. "Nice to meet you. You have a beautiful daughter." Terri reached out to shake her hand.

Sasha was a little hesitant, but she wasn't rude, so she stepped a little closer and shook her hand. "Nice to meet you, as well, and thank you." Taking her hand back and placing it at her side, she smiled. "I'm sorry, what's your name?" She looked over at Quamae, "Since my husband didn't tell me."

"Charge it to my mind, and not my heart," Quamae joked. "You know you my backbone when it comes to business."

"It's cool, boss." She looked at Sasha and replied, "It's Terri."

"Okay, nice to meet you, Terri."

"Hold the fort down for a few. We headed to my office."

"I'm on it." Terri immediately got back to work.

They walked off and Sasha couldn't help but wonder if Quamae was smashing his worker, nor could she pass up the opportunity to call him out on it. After all, he had no reason to lie since they weren't together.

"So, y'all sleeping together?" she asked boldly.

Quamae stopped in front of his office door and looked back at her. "Me and Terri?"

"Duh." She sucked her teeth,

"Hell nah. Me and her cool, that's it." He opened the door and allowed her to walk in first. "We're strictly business. I don't mix business with pleasure. That will never work out."

"Yeah, okay."

"My plate too full. I'm still trying to get you back." Quamae sat down on the sofa, placed the carrier at his feet, and patted the spot next to him so she could sit beside him. Sitting down beside him, she crossed her legs and placed her purse in between them.

"That don't surprise me at all," she grinned.

"Why is that?" He had a feeling as to what she would say.

"The grass wasn't greener on the other side. She was sleeping with more than one person, but you were so blinded you couldn't see behind the fake and the phony."

"Well, you moved on, too." That was the quickest comeback he could think of.

"Yeah, because you put me out the house even after you knew about my issues and checkered past." The tears began to well up in her eyes as she thought back to one of the worst days of her life. "What did you expect me to do?"

Quamae felt bad instantly as he watched her tears stream down her face. Normally he wasn't moved by them, but he knew he destroyed her when he pulled the rug from beneath her feet. Reaching inside his coat pocket, he pulled out his handkerchief and dried her tears.

"I'm sorry, and I don't know how many different ways I can tell you. I never meant to hurt you the way I did, but you betrayed me in the worst way imaginable." Placing his handkerchief back in his pocket, he too went back to the day he found out about what she had done. "You slept with my nigga, my right-hand man, and that shit wasn't cool. That would be like me sleeping with Carmen." Shaking his head, he continued, "You could've slept with anybody but him, and I would've forgave you easier. That shit hurt more than you know."

Understanding is what they lacked in their marriage, and she wanted to make sure she gave him that without the argument. The damage had already been done, so she put her tears and emotions in check. "Well, what's the difference now? Why do you want me back so bad? I can't undo what I've done." He had her mind already wondering about the motive behind his forgiveness.

The answer to her question was easy. In a few he would never have to worry about Chauncey again because he was living on borrowed time, but he couldn't tell her that.

"It's Christine. She's been helping me get past my own issues in order for me to deal with yours."

"That's your therapist's name?" It better not have been another bitch he was talking about her business with.

"Yeah, and I prefer to call her my counselor." It was nothing against Christine, but he preferred not to refer to her as that.

"Okay, well, some people say tomato, and some say to-mah-to, but whatever makes you comfortable." Dream started to whine, so Sasha pulled the pacifier from her diaper bag and handed it to Quamae. "Give this to her."

Quamae looked at it before he placed it into her mouth. "Why you giving her this fake-ass illusion like she really getting something out of it?" he asked, looking in her direction.

"What?" She held her palms up. "She loves her binky."

"Yeah, okay, but can we discuss the matter at hand?" He needed an answer now.

Folding her hands and placing them in her lap, she sighed. "I've been thinking, and it's only fair I give you the chance to make things right with her, because I already know the answer to that question."

Quamae placed his hand on top of hers. "And what about my chance to make things right with you?"

Sasha swallowed her spit as a small lump formed in her throat. The question shouldn't have been a surprise because she already knew he wanted another chance to make their marriage work. Giving Dream a two-parent home would be a godsend, but who's to say things would be better the next time around? That decision would take careful consideration, a lot of weed, and liquor. Finally able to look into his eyes, she smiled. "I'll think about it."

Quamae couldn't do anything but respect her wishes. "I respect that, and while you at it, think about coming to counseling with me, too?"

She nodded her head. "I will."

He was willing to do anything to get his family back, and God was his witness.

Chapter 11

Quamae had a good feeling about today's activities, but he was anxious at the same time. It was the day when he would put an end to their doubts, Blue in particular. His wish was finally being granted. It was sure to set him free and bring home the woman he loved. He was going to get a DNA test done for Dream.

After Blue went off about him asking for one, Sasha went against his word and agreed to get it done in order to silence him for good. It caught him off guard when she agreed, allowing him to get his proof.

The plan was to drive to a DNA testing center located in Ft. Lauderdale and have the three of them swabbed. There was no way she could risk being seen at a public location in Miami.

When he arrived at their destination, she was already there waiting on him. Her demeanor was completely different from the last time they saw each other. Sasha got out of the car and handed the baby over to him. They locked eyes, and that family moment felt so right, as if it was preordained.

"How are you doing?" he asked.

"I'm good."

"It don't seem that way." He was hoping to get some conversation out of her.

"I'm good, Quamae. Just a little tired," she lied.

"Hey, my little princess."

Dream smiled and cooed at him as if she was used to seeing him.

In her heart she knew he was the father, but after all the shit he put her through during her pregnancy, she gave his role to Blue.

He finally took his attention away from the baby and focused on Sasha. "You ready?"

"As ready as I'm gon' be." Sasha patted the top of her weave.

"If you stop wearing that shit, ya scalp wouldn't be so dirty," Quamae joked and walked off.

"Shut up, 'cause you used to pay for it," Sasha trailed behind him, yelling out.

"You absolutely right, 'cause I was paying for the human horse and still don't know what the fuck a bundle is."

They walked inside the building and all the joking stopped. Sasha filled out the necessary paperwork and gave the receptionist both of their driver's licenses. After a twenty-minute wait, they were escorted in the back to a secluded office.

"Have a seat, please," the counselor instructed. She appeared to be a tad bit young, but hell, it didn't matter as long as she knew what the hell she was doing. They sat down in the chairs positioned directly in front of the desk.

"Well, isn't she gorgeous."

"Thank you," they responded in unison.

She then went on to explain the process. "Now, after you receive the results and if they're not what you expected, we also provide counseling." She adjusted her glasses and stared back and forth between him and the baby. "Honestly, I don't think you have too much to worry about."

"Why not?" Quamae was curious as to what she was speaking on. Sasha wasn't interested or paying attention. She was too busy texting Nate.

"You have very strong genes. I observed that from the waiting area when I saw the two of you. I'm normally right about this type of thing. The only way she couldn't be yours would be from a bad test or a twin brother."

Quamae couldn't believe what he was hearing. To hear it from someone he knew was one thing, but from a complete stranger was another story.

"So, would you be leaving a down payment or paying in full?"

"Full. How much?"

"Four fifty, and it takes about 48 hours to get the results."

Quamae pulled a wad of money from his pocket. He could feel her eyes on him, but he wasn't paying her any attention. The only thing she could offer him was a rush order on the results, and nothing else.

"I'll call you personally when they come in."

"Good."

110

She was attracted to him, and it wasn't a secret. He was fine, and he had money. That was a double whammy. She tried making small talk, but she only came off as thirsty. "Is this the mother?"

Sasha took her eyes off the phone when she heard that. "Yes, I am her mother, and you can have him. He single and free to mingle."

"She lyin'. This is my wife," he responded.

That took her by surprise. "Oh, I apologize. It's very rare we get a husband and wife in here for a DNA test."

Quamae brushed her off quickly because he wasn't checking for her, point-blank period. She wasn't ugly, but he had enough problems as is. "Can we get on with the testing now?" He was clearly in a hurry.

"Sure," she responded. She stood up and walked them over to the lab. The technician swabbed the three of them and placed the sticks in separate tubes.

"We're all done. You'll receive a call in 48 hours to pick up your results."

Quamae walked out of the lab with Dream lying over his shoulder. She had fallen asleep right before the testing.

Looking at them and seeing how he cared for Dream made her feel bad, and she wished they had diffused the situation a long time ago.

***

Quamae felt like the President of the United States as he walked through his establishment. It was the night of his grand opening, and he was ready to open the doors. Starting his business was the best thing he could've ever done. With the help of Terri, everything had fallen into place, and on time at that. Being successful never felt so good, but it didn't mean anything if he had no one to share it with. Right now he was on top of the world, and all he needed was his family standing right beside him.

Making sure everything was immaculate, he walked the floor with his hands in his pockets, making observations. Terri was in her usual spot, but this time she was sitting on the opposite side of the bar on a stool. She smiled and stood up once Quamae was within arm's distance.

"Are you ready for the big night?"

"Ready as I'm gonna get. How about you?"

Terri rocked back and forth on her heels. "I'm very excited for you, and I know you're going to do well."

"You mean we, 'cause I couldn't have done all of this without you, and I appreciate everything you have done."

"Well, I'm proud of you." Terri leaned forward and wrapped her arms around Quamae.

"Thank you."

The sound of the front door opening put an abrupt end to their hug. Quamae quickly turned around to see who entered the building. Standing there were two men wearing all-black slacks and button-up shirts.

"Yes, how can I help you?" At first glance he would easily assume they were detectives, but since he knew better, that wasn't the case.

"Are you the owner?" the first man asked.

"Yes, I am." Quamae met the men halfway across the floor and stopped right in front of them.

"I'm Claude, and this is Jake." He pointed to his friend beside him. "We're the security detail Jerry sent over."

"Thanks for your early arrival. I'm Quamae Banks." They all shook hands. "So, doors open in an hour. I need one of you at the door with the bouncer, and the other can walk around and observe the area. This is a 25-and-up lounge, so there should be no issues in here. Everyone coming through those doors needs to show valid identification. I have a license scanner at the door, just in case anything goes wrong."

"I like the sound of that," Claude added while he and Jake looked around, observing the area. "This is a nice place you have here."

"Thank you. Let me show you around." Quamae extended his arm. "Right this way."

Quamae escorted them around the lounge and introduced them to the rest of the staff. Everyone needed to be on point so the first night could be a breeze. With the hottest promoters in the game on his team, he was guaranteed to have a packed house.

Taking them to his office, he opened up the door and let them in. "And this is my office. As you can see, I have surveillance everywhere. There are no gray areas. Except for the restrooms, of course."

Jake laughed and nodded his head. "I hope not, 'cause definitely an invasion of privacy."

"Yeah, that's a lawsuit, at best," Claude added.

"There won't be any lawsuits here." Quamae adjusted his jacket and walked toward the door. "It's time to go and cut the ribbon. Let's go."

Quamae and his staff stood outside of the lounge with news reporters ready to go live. To his left was a line full of patrons ready to come inside. In his hands were a pair of gigantic scissors. After the reporter gave the intro, they zoomed in on him to catch him in action.

"Good evening. It is my greatest accomplishment to open up my very first lounge, Dream's Palace, in honor of my daughter. This lounge is for the grown and sexy, which means you have to be 25 and up to party. We have a variety of food, drinks, and hookahs, so come on down after work, kick back, and enjoy yourself. Thank you."

Quamae placed his fingers inside the loops of the scissors and closed it, slicing the ribbon in half.

"The doors of Dream's Palace are officially open. Step on in and enjoy yourselves."

***

Sasha was in the middle of burping Dream when she received a text message. When she looked down at the screen, she sucked her teeth once she realized it was Carmen's number. The contact had been deleted, but she knew her number by heart.

"I know damn well this bitch ain't texting my phone." She was disgusted.

The love she had for Carmen was real, but the hate that had grown inside of her overpowered it. Sasha looked down at the text message.

954-661-3275: I know I'm the last person on earth you want to hear from, but I want to tell you again how sorry I am about what went down. I also wanted to tell you that Chauncey is in jail. It's all over Facebook, but I see you deactivated your page. I still love you, Sasha.

Sasha closed the message without responding and opened up the jail base link. She scrolled through the first few rows of mug shots while holding the baby's bottle. Chauncey's picture showed up, but his charge didn't make sense to her.

"Pre-meditated murder," she whispered. "Chauncey, what did you do?"

Her next thought went to Quamae, and she needed to make sure he wasn't in jail along with him. Sasha called his phone three times and he didn't answer. Her chest begin to cave in as she thought about the possibility of him in the same predicament. Multi-tasking wasn't working, so she propped Dream against the pillow with her bottle so she can call the county jail.

As she dialed the number, a text was coming through. She felt a sense of relief when she saw Quamae's number pop up.

Quamae: I'm taking care of some business. I'll hit you up when I'm done
Sasha: Okay

The beating of her heart slowed down once she knew he was okay. She was finally able to call the Broward County Jail to inquire about visitation. It was just her luck that visitation was the same day. Darlene was in her room, so she went over to ask if she would look after the baby until she got back from running an errand. Sasha left the house quickly, making sure she didn't run into Blue on the way out.

At the jail, Sasha checked in and waited in the lobby downstairs with the rest of the visitors until her name was called. Thirty minutes later she was walking down a row, checking each booth until she saw Chauncey sitting behind the Plexiglas. Sasha sat down and picked up the phone to start the questioning. It was clear he let himself go. He looked tired, as if he wasn't getting enough sleep and had missed a few meals.

Chauncey picked up the phone, cracking a little smile, but he was far from happy. "What you doing here?" he asked.

"Well," she smiled, "I came to make sure you're okay."

"I appreciate that."

"You know I don't want to see anything happen to you." She batted her lashes. "You know I have love for you."

Chauncey gripped the phone tight and looked away. His secret was killing him on the inside, and he was contemplating if he should tell her or not. "I have love for you, too." He had to change the subject. "How is the baby?"

"She's good. I left her with her grandma so I could come see you." She leaned in closer to the glass.

He chuckled. "Her grandma, huh?"

Sasha cut her eyes at him, unsure of what he was insinuating with his comment. "Yes, her grandma."

Chauncey rubbed his hand over his face. "Can I ask you a question?"

"Sure," she replied.

"Is there a chance it's my baby?" He knew there was a chance the baby was his, but he wanted to be sure. There was no way he could do his time knowing there was a possibility he has a child out here. Thanks to the nature of his charges, he knew it would be a while before he ever saw them again.

A huge lump formed in her throat, and she swallowed spit to try to push it down. Sasha adjusted her necklace and hung her head low. "No."

"Are you sure?"

"She's not yours." Her attitude was snappy.

"How do you know that? Did that nigga take a paternity test?"

Sasha sighed, hoping he could hear the irritation in her voice. "Why does that matter to you now?" He was taking her back to that awful day he snapped on her. "When you found out I was pregnant, you told me to do me. You also said you wasn't fucking with me and there was no way my baby could be yours."

Chauncey had his arm propped on the booth with his head in his hand. "I said that shit to hurt you, the same way you did me." His eyes became glassy. "That shit was dropped on me by someone other than you. How did you expect me to react?"

Sasha was not about to go back down that road with him. Dream had a father, and she wasn't about to go through the motions.

"Chauncey, that's a thing of the past, and I want to leave that alone." Tears stung the back of her eyes, making her vision blurry. "I'm in a good place right now, and I want to keep it that way. I only came up here to check on you and see what happened. I don't want to bring up old feelings and memories. Blue loves me, and I love him, too."

Hearing that name put him in his feelings. "So, it's fuck me, huh?"

"I didn't say that!" She paused. "If I didn't give a fuck, I wouldn't be here. All I'm saying is I'm not about to ruin my happy home on a possibility."

Chauncey shook his head slowly. Rejection was killing him. It was bad enough he killed his seed, but he killed the mother of his child as well. This situation with Sasha only added fuel to the fire.

"I can't sit back and say nothing. I need to know." He waited on her response, but she remained silent. "So, you want me to forget the fact she could be my daughter?"

Tears flowed down her cheeks because there was a point in time where she did love him, but those feelings were long gone. The only feeling she could share with him was friendship, and nothing more. Sasha was not leaving Blue for another man.

Bride of a Hustla 3

"Chauncey, please don't do this. Just let it go. You're in here for murder."

"It was an accident. I didn't mean to kill her."

Sasha was confused because she had no clue who he was referring to. "Who?"

"Monica."

"Wait. What?" That was the last name she expected to hear. "Monica's dead?"

"Yeah." Chauncey rubbed his head. "We got into a fight and she stabbed me. I chased her into the bathroom and she slipped and hit her head on the bathtub," he cried. "I didn't mean for that to happen," he repeated.

"Damn, Chauncey, I'm sorry to hear that."

He looked up with tears in his eyes. "She was pregnant, and I made her get an abortion. If I didn't do that, she would still be alive."

"So, that's the reason you wanna know if my baby belongs to you? To replace what you lost?" As insensitive as that sounded, she didn't care. "That just let me know if she wasn't dead, you wouldn't want anything to do with us." Deep down she knew if Monica was alive, they would've never had this conversation, and he wouldn't be worried about Dream.

Chauncey looked at her through hooded eyes. "You don't know that, so stop assuming what you can't prove. You used to love a nigga, but you let another nigga come in and take my place. That's fucked up."

"It's not fucked up because I didn't have to ask him to step up and be her father. He did what any real man would do because he knew he slept with me. So yes, he is her father, and that's all I'm going to say about it. Blue has been there since day one, and he's still here, and he's not going anywhere." Her intention of the visit went south really quickly. She never wanted to hurt his feelings, although he did her the same way months ago.

Chauncey's heart ached listening to her talk. "So, this what it's come to, huh? That nigga probably ain't her daddy." He couldn't let her get away with talking to him that way.

117

Sasha rolled her eyes and sucked her teeth. He was really getting on her last nerve. "Well, according to her birth certificate, he is."

"You gave her his last name, too?" He was disappointed.

"Yes, I did."

"What does your husband think about what you did?" That was a punch to the gut for her, and he could tell by her demeanor and the way she shifted in her seat. Chauncey tapped his temple with his finger. "Oh, I forgot he moved on and had a set of twins."

Sasha stood from her seat, obviously disgusted by his comment. "I'm going to leave now and forget about what you said. You enjoy your life sentence, and I hope it's filled with regret and pain."

Her words drop-kicked him in the chest, and he glared at her with anger. If he was close to her, he would choke the life out of her. Since he wasn't, he decided to attack back. "Before you go back to living your happy life, there is something you should know."

She placed her hand on her hip. "What now?"

A devious smirk spread across his lips. "I'm HIV positive. I hope you have a nice and painful life, too." He dropped the phone and walked away, smiling.

Sasha's adrenaline was pumping fiercely after hearing Chauncey's last words to her. All she could do was run out of visitation with smoke under her heels. His voice was on repeat in her head. *I'm HIV positive. I'm HIV positive. I'm HIV positive.* Just when she thought her life was perfect, life had a way of taking that away.

When she made it into her car, she sat down and released a loud scream from her gut, punching the steering wheel. "You win, God. You win. I was a horrible wife, I committed adultery, but I'm sorry. I don't want to die like this." After all of the lying, deceitful behavior and cheating, she was finally about to suffer the consequences. In her mind, God was punishing her for breaking her vows and lying in the house of the Lord.

Now was the time she needed a friend, but there was no one

she could talk to. India was dead and gone, and Carmen had become an enemy. There was no one she could turn to. Sasha cried non-stop during her hour drive back home. Normally it wouldn't take that long, but she took scenic routes to kill the time.

At a red light she put a few drops of Visine in her eyes to clear up the redness. Thoughts of Dream and Blue flooded her mind, making her weak. *What if she gave it to Blue? What would he say? Or better yet, do? What about Dream?* Those questions circling around in her head. Blue's truck wasn't in the driveway when she reached home, which was a relief in itself. There was no way she could look him in his eyes right now. Sasha needed a moment to regroup and get her thoughts together. All she wanted to do was hold and kiss her baby girl.

Sasha got her baby from Darlene and went to her room. She held a sleeping Dream close to her heart and rocked her back and forth. Her baby was so precious and innocent. She couldn't imagine Dream growing up without her.

"Dream, I am so sorry for everything you will have to go through when you get older." Tears fell from her eyes onto her shirt. "Mommy made a mistake, and it's going to cost me my life, and I'm praying it didn't affect yours. I just want you to know I love you and none of this was on purpose." Sasha wiped the fresh tears from her face. Some of them dripped onto the baby blanket. "I always wanted to be a good mother, the type of mother I didn't have, but one like your grandmother."

"And you will be."

Sasha looked up to see Blue standing at the door. She panicked because she never heard him come in. "How much of that did you hear?" Her heart was beating rapidly.

Blue walked over and wiped away her remaining tears. "Everything about you wanting to be a good mother." He kissed his baby girl on the cheek. "You're a great mother. Stop worrying so much. Everything will be okay."

Sasha nodded her head, ready to drown in her sorrows because she knew that was far from the truth.

Destiny

Chapter 12

The past 48 hours had been the longest hours in history for Quamae. He had finally received the phone call he was waiting on, and in his hands was the answer to his question. He gripped the envelope tightly as he sat in the car and took a deep breath before he opened it. After declining the counselor's offer to read them inside, he rushed back to his car so he could read the results alone.

Quamae's heart was beating fast, as if he was afraid of what the answer might be. His hands were trembling and sweaty because he knew the possibility was very strong.

Ripping open the envelope, he pulled out the paper and scanned over it slowly. His eyes were wide as flying saucers, with not a blink in sight. Staring at him dead in his eyes, in black and white was the answer he felt in his heart all along. He was 99.99% the father.

Feeling upset and happy at the same time, he hopped back on I-95 and floored it to Pembroke Pines. The guilt was heavy on his heart because he missed out on the most important part of his daughter's life: her coming into the world. That was something he could never get back. Just the thought of the way he treated his wife was killing him, and he knew there was nothing he could say to take back the things he had said and done to her. But he had a plan to gain her forgiveness. Instead of calling her, he decided to shoot her a quick text to meet up.

Sasha agreed to meet up with him at his house, so he went there to wait on her. While he awaited her arrival, Quamae fixed a glass of Hennessey and sat down on the sofa. He was so overwhelmed with emotion that he didn't know how to act. All he could do was keep looking at the results and smiling.

Forty-five minutes later there was a knock on the door. Setting his glass down on the table, he walked to the front door and opened it. There she was, just as beautiful as the first time he laid eyes on her a few months ago.

"Look at daddy's baby." Quamae relieved Sasha from carrying the heavy seat.

She sighed and shook her arm to get rid of the numbness. "This girl is heavy."

"You could've called me when you pulled up so I could come out and get her." He took a step back so she could come inside.

"I don't know, my mind is just." She paused and turned back to face him. "Hold up, you said 'daddy's girl.' Is that what the test said?"

"Go and look at it. The paper is on the table." Quamae locked the door behind them and followed her into the living room.

Sasha took a few steps forward and froze up. Her legs became stuck in place as she went back to the last time she was there. Quick flashes of an argument invaded her thoughts, then she heard a gunshot. Breathing heavily, she grabbed her head and tried to shake away the thoughts. "No!" she shouted.

"Are you okay?" Quamae placed his hand on her shoulder.

"I just had a flashback that we were arguing, and then I heard a gunshot. Everything went blank after that."

The sadness in her eyes hurt him to the core because he knew she was battling with the memory loss from when he attacked her. However, he couldn't pull himself to tell her the truth. If he stood any chance at getting her back, he couldn't tell her what really happened. "Come and sit down. I'll get you something to drink." Holding her arm, he walked her over to the sofa and helped her sit down with the baby seat at her feet before he walked away.

Sasha dug through her purse looking for her anxiety pills while she did exercises to even her breathing. Something didn't feel right about being in that house again, but she couldn't put her finger on it.

When Quamae returned, he handed her a bottled water. "Thanks." She put the tablets in her mouth and washed it down with water.

"You okay?"

"Yeah. I'm sure it's nothing." The papers were visible on the table. "Are those the results?"

"Yeah." Quamae picked them up and handed them to her while wearing a Kool-Aid smile. "Read 'em and weep."

122

Grabbing the results, she scanned through quickly until she saw what she was looking for. With the results clenched tightly in her hand, she nodded her head. "Read 'em and weep, my ass! 'Cause I told you it was your baby, but no, you didn't believe me. You took the word of a bitch you was fuckin' over mine, and she fucked you over in the end."

Thinking back to those torturous days brought tears to her eyes. From the moment she told him, he had denied their baby, and now he wanted to sweep it under the rug like nothing happened. Regardless of the fact she cheated, she knew who the father of her baby was the whole time. Sasha didn't believe she produced a baby with Blue, or Chauncey for that matter. In her heart she always felt it was her husband.

"You missed out on everything, and another man stood up in the paint when you just abandoned me like yesterday's trash." Sasha's emotions reared their head, and it was time for her to let him know how she really felt. "I know what I did was wrong, but you ain't no saint. You cheated on me on more than one occasion, but I stood by my vows and turned the other cheek. You didn't do that for me, and that's not fair. That shit with Chauncey didn't mean nothing to me. I was vulnerable and weak, and he was there during that moment."

It hurt him to know she felt the way she did, and all he wanted to do was fix it and make it all go away. "I know, and I'm sorry for everything I took you through."

"What do you mean, 'you know?'" Sasha tilted her head to the side and looked into his eyes. She needed to feel his words and examine his expression.

"Chauncey told me what happened," he sighed. "I forgive you."

"So, because Chauncey told you what happened, it's all good?"

"No." Quamae rubbed his hands over his face. "I told my counselor what happened and shed light on your situation."

"What did you tell her?" Living with her past was bad enough, but to keep reliving it was something she didn't want to do.

"I told her about my past, yours, our infidelities and marriage. She believes we can make it."

"Do you believe that?"

"I do." Saying those words took him back to their wedding day. He nodded his head and smiled. "I do once again."

Those were the words she had waited to hear for the longest time, but he waited so late in the game. "I don't know about that. You did me wrong, and I don't feel like I should move to the beat of your drum." On that last statement she rolled her neck hard so he would understand she meant business.

Quamae rose to his feet and opened up his briefcase that sat beside him. Sasha could see he pulled out something, but she didn't know what it was. As he walked over, he slipped something into his pocket and sat down beside her. Taking her hand into his, he held it tight and expressed his feelings. "I just want one last chance to prove to you I can and will be the husband you deserve. We can raise our daughter together and give her what we didn't have growing up."

Sasha dropped her head. "You mean what I didn't have growing up? 'Cause you had your parents."

"After my father died, I didn't have that anymore. It was just me, Emani, and my mom." That fateful night suddenly replayed in his head, causing him to choke up a bit. His tears were slowly building up as he saw his father's face. "Sasha, I just want to be the best father to our daughter. I don't want another man around her, let alone raising her. I couldn't sleep at night knowing another man was laid up in your house with access to Dream." Quamae bit down on his lip. "I would catch a body about her."

"I would never put our daughter in harm's way." She squeezed his hand a little tighter. "All I ever wanted was to be a family, but you didn't want that with me. You chose another bitch over me. I dropped a body for you, Quamae. I'm the reason you still here, but that doesn't mean anything to you."

"It does, and I want to make it up to you." Reaching into his pocket, he pulled out a card and handed it to her.

Grabbing the card, she noticed it was a bank card with her

name on it. "What is this for?"

"It's yours. I want you to get yourself situated, start you a business or something. It's my job to make sure you and her are taken care of, and I know you desperately want to have your independence."

Sasha was curious to know how much money was on that card, but it would be tacky to check the balance when he was being generous and trying to right his wrong. "Thank you. I appreciate that." She sat the card beside her on the sofa.

"You don't have to thank me. I'm doing what a husband would do for his wife and child," he replied.

Sasha leaned over and hugged him tight. "You don't know how much this means to me, and I don't know how I will ever repay you for this."

Quamae inhaled her scent as he held her in his arms. It felt good to be close to her once again, and better knowing he was one step closer to getting her back. "All I want in return is a second chance. Please allow me to make this right with the both of you. And if it's not too much to ask, I want you to come to counseling with me."

Sasha's head rested on his shoulder and she cried into his arms, wondering why he couldn't be this understanding months ago. True enough, she loved Blue and he had been there for her since the beginning, but he was slowly starting to show a new side she had never seen before. There was no more room for surprises in her life. It was time to get it together, and now Quamae just gave her something else to think about.

"Yes, I'll go with you and see what happens. I'm not making any promises, but there is a lot we need to work on."

"I can accept that."

Lifting her chin, he brought his mouth to hers and kissed her lips softly. His body yearned for her touch, but he didn't want to push it, and slow progress was better than nothing at all. Their kiss was sensual, sending tingles up and down his spine. The tip of his head began to throb and poke against his jeans. Sasha's nipples were hard, and she could feel a slight heartbeat in her panties. He had her aroused to the max, and on another night she probably would've opened her legs for him, but after Chauncey sent her world tumbling down a slippery slope, that wasn't gon' happen.

Dream's cries broke their kiss, and she was happy because they were saved by the bell.

***

Two weeks had passed since Chauncey hit Sasha with the devastating news. Since that day she forced herself to be abstinent in order to protect Blue. If he didn't have it already, she didn't want to increase his chances just in case there was a God who would bless him with a second chance. Her heart really ached for Nate 'cause he lived 15 years of his life pussy-free. The man hadn't been free a year yet and he was at risk of having the virus all because he trusted his cheating-ass baby mama. There had been similar cases, so she was hopeful for some good news today.

She sat nervously on the table at her doctor's office, awaiting the results so she could put all doubts to rest. The sleepless nights, uncontrollable crying, sickness, and lying to Blue just to avoid sex was finally coming to an end, good or bad. Sasha couldn't keep her nails out of her mouth. She was a nervous wreck.

The door opened and her heart dropped to the pit of her stomach.

"Hello, Mrs. Banks, how are you doing today?" Dr. Milan asked. She was a short Indian lady with long, dark hair and brown eyes. She was the sweetest.

"Nervous as hell," she responded.

Doctor Milan observed the bags under her eyes. "Have you been getting any sleep?"

"Not really."

"Is the baby keeping you up at night?" the doctor asked.

"Yeah, and these results have been haunting me like crazy."

She handed Sasha a piece of paper. "I have taken a look at the results, and I can only imagine what you're going through at this moment. Understand that many women have gone through the same thing as you. With a good support system at home, you will be just fine."

With the paper clutched tightly in her hands, sweat beads formed atop her forehead and the loud echo from her racing heart filled the room. The moment she had so desperately awaited had finally presented itself. Knowing it could only go two ways, she was banking on a not-so-happy ending. She had done so much bad shit in her life, so she felt like karma was that dark cloud that hung over her head continuously. Whatever the results read, she only had one choice, and that was to deal with it.

Sasha read the results and passed out when she saw the word *POSITIVE* in big, bold letters.

***

Blue was suffering from a bedroom drought since Sasha closed shop between her legs. With that being said, he became a tad bit too friendly with Emani. He wasn't sure if Sasha was cheating on him or not, but he knew she was capable of doing so. He didn't want to assume the worst in her, but there was no logical explanation.

Professor Stoudemire stood at the front of the class explaining the assignment. He was an older black man who wore glasses and suspenders. His voice was deep like the man on the Allstate commercial. Blue wasn't listening because he was too busy thinking about his family and what he could do to fix it. Dream and Sasha were his lifeline, and he had to fight for what he wanted.

The lights in the classroom went out and a video started to play. Blue felt a light tap on his arm. He looked to his right where Emani sat. Apparently she had scribbled something down on a piece of paper for him to read.

Do you want to come to my place after class and chill? We can work on Anatomy and Physiology.

Blue thought long and hard about his response before he wrote it down. He handed the paper back to Emani and she smiled at the answer.

Yeah, I'll slide.

After class was dismissed, Blue followed Emani to her apartment. His heart told him to go home, but his mind kept telling him to take her up on her offer. He knew damn well she didn't want to do no damn homework. She wanted him to beat the brakes off that pussy, and the way he was feeling, he was ready to handle that. Emani was cute in the face and she had a nice shape. He scoped her body out a long time ago, but never pursued her. Blue knew he could've had her on the first day of school, fresh out of the gate, but he didn't have a reason to cheat. Sasha was handling business in the bedroom, so he was satisfied. That wasn't the case now because he ain't got no pussy in two weeks. He couldn't understand how men lived with their chicks going through the drought. That's what single niggas went through, but Emani was trying to end that today.

Before he got out of his truck, he gave it a little more thought. Going home right now was a teaser because no matter how hard he tried to make love to her, she wasn't giving it up. The only good thing about going home was seeing his princess smile and coo whenever she saw his face.

Blue crossed the threshold of Emani's place and was impressed with her bachelorette pad. The place was decked out, far too expensive for a college student. Everyone knew college kids were broke unless they came from money, or in Blue's case, they studied Hustlenomics 101. So, he figured she came from money.

"So, this how you living, huh?" he smiled.

"Yep." She looked over shoulder. "Not bad for a college girl with no job, huh?"

"It depends."

Emani stopped in her tracks and turned around to face him.

"Depends on what?" She folded her arms across her chest.

"If you have a sugar daddy or not?"

"You tried it, Darian," she replied, poking out her lip.

"I'm just saying," he shrugged his shoulders. "How you paying for all of this with no job? You gotta be doing something to pay the rent." Blue thought to himself that maybe coming home with her was a mistake after all. He had no clue about her lifestyle, and to be honest, he could care less.

"So you think I'm a whole ho out here?"

"I never said that. You did!" Blue looked her up and down, stopping at her hips. She was wearing a fitted skirt that exposed every curve on her body. His mind drifted to him lifting that muthafucka up and bending her over on the couch. The blood was rushing from his brain to his dick, causing it to throb.

Emani smiled. "You right, but to be honest with you, my brother pays for all of this in exchange for good grades."

"That sounds better." Blue played with one of her braids. "'Cause you seem like a good girl, but one can never be so sure."

"You funny," she smiled. "Follow me to the kitchen. We can work in there."

Blue sat his Gucci backpack on the table, along with his book. For the first hour they discussed the assignment and put together an outline. Emani was turned on by his bad boy image, but finding out he was smart turned her on even more. Blue caught her eyeing him a few times, but all he did was smile and suck it all in. It felt good to be desired, especially since his woman wasn't showing much interest these days.

Awkward silence fell over their study session, but Emani killed that quickly. "Do you want a drink?"

Blue sat back in the chair. "What chu got in there?"

"Patron." He chuckled a bit. "What's funny?" she asked.

"Nothing. I'll take mine straight with one ice cube." He would normally drink it straight, but he couldn't be too lit when he made it back to boot camp, referring to his home. The way he was on restriction at the house felt like punishment.

Blue licked his lips as he watched Emani sashay to the

kitchen. She pulled the bottle from the cabinet, along with two glasses and fixed them a drink. The way she bent over confirmed his assumptions about her wanting to fuck. He tilted his head to the side to get a better view of the new booty in front of him. His dick was getting harder by the second staring at her thick thighs.

Emani walked back over and handed him his drink with a Kool-Aid smile plastered on her face. "Here you go."

"Thanks." Then he took a sip.

Three cups later they were relaxed and discussing everything except homework when Blue's cell phone starting to ring. It was Sasha, so he let her go to voicemail. After her fourth attempt to reach him, she sent him a text message.

> *Wifey: I know you see me calling you*
> *Hubby: In class*
> *Wifey: I don't like how you've been acting and it's bothering me. Since you started going to school you've changed. Do you not love me anymore? I just feel like you're advancing in life and I'm stuck being a single parent and that's not fair to me and OUR DAUGHTER!! Don't keep me in the blind about your plans.*

After reading the paragraph-long text, he closed it and placed his phone face-down on the table. Emani watching his every move.

"Is everything okay?" She was genuinely concerned.

He nodded his head. "Everything cool."

"You don't look like it," she probed further. "We're friends, so you can talk to me."

A tipsy and emotional Blue took another sip from his cup and confided in his newfound friend. Sasha had him fucked up because he wouldn't never have discussed his relationship problems with the next female.

"I think my girl cheating on me, but she texting me all this bullshit like I'm the problem. I never cheated on this girl." Then he paused. "Well, I semi-cheated."

Emani laughed, holding her hand up. "Hold up! What's 'semi-cheated?' You either cheated or you didn't."

"Damn, you sound just like her. But this chick I used to fuck with gave me head. That's all that happened between us."

"And that's called cheating, sir."

"I guess." He exhaled and took another sip from his glass. "I told her about it right after it happened because I felt bad."

"That was an honest move."

"Now it's her. We haven't had sex in two weeks, so I know she cheating."

Emani's eyebrows shifted down. It was uncomfortable, hearing him talk about her, especially since she was interested in doing more than studying. Maintaining her composure was important. She didn't want to seem jealous over a female. "Maybe it would be different if y'all lived together. That would make the sex stronger, don't you think?" She was trying to slide in a few questions on the low.

"We do live together."

Emani lost her breath for at least five seconds. In her mind she was repeating the answer. *What the hell he mean they live together?* She definitely need a quick pep talk with her inner self. *Girl, stop acting crazy before you scare this man off.*

She pretended to be interested. "Well, maybe you're just paranoid." Discussing his girl was not something she wanted to do, but because he was so damn fine, she would engage in any type of conversation as long as they were having it in her place. Emani knew he had a girl because he was too fine to be single. It was either that or he was a bachelor. She just hated the fact they lived together, but she had her own place where he could crash, so it was all good. At the rate his girl was going, she was liable to lose him real soon, 'cause if she sunk her nails in him, it was a wrap for them as a couple.

"Nah, it ain't that. We had a baby not too long ago, and she's been stressed out lately. I don't know what to think when it comes to her."

If he was paying close attention to her, he would've caught her facial expressions. Emani couldn't believe what she was hearing, but her heart was registering the details just fine. *Hell nah, you mean to tell me they live together and have a baby? I can't compete with that.* Blue was slowly breaking her heart without knowing it. One thing she knew was there was no destroying a relationship with a baby mama. No matter what, them dudes would always find their way back to the mother of their child. No matter how bad his situation sounded, it didn't turn her off from him. It made her want him even more.

Before she got the chance to respond, his phone alerted him that he had another text message. It was Sasha again.

Wifey: You need to get here quick. I have something to tell you.

Blue looked at Emani. "She just texted me saying she has something urgent to tell me. I think I better head home." He wasn't sure what to expect from her.

Emani was disappointed, to say the least. *Whoever this chick is, she has him messed up,* she thought to herself. Emani needed to think quickly on her feet because she had come too far to let him leave so easily.

"Okay, give me a second and I'll walk you to the elevator." Taking a step, she walked away and disappeared into the bedroom.

Chapter 13

Blue took one final shot to get him through the news Sasha was about to tell him. His only concern was if she cheated or not, because if she did, it was over. Blue was tipsy as hell, so he leaned forward with his elbows on his knees and eyes closed.

Emani caught him off guard when she tapped his shoulder. "Do you need to rest before you go home?"

"Nah, I'ma head to the house 'cause I don't know what I'm walking into." Blue eased up slowly, and standing in front of him was a half-naked Emani. She was wearing a hot pink lace bra and panty set. His dick rocked up immediately from the beautiful sight. Her brown skin was flawless, and the gap between her legs exposed her pussy print. The cat had his tongue, so he was speechless.

Emani stepped closer and stood in between his legs. "You sure you wanna leave?"

He didn't reply. The silence bestowed upon them gave her the answer she was hoping for. Emani ran her fingers through his dreads, tilting his head backward before kissing his lips.

Blue contemplated telling her to stop, but he couldn't pull himself to do it. This was what he lacked at home, and it felt good at the same time. The evidence of the Patron was present, and it was doing its job. Blue engaged in the kiss easily, gripping her ass in the process. Without breaking the kiss, she straddled him and grinded on his lap. Caressing her C-cups, he placed his mouth over her breast and sucked gently on her pierced nipple, causing her to moan. Emani could feel the juices soak the seat of her panties as she grinded against his thick, hard dick. Her body was anxious to feel him inside of her.

Not wanting to waste any more time, she reached inside his shorts and pulled it out. He definitely had inches for days, and she couldn't wait for him to bust her open. The last dude she dated was half of Blue's size. There was no way he could leave her disappointed with that big-ass package he was carrying around.

Emani slid her panties to the side and tried to ease down on him, but he stopped her. "What's wrong?" she asked.

Blue pulled a gold wrapper from his pocket. It ain't like he was issuing out community dick or no shit like that. On the way to Emani's house he stopped at the store and picked them up. He and Sasha didn't use condoms, so there was no need in carrying them. She would definitely lose her mind if he came home with them.

He pulled his shorts down to his knees and Emani removed her panties. Once he was strapped up, he sat back down on the couch so she could mount up. Following his lead, she climbed on top of him and eased down slowly. The constant flow of her juices made it easier to take every inch.

"Ah," she cried out. "Shit." Emani rode him slowly while she got into her zone.

"Damn," Blue moaned. He didn't have time to be gentle with her. It was bad enough he was backed up, but on top of that Sasha kept sending text messages and calling. She must have felt he was doing wrong because she hasn't done that since his slip-up with Red.

Gripping her waist, he lifted her up and down so she could bounce on it. He bit his bottom lip and thrust his hips forward. The way she gripped his dick was causing that nut to build quicker than he wanted it to.

Blue lifted her up, stepped out of his shorts, and carried her to the counter. She wasn't about to ride him to death. He needed that pound game right now. He had a lot of pressure, so she was in for a world of trouble.

Standing in front of her, he spread her legs and slipped into her tunnel. Skin smacking and loud moaning filled the room, but that was short-lived when the phone starting ringing back-to-back. He already knew who it was, and she wasn't about to mess up his nut.

Blue removed his yellow diamond necklace and tank top, placing them both on the counter. Using his hands to pin her thighs down, he dug deep, making her scream.

"Ah! I wanted to do this since the first time I saw you," she said in between breaths.

"Oh yeah?" he bit down on his lip.

"I knew it would be good." Her breathing became shallow. He was wearing her ass out. "I knew you would fuck me good." Emani surprised him when she showed him how flexible she could be by using both hands to spread her legs into a split.

"Bust that shit open."

"Fuck me like you want me," she shouted.

One round wasn't enough for him, so thirty minutes later he got off for a second time. He couldn't lie, Emani was worth that cheat. The pussy was A-1. Another round would've been nice, but he had to clear it. He may have relieved his sexual tension, but another type of tension was waiting on him at home, and her name was Sasha.

***

Blue walked into the house lightly buzzed, tired, and ready to go to sleep. When he opened the room door, Sasha looked at him in utter disgust. The white parts of her eyes were red, so he knew she had been crying. He also knew he wasn't about to get any sleep, especially when she put the baby in the crib with the quickness.

"Where the fuck have you been?" she snapped.

Blue kicked off his shoes, dropped his backpack and keys on the floor, and attempted to climb into bed, but Sasha blocked his path. "I'm talking to you. Where the fuck have you been?"

"Bruh, g'on playin', 'cause you know I was at school." That was his story, and he was sticking to it.

"Not this long. You should've been home a long time ago."

"I was in the library studying for a group project."

Sasha placed her hands on her hips. "Then why haven't you answered my calls or texts?"

"I just said I was in the library." He chuckled a little bit because she was so over the top. "You can't use your phone in there."

Sasha didn't think it was amusing, so she grabbed his face.

"Have you been drinking?"

Blue slapped her hand away. "Sasha, chill the fuck out. I'm home. What you wanna talk about?"

"You've been acting funny lately," she pouted.

"I wonder why." The sarcasm dripped from his words, but he wasn't angry.

Sasha knew this all reverted back to her not fucking him, but if he only knew she was doing it for his own good. Taking a seat next to him, she took a deep breath and prepared herself to deliver the news. In her hand she clutched the test results tightly, afraid of what he was going to say. Placing a hand on his knee, she prepared to deliver the news. "You know I've been sick."

Blue cut her off immediately, not giving her a chance to finish. "So you been sick for two muthafuckin' weeks?" he held up two fingers. That weak-ass excuse caused him to sober up quickly.

"Yes. Why don't you believe me?" she yelled loudly, scratching her throat in the process.

"You must be fuckin' another nigga," he spat furiously at the thought she could betray him after everything they'd been through.

"Why would you say that?" By this time she was belligerent and loud. "I never cheated on you, and you know it." Sasha was determined to get her point across.

Blue patted his chest. "I ain't gettin' the pussy, so somebody hittin' it."

"I never cheated on you," she screamed, trying to make a point and knowing damn well she recently cheated with Nate.

He pointed his trigger finger at her. "Aye, stop yelling before you wake up my baby."

"Oh, so now you worried about her?"

"I'm always worried about her. Don't get that shit twisted." He sat upright so she could look into his eyes when he spoke. "Me not answering your calls has nothing to do with her."

She was heated. "Whatever, Blue. Fuck it. If you don't care, I don't either."

"You think I would be arguing with you if I didn't care? You don't recognize a good nigga when you got one. You so used to dealing with fuck-niggas you don't know how to treat one." He pointed in her direction. "Keep on and you gon' push me away."

"You threatening me now?"

Blue shook his head from side to side. "Take it how you want to, but you heard what I said."

Just hearing him talk that way frightened her because he didn't talk to her like that. She had no intention of losing him, and she definitely wasn't losing him to another bitch. He may not have said it directly, but she could read between the lines. Tears begin to cascade down her face as she grew more emotional than before. "Blue, don't do this to me. I love you so much. You just don't understand what I'm going through."

Seeing her cry always made him weak, but he was beginning to think she knew this. Blue massaged his scalp with his forefingers before scooting beside her. "I love you, too. I just don't know what's up with you. We haven't had sex in two weeks. How do you think that makes me feel? Every time I try to touch you, it's always an excuse. Then if I get outside pussy, it's a problem. I don't know what you expect me to do, Sasha, but I'm a man, and I have needs," he explained after taking the bass out of his voice.

Sasha rubbed her wet eyes and sniffled. The anticipation built up in her chest, and she knew it was now or never. She had to tell him about her test results before it was too late. "I went to the doctor, and I need to show you something."

"What's wrong?" he asked.

Sasha raised her shaky hand that held her fate and gave him the paper. Blue scanned the paper to its entirety, his eyes moving back and forth. He looked up with a blank stare, taking a moment to register the answer he had been searching for.

"Damn!" Blue was in disbelief as he stood to his feet. Everything finally made sense, and now he knew the reason behind the drought. "How long have you known about this?"

"Not long. I just got the results today." Playing with her fingers, she avoided all contact until he was done questioning her.

"Come here." He held his hand out, and when she accepted it, he pulled her close to him and wrapped his arms around her.

"Damn, I can't believe we having another baby. We gon' have to move out soon."

Sasha dried her eyes as she cried tears of joy. "I know. I was saying the same thing." It was such a relief to know her HIV results came back negative. She could finally breathe again, although she wasn't expecting a positive pregnancy test, either. However, she would take those results any day over the other.

Blue continued to rock her in his arms. "I guess we made a Puerto Rican baby, huh?" he laughed and released his hold from her.

"I guess so," she replied.

"I'm going to the shower. I'll be right back."

"Okay."

Blue walked out of the room with his phone in his hand and put it on silent just in case Emani decided to call or text. That wasn't her normal behavior, but he didn't want to take any chances on getting caught. The way he put that dick on her, she was liable to lose her mind.

After a long, hot shower he went back into the room and cuddled up next to Sasha. He now understood the reason behind the drought, but that would never change the fact he cheated.

The shower had him so relaxed he could barely move once he lay down. Sasha extended her arm and played with his dreads. "Did you cheat on me?" she asked, catching him off guard.

"Huh?" he asked, acting as if he didn't hear her the first time.

"You said you had needs and I wasn't fulfilling them, so I'm asking did you cheat on me?" Sasha took a deep breath. "Please don't lie to me."

Lying to her wasn't what he wanted to do, but hurting her again was something he couldn't handle. The last time he was truthful didn't go so well, so he kept it to himself. "No, baby, I didn't cheat on you."

Pulling her closer, he held her tight in his arms until they both fell asleep.

***

Sasha rolled over and stretched after a good night's sleep. Blue's side of the bed was cold. Slowly opening her eyes, she looked around to see if he had taken his belongings. That meant he went to class, since his keys and phone were missing. Reaching for her phone, she glanced at the time and could see why she was alone. It was almost noon and she was just getting up. It had been a long time since she slept in so late.

Dream wasn't in her bed, either, but she had a feeling she was in the room with Darlene, the woman who had played the grandmother role since day one. Ever since she got the results from the DNA test she had contemplated being with Quamae, but now that she was pregnant with Blue's baby, she was more confused than ever.

Letting out a huge yawn, she covered her mouth and shook her head. Sasha was drained mentally and physically. The entire ordeal with her health is what really led to all the exhaustion. Dying from a deadly disease was not how she planned on leaving the earth. Going forward, it mas mandatory to stop being so careless and make her health her number one priority, especially if she planned on being there to raise her kids and grandchildren. Chauncey had really opened her eyes, and that shit wasn't kosher.

Sasha finally decided to pull herself to the edge of the bed, placing her feet on the floor. Taking a deep breath, she closed her eyes for a few seconds, and when she opened them up they were filled with water. After a few blinks the tears were moving quickly down her cheeks. The pain she felt in her heart made her weak. Her breathing was shallow, and she began to hyperventilate. The snot tried to escape her nose, but her sniffles managed to bring it back up, avoiding her lip.

Last night's news was supposed to bring her and Blue closer, but she had a feeling it did the opposite. All they did was cuddle and go to sleep. Not once did he try to slide in and end their no-sex streak. Those actions meant one thing to her: he had gotten some pussy from someone else, and in her mind and heart she knew that was a fact. If Blue had even gotten a whiff of the truth, she had a feeling he would have a hard time trusting her, let alone being with her.

Wrapped up in her emotions, the tears grew heavier and the sobbing came into play. Her woman's intuition would not let her mind rest on Blue's infidelities, and she wasn't crazy by a long shot. Nor did she need a lie detector test to prove it.

Then there was Quamae. Yes, she still loved her husband, and if he changed the way he said he did, then she knew they could be happy once again. The new bank account he gave her with $100,000 was an added bonus, but the fact he started going to counseling to become a better man was something she was proud of, and that was the reason she was going with him that afternoon. It would give her insight on if they could conquer their storm and keep their vows as promised. Quamae wasn't perfect, and neither was she, so it was definitely worth the fight.

Slowly rising from the bed, she gathered up her items to go and take a hot shower before meeting up with her estranged husband.

***

It was a quarter to two, and Sasha was sitting in the parking lot waiting on Quamae to pull up for the session. While she waited on him to arrive, she pulled out her kindle and tried to finish up a book she was reading. A few minutes passed and she was completely wrapped up in her reading. There was a tap on her window, causing her heart to drop to her ass. When she looked up, Quamae was laughing. She pushed the car door open with force.

"That is not funny, jerk." She couldn't help but smile. "You scared the shit out of me."

"Yeah, it actually was. If you saw your face, you would've laughed, too." He looked in the backseat. "Where is my baby?"

"I left her at the house." Sasha tried mumbling her words 'cause she knew he was about to say something about her leaving the baby behind.

"You left her there with that nigga?" Quamae propped his arm on the car door, mugging her slightly.

"His mama is watching her for me. You know she ain't gon' stay quiet in there, and kids not allowed, anyway." Sasha grabbed her bag and placed her kindle inside. Taking her keys from the ignition, she got out of the car and closed the door.

"You thought I was gon' be okay with that?" The volume in his voice raised a few notches. "You know me better than that."

"Yeah, I know that, but what do you expect me to do? That's all she knows right now. They've been there from the beginning."

"I don't care, that's not her father." Quamae hit his chest. "I am. What, you didn't tell the nigga it wasn't his baby?"

A shouting match was not what she was expecting, but then again, this was Quamae she was talking about. Leaning against her car, she dropped her head. Once again he managed to hurt her feelings, and because she was so hormonal, it didn't take much to make her cry.

"Quamae, you abandoned us, and that's who took us in without judgment. You put me out, remember?" Hopefully the reminder would get him to tone it down a bit.

Making her cry wasn't in his plans, but he needed her to answer his question first. "Did you tell him that's not his daughter?"

Sasha shook her head and whispered, "No."

Suddenly Quamae snapped out of his angry stage and stepped closer to her to wrap his arms around her, but she flinched. "Sasha, please don't be afraid of me. I promise I will never put my hands on you again, and that's my word."

"Okay." Her voice was a tad bit shaky.

The car keys were still in her hand, so he grabbed them and placed them into his pocket, then took her hand into his. "I'm sorry for yelling at you, and I don't want to see you cry. Just understand where I'm coming from. I don't want another man raising my daughter, and I don't want her comfortable with them." Quamae rubbed her back and kissed the top of her head. "I love you, Sasha, and all I want is for you and my daughter to come home. I'll buy another house if I need to so we can create new memories. Just tell me what you want."

"I don't know what I want," she admitted.

"Okay, take your time, but right now we need to get inside and start this session."

"Okay, I'm ready."

***

"Thank you so much for coming, Sasha, and again it's a pleasure to meet you. I advised Quamae to bring you because that would be good for his healing process. There is so much you don't know, but that's where he is going to come in and fill you in on his past. I'm going to sit in silence and allow you two to talk."

Christine put on her glasses and crossed her legs with her notepad in her hand, prepared to take notes. "You may begin, Quamae. Let her know why she's here, and then explain the birth of your insecurities."

"Okay." He took a deep breath before he started. "I brought you here because I never told you how my father really died. After I tell you the story, then you will understand why I had a hard time trusting women."

Sasha nodded her head to let him know she was listening. The truth is what she needed to hear because she knew there was a reason behind his insecurities, but he never disclosed that information to her. He always made it seem like she was why he snapped off for no reason at all. If she was going to take him back, she needed the whole truth and nothing but the truth.

"When I was younger, my father used to work late at night. He and my mom used to argue all the time because he spent so much time away from home, but he was the breadwinner in the family. After a while my mom got tired of being second to his job and started seeing another man. They would have sex in the house my father paid for without any regard to her kids being in the home. One night my father came home early and caught my mother's boyfriend in the house." Quamae paused due to the sensitivity of the story for a few seconds. This was the part of the story that caused him to grow weak and breakdown. Their bond was tight, and he had been robbed of growing into manhood with his father by his side and guiding him in the right direction.

"That was the first time I ever saw my dad hit my mom," Quamae sniffled as he tried to continue the story. "After that my dad and her boyfriend started fighting, and then there was a gunshot. I watched my dad collapse to the floor, bleeding from his stomach. As he lay on the floor dying, I held his hand for dear life. He knew he was about to die, and that's when he made me promise to take care of Emani."

Sasha slid closer to her husband to console him. She slipped her fingers in between his and looked deeply into his eyes. "I'm sorry, Quamae, and I wish you would've told me this sooner. The same way I should've told you about my past."

"My mother is the reason I don't trust women. You can give a woman your all, take care of the home and the kids, and they will still step out on you. She did this to me, and her ho-ish ways is what got my father killed. I never forgave her for that, and I never will."

"I understand you completely now after hearing this, and now I know I didn't make it better for you." Sasha used her finger to wipe away the tears from both of his eyes. "And I'm sorry for everything I did to you. I should've never used your absence or business as an excuse to cheat."

Christine knew she could save their marriage, and she was determined to help them get past their faults. "That was really good for the both of you, and I believe we can make this work together, as long as both parties want this. Is that the ultimate goal here?" Her attention was on Sasha.

"I'm willing to see where it goes," she replied. "There is so much damage from the mental and physical abuse."

"Yes, I can understand that, and I have spoken to him about that. Quamae has made tremendous progress for not only himself, but for you. This marriage is worth fighting for." She then looked at Quamae. "How do you feel about what she said?"

Looking into Sasha's eyes, he made sure she understood what

he meant by his words. "I'm going to do any and everything it takes to get my family back, and I mean that." Quamae gently pulled his hand away from his wife and looked over at Christine. "I need to step out for a minute. I'll be right back."

"Okay." She then turned to Sasha. "So, tell me a little bit about you until he returns."

Quamae walked through the parking lot quickly to his truck. Time was of the essence, and he needed to utilize every moment of it. Killing the alarm, he snatched open the door, opened the glove box, and removed the envelope and device he had for Sasha. Every word he told her was the truth. No matter what he had to do to get her back, it would be done, and he put that on his father's grave. When all was said and done, someone was going to hurt, but it wasn't gon' be him.

Slamming the door behind him, he jogged to her car and pulled her key from his pocket. Opening up the door, he opened her glove box and placed the envelope inside. "Sasha, baby, get ready to come home to daddy. It's the gift that keeps on giving."

Quamae closed the door and walked to the front of the car. Kneeling down, he placed the GPS tracker underneath the car inside the bumper, rose to his feet, and walked off.

Chapter 14

Blue jumped up from a deep sleep. Looking at his phone, he realized it was 8:25 a.m. Springing to the floor, he grabbed his boxers and slipped them on. "Shit!" he shouted.

"What's wrong?" Sasha rolled over with sleep in her eyes and yawned.

"I overslept, and my damn class starts at 9:15 a.m." He grabbed his towel and ran out of the room to take a shower. There was no way he was going to school with a sticky dick. Blue hated to rush when he got dressed, but he was on borrowed time 'cause he definitely didn't want to be late for class. Since he'd been back he made every single class and was never late. Education was everything to him, and he took that seriously. Becoming a doctor would keep him out of the game forever.

Jumping into the shower, he turned on the water and it was cold as shit hitting his skin. Chill bumps surfaced instantly. "Damn, that's cold," he shivered. Dropping some Axe shower gel onto his rag, he lathered it up and washed himself from head to toe. "A ho bath gon' have to do today."

Blue stood underneath the shower and rinsed himself off, then turned off the water. His movements were quick as he headed to the sink to brush his teeth and wash his face. When he was done, he went into the room to get dressed. Sasha was lying in bed, but he could see she laid out his clothes.

"Thanks for getting my clothes out."

"You're welcome, baby." Sasha watched him apply cocoa butter to his flawless skin and pretty dick. Licking her lips, she salivated over the way his piece glistened. "Too bad we couldn't get a quickie."

"That's the reason I overslept in the first place. That li'l coochie should be tired after the way I dug up in them guts last night and put that pound game on her ass." Blue pulled his shirt over his head, then sat down on the bed to put on his socks and shoes.

"Grown-ass women don't have coochies. We have a pussies,

thank you."

"Yeah, I hear that, but yo' grown ass was in here whining like a little-ass girl while this dick was up in ya."

She couldn't argue with that 'cause it was the truth. Instead she laughed it out. "So that's why you gon' have a backward-ass day, 'cause you put your pants on before your socks."

Blue looked over his shoulder and laughed at the foolishness she was spitting. "What?"

"You supposed to put your socks on first, and then your pants, college boy."

He leaned back and kissed her. "Yeah, yeah, I hear you, old lady. I gotta go before I'm late for real."

"Okay."

On his way out, he kissed Dream on her head and left. Time was ticking, and he had 25 minutes to get to class. Blue rushed to his truck and unlocked the doors. Just as he opened the door, he saw his tire was flat. "What the fuck?" He was frustrated right away. "You got to be fuckin' kiddin' me." He took a look at the tire and realized there was a cut on the tire wall.

Rushing back into the house, he ran to the room where Sasha was sitting up watching T.V.

"What did you forget?" she asked.

"I need to borrow your car 'cause my damn tire flat."

"Look in my Louie bag on the hamper."

Blue looked through the purse until he found them. "Okay, I'm out."

Blue was hauling ass trying to get to class on time, and when he came up to the light it had just turned red. He was already speeding, so there was no need to slam on the brakes, so he kept going. Seconds later he could hear sirens behind him.

"Fuck!" He hit the steering wheel. "The last thing I need is a muthafuckin' ticket." Throwing on the hazard lights, he pulled over on the side of the road and slipped on his seatbelt. A speeding ticket was more than enough. He didn't need a seatbelt ticket, too.

The officer walked up with a nasty scowl on his face. With his hand on his holster, he tapped on the window. Blue rolled down the window and made sure his hands were visible. There were so many killings that had taken place with law enforcement, so he made sure he was cautious. He wasn't being a statistic today. Not on his watch.

"Where you headed in a hurry?" The officer was chewing hard on some gum.

"I'm late for class."

"Oh, really? What class would that be?" Realizing he wasn't a threat, he took his hand off his holster and placed it on the hood of the car.

"Anatomy and physiology at the University of Miami. Here's my ID card." Blue picked up the badge on the seat and showed it to him.

The officer smiled. "What you going for?"

"My bachelor's degree. And when I'm done, medical school."

"You wanna be a doctor?"

"I'm going to be a doctor just like my mother."

"Well, good luck to you, and make sure you be on time to all your classes," he chuckled.

Blue laughed as well. "I will."

"I tell you what, I'll let you go with a warning as long as you have your license and registration."

"Sure, that's not a problem." Blue unfastened his seatbelt and leaned over to get the registration from the glove box. As soon as he pulled out the registration, an envelope fell on the floor. Sitting up, he handed it over, then pulled his wallet from his pocket to retrieve his driver's license.

The officer looked at both of them and handed it back to him. "Go ahead and get to class. Good luck, young man."

"Thank you, I appreciate that."

As soon as he walked off, Blue picked up the envelope from the floor and opened it out of curiosity. The first thing he noticed was the letter heading, and his heart sank to the pit of his stomach. In bold letters he saw Sasha, Quamae, and his baby girl Dream's name. Blue's heart was beating out of his chest as he continued to read, praying his arch nemesis wasn't the father.

The moment he began to read the numbers and then the words at the bottom of the letter, he wished he could undo what his eyes just saw. Filled with so much anger and rage, he threw the letter in the passenger seat, put the car in gear, and pulled off. There would be no class today 'cause Sasha was about to straighten him. She had really gone against the grain. Out of everything she had been through with her husband, she would fall back into his trap and disobey the man who had been there for her and the little girl he knew as his daughter?

When Blue finally made it to the house, he rushed inside, leaving his book bag behind and slamming the door behind him. Sasha was so engaged in her phone conversation with Lelah when he walked into the room that she didn't notice him come in.

Suspicious of who she was on the phone with, he snatched it and put the phone to his ear.

"What are you doing?" she yelled.

"Who is this?" Blue barked into the phone.

"It's me, Blue. Lelah." She was so confused at what was going on.

"She'll call you back." Blue hung up the phone and stood there. His chest was heaving, breathing like a fucking dragon.

"What the fuck is wrong with you?" She was clearly confused because not too long ago he seemed to be fine.

Now he had her attention. Blue threw the results in her face. "What the fuck is this?"

Sasha jumped back. "I don't fuckin' know."

"Open it." Blue was so loud he scared Dream and she started crying, but he couldn't pull himself to look in her direction.

Sasha handed her a bottle, then proceeded to pull the papers out of the envelope to see what had him so upset. When she saw the DNA results, she wanted to die right then and there, but she had to make things right. "Let me explain." She stood up and took two steps toward Blue, but he backed up.

"Yeah, explain why you went behind my back with that fuck-nigga and got her tested anyway." In his mind he wanted to slap fire from her ass, but he couldn't do it. It was bad enough he broke his promise to never put his hands on her. Since she was carrying his baby, she was safe.

"I didn't have a choice. I'm sorry." Sasha tried to reach for his hand, but he moved it from her grasp.

"You had a choice 'cause I told you not to do it." Granted he knew there was a possibility he wasn't the biological, it just hurt to know the truth. He would have preferred to continue on with the way things were going.

"He had a right to know, and regardless if I agreed to do it or not, we still have to go to court for the divorce. All that was gonna do is make things bad for me," Sasha pleaded, trying to call him down. Her mind was racing, but there was only one explanation to how he got those in his hand, and that was Quamae.

"Bad for you?" Blue leaned against the dresser with his arms folded. "What about me? Fuck my feelings, huh?"

"No, it's not like that. I love you, and you know that. But I know Quamae, and he would've filed for full custody if I didn't do it. What would you have done to make sure the courts didn't take my baby? I don't have a job, and you don't either." Sasha paused. "Wait, where did you get this from?"

"The same place you left them. In your fuckin' glove box."

At that point she knew Quamae put them there, and he did make it very clear he would do anything to get her back.

Blue wasn't trying to see the bigger picture. His only focus was the fact he was betrayed by the woman he professed his love to and shared his bed and home with. "You think I would've allowed that? And secondly, he would have to prove you unfit. And thirdly," he drops his arms and patted his chest, "I signed her birth certificate. Or did you forget that, too?"

"I'm sorry." She walked up to him and they stood eye-to-eye. "But we're gonna get through this. I'm carrying your child now. Everything is gonna be okay. We live here with you, and she knows you as her daddy. Her DNA shouldn't ruin the way you feel about her. The bond is too strong."

Blue teared up, but he refused to let them fall. Sasha peeped it and hugged him tightly. "I'm sorry, baby. Please believe me. I didn't mean to hurt you."

Sasha's apology didn't mean shit to him. Instead of responding, he placed his hands on her arms and pushed her gently so she could let him go. When he was free, he walked to the closet and grabbed his duffle bag.

Sasha watched him as he filled up the bag and reality set in on what was going on. "Where are you going?" she asked softly.

Blue ignored her and continued to put his personal items inside. When he was all packed up, he suddenly remembered one of his tires was still flat on the truck, so he had to hit up his boy. He took his phone out of his back pocket and dialed his number.

"Wassup homie?" Chico answered.

"Aye, come pick me up from the crib and take me to the rim shop. I need a tire."

"You in luck, my boy, 'cause I'm by you."

"Good. I'll be outside waiting."

"A'ight."

Blue hung up the phone and threw the duffle bag on his shoulder. On his way out of the room, he didn't look Sasha's way. A few seconds later he could hear her footsteps behind him, but he kept going.

Sasha ran out of the house as quickly as possible so she could catch up with him. "Blue, wait."

Sasha grabbed his arm, but he snatched away from her. He turned around and saw she left the baby in the house. "Sasha, stop and go back in the house with the baby."

"Oh, so that's how you refer to her now? As 'the baby?'" She had her hands on her hip.

"Man, g'on with all that, 'cause you can't flip the script on me."

Blue received a notification that he had a text message, so he went over to his truck and sat the bag in the driver's seat. When he looked at the phone, he saw it was Emani.

Admissions: I missed you in class today ☹
Blue: Yeah, I know. I'ma come spend the night with you

Admissions: I like the sound of that
Blue: I'll be over after I leave the tire shop
Admissions: Okay, I'll be waiting

Blue put his phone up in time, 'cause when he looked up Sasha was within a few feet from him, walking fast with a unit on her face.

"Don't put it up now." She pointed her finger in his face. "Who you texting? One of yo' hos?"

He moved his head to the side. "Come on, don't put your hand in my face. I don't have hos."

"So why did you put your phone up when I walked over here?"

"'Cause I was done texting." Blue tried to move her from in front of him, but she grabbed the steering wheel. "Come on, man, move and stop playing."

"I'm not playing with you, and I know you going to a bitch's house, too. You think I'm stupid and shit."

Sasha was really testing his patience, and he was trying so hard to be patient with her. The sound of a truck was coming up the block, and he was happy to see it was Chico in the tow truck. "Watch out, 'cause my ride here." Sasha stepped to the side and allowed him to walk away, but it wasn't over between them. Blue stood on the sidewalk and waited on Chico to get out.

"What's up, bruh?" They slapped hands and G-hugged.

"Trying to get up outta here. This crazy-ass girl trippin' hard."

"Damn, sorry to hear that," Chico laughed.

"Come on and hook my shit up so we can bounce before I get booked downtown."

"Damn, it's that bad?"

"Hell yeah."

"A'ight. Let me back it in, then."

Blue stepped to the side and watched Chico back the tow truck up to his and lower the slab. It took about 15 minutes to get it up there, and as soon as he started to strap it up, Sasha went to flipping out again.

"So, you not coming back home?" She stepped in his face again, doing all that yelling.

"Sasha, get out my face. I don't understand why you trying to provoke me." Cutting his eyes to the side, he looked up at Chico. "Bruh, please hurry up so we can go."

"Answer my question. Now." She rocked back and forth on her heels.

"I don't have to answer shit. You do what you wanna do, so I'm doing what I wanna do. I come back, then that's what it is. If I don't, then hey, that's what it is. Go call your husband and reconcile. You want that nigga back, anyway."

That comment made her flip and take wild swings at him. Blue tried hard to restrain her, but she was very strong at that moment. "Fuck you, Blue. Let me go. You ain't shit!" she yelled.

"This is all your fault, and you mad at me. Get the fuck outta here, bruh."

His laughter only pissed her off even more.

Chico could no longer stand back and just watch, so he jumped in and tried to calm her down. "Calm down, ma, you pregnant." He held her hands. "I don't know what's going on, and I don't wanna know, but you got to stop."

"Yo' friend ain't shit, trying to sneak off and stay with a bitch." Sasha tried to escape his grip, but his ass was cock-strong. She could see Blue looking at her, shaking his head.

"You think you got all the sense, but you don't."

Chico managed to get Sasha to the front door while Blue got inside the truck. "Go in the house and cool off, ma, for real."

"Tell him I'll be gone when he get back." Sasha walked into the house and slammed the door behind her.

Chapter 15

Sasha walked into the room and saw Dream was asleep in her bed with the bottle still in her mouth. Easing it from her mouth, she sat it on the dresser. She was happy she went back to sleep because Blue had just put her in a foul mood. The suspicions she had about him cheating had just been confirmed.

Crawling into bed, she bundled up underneath the covers and cried into the pillow. It was obvious a faithful man wasn't in her deck of cards. She went from a bad marriage to a bad relationship and lost two best friends all in one year. The only good thing to come from all of it was her daughter, Dream, and her newfound relationship with her son, NJ. Just when she thought things were good, that bitch Karma always showed up and showed out. She just couldn't win for losing, and it made her wonder what she was doing wrong. Another heartbreak is what she couldn't take.

Sleep was what she needed at the moment, and after that she was out of there. When she woke up, she planned on going to spend the night with Quamae since Blue wasn't coming home.

Sasha had been asleep for a little over an hour when her phone rang, waking her up. "Hello."

The voice on the other end was loud and she couldn't make out what the caller was saying. It was a female for sure, though. "Who is this?" she asked.

"Jazz," she cried.

The first thing that came to mind was, *What the hell did NJ do to this girl now?* "Calm down so I can hear you."

"NJ is in the hospital. You need to come here. It's bad." There was a lot of rumbling in the background.

"Jazz?" she called out, but she didn't say anything. Now she was anxious and aggravated at the same time. Sasha hung up the phone and called Nate.

"Hello," he answered on the second ring.

"What's going on?" she panicked.

"NJ got jumped by some niggas." Nate tried to remain calm, but all he wanted to do was lay down whoever harmed his son.

Sasha stood up and paced the floor with her hand on top of her head. She could feel a migraine coming on strong. "What happened?"

"I don't know. I'm on my way to the hospital now. He's at Broward General."

"Okay, I'll meet you there."

"A'ight."

Sasha hung up and called Quamae. The tears were running down her face heavily. "Why is all this happening to me at once? I just don't understand."

Quamae's phone kept ringing and ringing. When he didn't answer, she called him right back, and this time he answered. "It's been a long time since you called me back-to-back. What's going on, wifey?"

"I need you to watch the baby while I go to the hospital," Sasha sobbed.

Hearing the brittleness in her voice let him know that whatever happened was serious. "What's wrong?"

"My son is in the hospital. He may not make it, and I need to get to him, and I don't want to take the baby."

"Damn, I'm sorry to hear that. Drop her off to the house, and drive safe, please."

"Okay, I'm on my way."

Sasha packed Dream's bag quickly, strapped her in the car seat, and headed out the door. Her son needed her, and she had to get there fast, but in one piece.

**

When Sasha arrived at the hospital, the waiting room was packed with people. She could hear a woman screaming at the top of her lungs as she got closer to the nurses' station. There was a small crowd standing around the woman. Apparently they were trying to hold her up.

More concerned with her own journey, she looked around the room for Nate and Jazz. Finally spotting them in the corner, she

154

ran over to them. Nate stood up when she was within arm's distance.

"What's going on? Is my baby okay?" Sasha couldn't stop the tears from falling.

Nate took her by the arms and led her to the seat next to him. "He's going to be okay. I promise," Nate assured her while drying her tears.

"He's all we got. We can't lose him like this." Sasha's eyes were bloodshot red and her hair was mangled. The sadness in her eyes and the puffiness around them made it look as if she hadn't slept in days. "Has the doctor been out here yet?"

"Yes."

"What did he say?"

"He was unconscious when they brought him in. Once they have him stable, they will give us an update."

"Nate, I'm scared."

Nate rubbed her shoulders while she buried her head in his chest. "I'm here, and everything will be okay. God's got him."

"I hope so."

"Have faith."

The whole hospital thing was a fiasco, a waiting game, and they were getting more and more impatient by the second. Jazz was still hollering. Nate looked at her. "I'ma need you to calm down before you get admitted next."

"I'm trying, but I love him so much. I don't know what I would do without him."

Nate pulled her close to him as well, giving her his other shoulder to cry on. Now he had to be strong for both women.

Two hours later the doctor walked into the waiting room and in their direction. Sasha immediately started to panic. Nate was cool, calm, and collected as always.

As soon as the doctor began to speak, Sasha closed her eyes and squeezed Nate's hand tight.

"I have great news. Your son is going to be just fine. I have him stable. He needed a lot of stitches, but he's going to recover just fine."

"Oh, thank you so much." She finally felt a sense of relief. It wasn't time to let go of her son yet. They were just getting into the bonding thing, and they had so much further to go. "I wanna see him. Please let me see my baby."

"Right this way," the doctor responded.

***

Blue and Emani were lying in bed, Netflix-and-chilling. His mind was still fucked up after finding out the results of the paternity test. It was one thing to find out when he knew it was coming, but to be caught off guard hurt like a muthafucka.

Emani was cuddled up under him closely, listening to his heartbeat. She knew something was on his mind because he would space out every now and again. She rubbed her hand over his chest. "Are you okay?" she asked sincerely.

"Yeah, I'm good," he lied.

"You sure? 'Cause you're awfully quiet." Emani really liked Blue, and she was genuinely concerned about him. However, she knew there was trouble at home, being as he never spent the night. No matter how long or hard they fucked, he always managed to go home. This night it was different, and he came with an overnight bag.

Just as he was about to answer her question, his phone rang. Reaching over to the nightstand, he picked up the phone and saw it was Joker calling.

"What's up, bruh?"

"Aye, we handled that shit for you tonight. That nigga in the hospital right now."

"A'ight, fam. I'll slide up on you tomorrow."

"Oh yeah, I think you should know your cousin up there with the nigga mama and daddy. I don't know, my boy, we might've did that shit for nothing 'cause she ain't gon' stop fuckin' with the nigga."

"A'ight. I gotta go."

"Yeah."

After hearing that he wasn't happy at all, but he would deal with Jazz another day. Right then he had pressure he needed to get off. Blue put his phone back where it was and removed his boxers, tossing them on the floor. He then pushed the comforter off of him to get free. Using his right hand he stroked his dick, and with his left hand he rubbed his fingers across her lips. "Get him up for me."

Like the good girl she was, Emani sat up and took his dick into her mouth. Whatever she needed to do to win his heart and make him happy, she was down for it. The fact he was there with her showed progress. Her relationship goal was to take Blue from his woman and make him her man.

***

After being at the hospital all night and a majority of the morning, Sasha finally made her way home. When she walked into the room she knew Blue never came home. The bed was still made and everything was still in place from the day before. She was grateful Quamae volunteered to keep Dream while she spent time at NJ's bedside because seeing her firstborn battered and bruised had her furious, hurt, and confused.

Dealing with the bullshit with Blue and now NJ had her on beast mode, and she was liable to snap at any given moment. Kicking off her shoes, Sasha threw her keys and purse on the floor. "This bitch think he slick 'cause I know he stayed with a ho last night."

Too tired for a shower, she pulled off her clothes and tossed them on the floor as well, then climbed into the bed wearing her bra and panties. As soon as her head touched the pillow, she closed her eyes. The comfort and coolness of the bed was exactly what she needed. Her body sunk into the mattress like she was lying on a cloud.

Approximately ten minutes later Sasha jumped up fuming. "Nah, he got me fucked up." Springing off the bed, she landed on her feet like a feline. "If he think he about to try me like this, he got another fuckin' thing coming."

Her cell phone was still inside of her purse, so she pulled it out and went through her call log until she located his number. Blue's phone rang a few times before it went to voicemail. "Answer this phone, stupid," she continued to rant. "You better answer this phone before I flip the fuck out on yo' ass, and I swear you don't wanna see this 'cause you fuckin' with the wrong bitch."

Sasha called him several more times, but each and every call went to voicemail. "That's okay. I'll call Lelah 'cause I know she'll tell me if you was there or not." She couldn't dial her girl's number fast enough to get the scoop.

***

Two days had passed, and Blue hadn't stepped foot back in the house because he was too busy digging all up in Emani's guts. The two of them stayed indoors during their little impromptu sleepover, getting to know one another on a more physical and personal level.

"When I say my body is tired, I mean that shit," Emani yawned while rubbing Blue's chest.

Blue kissed the top of her head as he played in her hair. "I had a lot of built-up pressure that had to be released. I'm going through it right now. I had to take it out on somebody."

Hearing him laugh made her do the same. "Well, I'm glad I could help you out with that."

Staring up into his eyes, she felt as if he was the one for her. Emani was so intoxicated by his swag and sexiness that she wished she could have him to herself. It was a stretch, but she figured with time and patience she could win him over, especially since his girl was tripping and he ended up staying with her and not going home. He wasn't even answering her calls, so she knew she was making progress.

"I wish this could last forever."

"Oh yeah?" Blue wasn't sure where his relationship was

going, but there were underlining issues with the woman he shared his bed with, and now the mother of his first child. True enough he wanted to be with Sasha, but without trust there was no relationship. If she could lie about something so serious and defy him, there was no telling what else she would do behind his back.

"Yes. I like you, and we have great chemistry. I know we would make a good couple."

"I like you, too, but shit is real complicated right now. We gotta take this slow."

That was a true statement, and there was no need in her battling his decision. Emani looked down and stared at the blanket. She was a little disappointed since she was trying to put it out in the universe. She believed in the Law of Attraction, so it was mandatory to speak positive on their situation-ship. Whatever she thought and felt would come to her just the way she imagined it.

"I respect your honesty." His response hurt her feelings, but she didn't let it show. Emani took that to the chin and let it go. The most important thing was he was there with her at that moment.

"All I know to be is one thousand. You deserve that much from me."

"Yeah, I do."

This time she looked up at him and kissed him on the mouth, and he didn't resist. His warm tongue entered her mouth and she sucked on it softly. Just a moment ago she complained about her body being tired, and here she was ready to go another round. Blue rolled over on top of her already-naked body and positioned himself in between her thick-ass thighs while they continued to kiss one another.

The intensity of their chemistry automatically made the tip of his head throb as if it had a heartbeat. With his left hand being used to prop his body up, he used his right hand to rub his head up and down her slit. On contact Emani rolled her hips. She was ready and super wet, just the way he liked it, but he wanted to tease her just a bit more. For the next minute or so he kissed on her neck and let his bare dick press up against her lips.

"Put it in," she moaned.

"You ready?" he asked, although he knew the answer judging by the way she kept grinding against him and wrapping her legs around his waist.

"Yes, so stop teasing me. I want it." Emani wanted this time to be special, so she reached over to grab her phone and looked for the mix she created just for her and Blue. Once she found it, she pressed play and sat it back down. A few seconds later *Pushin' Inside of You* was playing by Sons of Funk.

Blue used his hand to guide his rock-hard dick inside of her juicy opening slowly. He wanted to take his time since he wasn't in a rush. As soon as he sank deep inside, hitting the bottom, she gasped and wrapped her legs around his waist once again. His strokes were slow, yet deep, going along with the rhythm of the music. Emani squeezed her muscles tight, as well as her eyes, and enjoyed each and every thrust.

His dreads constantly smacked against her face, so she rubbed her hand through them before taking a handful into the palm of her hand. "Oh my God, this feels so good," she cried out. "Go deeper."

"That's how you want it?" he asked.

"Yes," she moaned.

Blue was gon' give it to her just the way she wanted it. Lying on top of her body, he put an extra oomph in his thrust and dug deep inside, finishing up with a hard grind. Emani's nails went straight to his back, but he didn't pay it any mind. He had a mission to complete.

The way he was putting it down, he could've moved in right then and there for all she cared. As long as he was delivering hard-hittin' sex, he had the green light. Emani felt every inch he owned in her stomach and all the way down to the bottom of her ass, but she still didn't want him to stop. There was no doubt he wasn't making slow, sweet, passionate love to her by the way he slowly wound with her frame. Unable to contain the tears, they flowed heavily out of both eyes and toward her ears while she sang along with the song.

Sho' feels damn good to me

160

When I'm pushin' inside of you.
Can't explain the way it feels.
All I wanna do is be with you.
Sho' feels damn good to me
When I'm pushin' inside of you.
Can't explain the way it feels.
All I wanna do is be with you.

Hearing those words really pulled at her heartstrings and played with her mind, making her more emotional than ever before. All she wanted was for Blue to move in with her and make love to her every night with no restrictions. They hadn't been together for a long time, but the longevity didn't mean shit when her conscience was telling her something different, and she was sure he felt the same way, without a doubt. No matter what he told her.

The feeling of urination settled in, and she was ready to let it go. Gripping Blue by the waist, she pulled him closer to her and threw it back on him hard. "I'm cummin'." The shallowness of her breathing was confirmation.

"Let that shit go," he demanded.

"I am."

"Cum all over this dick." Blue applied the rest of his body weight on her and pulled one of her legs off of him, pushed it toward the headboard, and beat up the box.

"Ooh," Emani's voice cracked. "I'm cummin', I'm cummin', daddy. Fuck me just like that."

"I'm cummin', too. You better get yours," he warned her, 'cause after that he was out of gas.

A few moments passed and Emani was creaming all over his dick and shouting like she just caught the Holy Ghost. Blue drilled her ass for a few more minutes until he felt that tingling sensation. Once it reached the tip of his head, he pulled out of the pussy and jacked his dick, cumming all over her stomach.

"Ah," he grunted. "Shit. Ah."

After that he wasn't good for shit but a nap. Since he'd been there, all they did was eat, drink, fuck, and sleep. He lay down on his back and looked up at the ceiling. "You trying to make me overdose on pussy."

Emani laughed. "No, I'm not. I'm just trying to satisfy you and me, that's all." She then got up to use the bathroom and clean the babies off her stomach.

It wasn't a whole two minutes before his phone started ringing. Something on the inside warned him it was Sasha's crazy ass, so he didn't bother to move. The phone continued to ring off the hook, so after the third attempt he looked at the screen and saw it was Zoe. Thinking it could be an emergency, he picked up the phone. "Wadup, bruh?"

"Shit, tryin' to catch yo' ass."

"What's goin' on?"

"I need to talk to you." Zoe hated what he was about to do, but something needed to be done.

"About what?"

"It's about your girl," he coolly stated.

Blue needed privacy, so he got up and went into the bathroom and closed the door behind him. Emani was interested in who he was talking to, so she got up and walked over to the bathroom as well. Gently placing her ear to the door, she could hear him talking.

"Man, Sasha is crazy, and that's why I'm not there now," Blue exclaimed.

Emani cut her eyes because she didn't know too many Sashas from their area. "I know damn well he ain't talking about my sister-in-law. We gon' have to get to the bottom of this."

Chapter 16

Monday mornings were laid back, being that it was a weekday and fresh from the weekend rush. The doors wouldn't be open until noon for lunch, so he had plenty of time to get everything in order. Business had been booming since the doors first opened. Quamae leaned back in his chair and smiled.

"Boy, this the best investment that money could buy. I'm a goddamn genius, if I must say so myself," he smiled, boasting proudly. He was alone in his office, so his conversation was a solo one. Over the weekend alone the lounge raked in a little over $60k. That was a lot coming from a new, yet legit business. As long as he continued to thrive and exceed all expectations, he would be a legal millionaire before he knew it.

Quamae leaned forward in his chair while continuing to make sure his financial books were in order. Over the years he played many games, but when it came down to his money he didn't play that shit. His number one goal was to stack his paper so he could make sure his family was straight. In his eyes it was family over everything, and he owed that to Sasha and Dream.

Once the final numbers were jotted down, he placed the folder inside his drawer and locked it up for safe keepings. Pushing the chair back, Quamae pushed himself up from his seat and onto his feet, ready to leave the office. Just as he made it to the door, placing his hand on the knob, his cell phone rang. A huge smile spread across his mouth while his heart skipped a beat at the thought of Sasha calling him. Hearing her voice on a regular basis had become second nature, and that was a good sign.

As soon as he pulled the phone from his suit pocket and looked down at the screen, he was quickly disappointed. It was an unknown number, but he knew exactly who was calling. This was the last person he expected to place a call. "I'm not in the mood to talk right now," he mumbled while silencing the phone and putting it back into his pocket.

After that he walked out of his office and closed the door behind him, but as soon as he walked down the first few steps to the bottom floor it rang again. This time he pulled out the phone and answered the called. "Hello," he said with an irritated tone.

"You have a collect call from Chauncey." Quamae waited until the recording prompted him to make his selection.

"What's up, bruh?" Chauncey asked.

"Nothing much, just working. What's going on?" He walked over to the VIP section and took a seat on one of the cushioned chairs, crossing his legs to get comfortable for the 30-minute phone call he just accepted.

"Oh yeah, that's right, you opened up your spot. That's some big shit. Congrats, man." Chauncey was elated that his boy was making boss moves.

"Thanks, bruh, I appreciate that."

"No sweat, bruh. I'm just proud of you. That means you officially out the game?" He was curious to see if he went back on his word.

"I'm a business man," he replied, not feeling the fact he would mention him being in the game on a recorded call. "Everything I do is legal and by the book."

"Well, I was calling 'cause a nigga getting shipped up the road tomorrow, and I want you to come see me before I go." Chauncey paused for a few seconds. "Now, before you say no, just consider the fact you won't be seeing me for at least 15 years, 'cause I already know how you feel about visiting jails and prisons."

Quamae thought about what he was saying, and he did make a valid point. There was no telling if he would ever see him again in life until it was time for him to pay his respect at his funeral. Twenty years wasn't promised to anybody, not even him.

"A'ight, bruh, since you put it that way, I'll be there. What time is viso?"

"Be here at five."

"Okay, I'll be there."

"Well, I won't hold you up for long. I'll just see you later. One."

"One."

Quamae hung up the phone and slipped it back into his pocket.

"I wouldn't miss this final visit for the world," he smirked.

***

Quamae took slow, paced steps past the guard's station, hooked a left, then continued down the aisle, looking inside every booth until he came across Chauncey wearing an orange jumpsuit. Over the course of time he'd been there, it was obvious he picked up some weight, and his skin tone was a shade lighter. Despite his situation, he had a huge smile on his face.

Quamae sat down on the metal stool, then picked up the phone and wiped the mouthpiece on his pants leg before putting the receiver to his ear.

"What's up, bruh? You clean as fuck," Chauncey laughed while admiring his brother's nice threads.

"Yeah, I'm a dapper young nigga." Quamae popped the collar on his jacket and smiled. "Catch me on the cover of a magazine in a few."

"Shit, send a nigga the magazine when it drop."

"I gotchu, bruh," he nodded his head.

Regardless of what happened between them, he still loved Quamae. The shit that happened between him and Sasha should've never happened, and for that he would feel bad forever. Quamae still didn't know that it happened on more than one occasion, and that's the way he planned on keeping it in order for him to maintain their friendship.

Two hours flew by quickly, and the officers made sure they were aware of the time. "Visitation will end in ten minutes, so wrap it up," the female guard shouted as she strolled slowly behind Chauncey with her hands at her belt. When she stopped in her tracks and licked her lips, Quamae knew she was checking him out, and he couldn't blame her. He was looking like Zaddy right about now.

"Aye, bruh, I won't hold you up any longer, but I appreciate you coming down here before I check out in the morning."

The sound of Chauncey's voice redirected his attention back

to him. "It ain't no thang. I had to come and see you off. A lot is about to change, and I don't want no regrets."

"Yeah, this shit crazy, bruh. Out of all the shit I did in my life, I'm going down for some shit that wasn't intentional." Chauncey dropped his head 'cause he could feel himself become emotional as he choked up on his words. He could feel the tears settling in. "I loved that girl, but I just didn't know how to treat her. Or how to love her, for that matter."

Being sober over a long period of time made him weak and really reflect on the way he threw his life away in the blink of an eye. If he could go back in time, he would bring Monica back and apologize for making her get an abortion. Maybe if he allowed her to carry the baby she would still be alive and he wouldn't be headed to prison on a long bid. One thing for sure, he would never know now. It was a little too late.

Quamae allowed him a few moments to himself before he finally spoke up. "You good, bruh?"

Underneath the surface Chauncey was broken, and he knew things would never be the same. The nightmares had resurfaced, and sleep wasn't an option anymore. Monica was riding him hard as hell at night. He looked up at Quamae, but all he could see was a blurry body in front of him. The fresh coat of tears affected his vision. "This shit hurts, and I just don't know how to handle all the bullshit I brought on myself." Chauncey wiped both of his eyes and sniffled. "I fucked up big time. I even fucked up your marriage, and I'm sorry about that. I crossed that line, and honestly I never thought you would forgive me 'cause I know how you feel about loyalty."

This was Quamae's moment to be honest with him, and since Chauncey was being honest, the timing couldn't be better. 'Cause just like his friend, he, too, had been keeping secrets, and it was time he came clean and cleared his conscious. Quamae sat erect on the stool and made strong eye contact with him. He needed Chauncey to hear every word and feel every emotion he was about to evoke. "All of that sounds good, but you reap what you sew, and that's why you going through what you going through."

Sitting on the opposite side of that glass and hearing his boy talk crazy had him confused as hell. True enough he made some mistakes, but he was trying to right his wrongs. "Shit, tell me how you really feel."

Quamae's bottom lip curled up just a smidgen and an evil smirk appeared on his face, just like the Grim Reaper taking a soul.

"Oh, I am." He cleared his throat. "Loyalty isn't gray. It's black and white. You either loyal completely, or not at all, and the only people I owe that to are the ones who never made me question theirs."

Chauncey was about to say something, but Quamae leaned to the glass and pointed his finger, cutting him off. "Let me say what I need to say."

He listened and confirmed it with a head nod.

"When I found out you betrayed me and broke the code, I wanted to kill you on site. I confided in you everything that went on in my marriage, and you would turn around and do that to me? I been down with you for years, and I never crossed you like that." He nodded his head once more. "Never even thought about it."

Chauncey felt his pain, and he wasn't denying the fact he was wrong. He owned up to it. "I know, bruh, and I'm sorry."

"Not as sorry as you gon' be after you hear this." Not giving him a chance to speak, he continued with the conversation. "You are going to die a slow, painful death over the next few years, and the next time I see you will be in a pine box provided by the state."

"Fuck you talkin' 'bout?" Chauncey was heated now, exposing his evil scowl.

"Yo' girl Ayesha."

"What about her?" he asked.

"I hired her to seduce and fuck you so you can contract that shit. See, putting a bullet in your head was too risky and messy, and I would've had to cover my tracks, yadda, yadda. I knew pussy made you weak and it would be your downfall, so I set you up knowing she had AIDS."

Chauncey completely snapped and hit the phone repeatedly

against the window that separated them. He'd known he was HIV positive for a little while now, but hearing it was on purpose – and from Ayesha, no less – threw him over the edge. "You nasty muthafucka," he screamed furiously.

Quamae smiled. "Calm down, bruh. Take it easy."

"Fuck you, Q!" He shouted that shit from the mountain top, and before he knew it the guards were on his ass trying to calm him down.

Quamae stood up and watched them tackle him and throw him to the floor, slapping cuffs on his wrist. Hanging up the phone, he adjusted his tie and took a step back so he could get one last look at the nigga who was supposed to kept it a bill at all times.

"You never bite the hand that feeds you, or the one that put you up on game, ol' sucka-ass nigga." Quamae smiled one last time and walked off. He had dreamed of the way to reveal his truth, and that was the perfect execution.

***

Blue dropped the full condom into the toilet and flushed it before stepping to the sink to wash his hands. Standing in front of the mirror, he splashed water onto his face and sighed heavily. The guilt from his ongoing fling was finally taking a toll on him. He was surprised he was able to keep it under wraps for so long without getting caught up in any bullshit. Well, at least nothing Sasha could prove. Emani knew her role, and she played it to a T, so their relationship stayed under the radar.

After Zoe called and put things into perspective about his relationship, that had him feeling real shitty about leaving the house for days and not answering any of her calls. Regardless of their present problems, he still wanted to build a family with his woman. He wanted a son and the daughter he had grown to love to have what he always wanted, and that was a two-parent home. Blue took another moment to clear his head 'cause he knew what he had to do.

Stepping from the bathroom, he walked over by the dresser

man she had been with in a while walk away so easily. "Darian, please don't leave me." Emani grabbed his arm, but he snatched it away and turned to face her.

"Emani, stop!" he yelled with his hands extended forward, trying to keep distance between them. "You making this harder than it needs to be."

"How could you walk away from me like this? I love you."

Moving forward, she grabbed ahold of his shirt. The love she had for him outweighed her pride, and she wasn't embarrassed about begging him not to leave her. If that's what it took to get him back, she'd do it in front of a live audience. A fire stroke-game would have the baddest bitches begging for the dick.

The grip she had on his shirt was tight when he tried to move her hand. All he could do was shake his head 'cause the conversation was going nowhere. The woman had zero understanding and she refused to let go. "And that's why I have to end this. You in this too deep when I can't give you what you desire. You gotta let me go." His hand was on hers, still trying to get free. "My heart is with her, and that's not fair to you."

"So fuck me and my feelings?" Emani cried harder than before. To hear him admit she didn't hold a place in his heart was painful.

"I'm trying to spare your feelings," he shouted. All he wanted was for her to get that through her head, but that shit wasn't registering at all.

Emani finally let go of his shirt, and that was when he walked off in the direction of the front door. "Just let me go."

Blue reached for the doorknob, but when he turned it she was right there to make sure he didn't open it. Emani put her foot against the door to keep him from leaving. "I can't let you go."

Taking one last look at her didn't help the guilt. He had never seen her in such a vulnerable, pitiful state of mind. The red marks in the corners of her eyes were confirmation she was truly hurt, and he was responsible for taking her down that road.

When he decided to continue his fling, there was no intention of staying with Sasha because she went against everything he told her. Dream wasn't his daughter, but he had been there since day one. He was there for her birth, she carried his last name, he watched her crawl, take her first steps, and she referred to him as Dada. Finding those results was the worst day of his life, and it was Emani who he ran to. Now that Sasha was pregnant with his child, that was all the more reason for him to stay with her.

"Listen to me." Blue grabbed her hands for the last time and kissed them. "I never meant to hurt you, and believe me when I say I'm truly sorry. My situation is fucked up, and under different circumstances we could've been together. With a new baby on the way, things will only get crazier from here, and I can't leave her alone to raise my kids."

Emani placed one finger on his lips and leaned in close to his face. "I understand. All I want is a goodbye kiss, and you can leave." Placing her lips on his mouth, she parted his lips with her tongue, and he didn't fight it. Their last kiss was deep and sensual. Pressing up against his dick, she got to feel what hooked her in the first place.

Breaking their lip lock, Blue released her hands from his and opened the door once again. This time Emani allowed him to walk away with no resistance.

"Take care," he said, closing the door.

Emani put the top lock on and walked into the kitchen. Sitting on the counter was the bottle of Patron the two had consumed before hours of what she now knows was break-up sex. Picking up the bottle, she turned the last little bit up to her mouth and drank the rest. After it was empty, she gripped it tight in her hand and chunked it against the wall, shattering it into tiny pieces.

"If you think I will let you walk away from me that easily, you must be a goddamn fool." In the sink she saw a glass, so she picked that up and threw it, too. It hit the wall and shattered. "On my mama, I am going to ruin that make-believe-ass family you got with that cheating-ass bitch you can't leave." Dropping to her knees, she screamed at the top of her lungs. "I gave you my loyalty, nigga, and you would play me like that? You got me fucked up, Darian. This shit ain't over."

Chapter 17

Sasha was sitting at the house she no longer considered a home doing something she hadn't done in a long time, and that was drink. Her baby was on her mind heavily, but the way she was stressing would definitely harm her unborn. So, as a liquor replacement, she chose red wine. According to the doctor the baby would most likely be fine as long as she didn't partake in a wine overdose. That was good news since she was mentally drained when it came down to Blue and his fucked-up ways. In the beginning he was schoolboy Blue, the man she fell in love with. Now she had no clue about the imposter who showed up and took over his soul.

The man she loved was gentle, sweet, caring, and faithful. He didn't stay away for days at a time with another bitch, so it was time to figure out what she was going to do about her current situation. Sure she could go back to Quamae, but that would be too easy. If she wanted the men in her life to take her seriously, she had to set boundaries and stand ten toes down on them. Whenever Blue came back, he was in for a rude awakening if he thought everything was going to be peaches and muthafuckin' cream when he strolled his happy ass in the house. The future was finally looking bright for her, and she refused to allow him to check her back into heartbreak hotel.

It was taking everything in her soul to not call him and curse him out from A to Z because he tried it. The fact she hid those details was a reason to be mad, but establishing the paternity of her daughter was warranted. Quamae deserved to know if that was his child in order to be the father he always wanted to be. She couldn't fathom the thought of allowing Blue to keep that away from him.

Sasha shook her head. "This nigga is really trying me, but I see right now I might have to bring the old Sasha out of retirement and let him know I ain't shit to be fucked with." A sudden thought popped into her head. "Shit, I need to check on my kids." Sasha snatched her phone up with the quickness and hit Quamae up.

"What's up, wifey?"

She could tell he was smiling when he said that. "You just insist on calling me that, huh?" She grinned just a little.

"Yep. What's up, though?" he repeated.

"I was calling to check on my baby. How is she?" Not that she didn't trust him alone with her.

"She's running a fever, but other than that she's okay," he replied.

That suddenly made her panic and hike the volume in her voice. "Why didn't you call and tell me?"

"Relax, I know what I'm doing. And besides, I know you have a lot on your plate with your son and all. Let me worry about her."

Sasha wasn't trying to hear that. "But she needs to go to the doctor."

"We're going inside the emergency room right now. I will keep you updated, I promise. Try to get some rest, 'cause you dealing with a lot right now."

"Are you sure?" It was hard to take no for an answer.

"Let me be a father, please. I know what to do," he replied.

"Okay. I'll talk to you later."

"A'ight."

Sasha hung up the phone and checked on NJ next.

"Hello," Nate answered.

"Hey, how is my baby?" Sasha fixed herself another glass of wine and took a sip.

Nate chuckled 'cause NJ was going to be a father. His baby days were over, and both of them missed out on that, but he understood her logic. "NJ is not a baby, but he's okay. They will be discharging him today."

"Hush, 'cause he will always be my baby. And that's good news. I can't wait to see him." It bothered her deeply because she didn't know who was behind the attack, but God as her witness if she found out who it was, she was gon' body that ass.

"I'm waiting on the doctor to draw up the discharge papers, then we out of here." Nate stroked his chin. "You coming to the house?"

Taking another sip, she replied, "Yeah, I'll be there. Just text me when you get home."

"I can get some of that today?" Nate hadn't touched her in a while, so he was anxious to drop that pipe off in her once again.

Sasha smiled, but before she could say anything the room door opened and in walked Blue carrying his duffle bag. The two of them made eye contact, but didn't say a word to the other.

"Yeah, that will work. What did the doctor say?" She needed to throw the conversation for a second, and she most definitely wanted to get a little payback in 'cause she knew he was with a bitch. She could cheat just as well as him, and better.

"The doctor just walked in, so I'll text you soon."

Saved by the bell, she thought to herself. "Okay, I'll be there." Sasha hung up the phone and sat it face-down on the bed. When she looked up, Blue was standing in front of her.

"We need to talk."

Rolling her eyes, she shifted her body away from him and looked toward the wall. She needed him to know she wasn't interested in nothing he had to say, but that didn't stop him from talking.

"I know you mad at me, and I'm sorry, but I was mad at you, too. We both took this too far, especially me." Her head was still turned, so he placed his right hand underneath her chin and turned her head toward his. "Look at me."

Sasha moved his hand. "I don't want to, so leave me alone."

"Bae, I'm sorry. I overreacted." This was the time to express his true feelings. After the long conversation with Zoe, it allowed him to put things into perspective. The guilt of being with Emani weighed on him heavily as well.

Blue kneeled down in front of her and grabbed her hand. "I had a lot of time to think about what happened, and I should've never let it get that far. True enough, I told you not to give him the paternity test, and I believe the reason behind that was because I knew she wasn't mine. I wanted her to be, but deep down inside I already knew." Everything he said was true, even if it took Zoe to point it out for him, but he would never tell her that.

Meanwhile, Sasha wasn't paying his ass no mind. She was too busy playing with her hair.

"And before you get the wrong idea, I wasn't wit' no bitch. I was staying at the hotel alone so I could clear my head and figure out a way to get past this."

Sasha sucked her teeth and rolled her eyes. "And you expect me to believe that shit?"

"I'm telling you the truth, and that's why I came back today, 'cause I was wrong for leaving in the first place. I love you, and I just want to make this family thing work." Blue grabbed her hand once again, and this time she didn't pull away. He was convinced he was making progress.

"All of that sounds good, but when you left here for days you didn't answer any of my calls or respond to any of my text messages. Do you care how that made me feel? Or the way it made you look?" Sasha rolled her neck, and had she done it a little bit harder it would've fallen off.

"I care, and that's why I'm here." Blue's knee's had finally grown numb from being on them for so long. Back on his feet, he sat down beside her on the bed. "I won't ask you to forgive me right now since I don't deserve it and it's not fair to you. All I ask is that you think about it."

Nodding her head in agreement, she said, "We'll see about that."

"That's all I want." He hesitated. "There's something else."

Instantly her mind went to wondering what he could possibly lie about next. "What?" she asked in a disgusted tone.

Blue wasn't dismayed by her attitude. It was pretty much expected. "I think it's time for you to go ahead and start your own business and gain your independence."

"You late because I already started looking for a place. I have an appointment with a realtor to look at some properties." Giving him the chance to think he held her independence in his hand wasn't happening. She needed him to know she was about to stand on her own two feet. If she didn't learn nothing else from being married to Quamae, she learned she needed to have her own if she didn't want to be controlled. Too bad she didn't take heed to what India tried telling her on several occasions.

"That's cool and all, but I'll give you the money to get it up and running." This was his way of making things right.

"That's okay, I want to do this on my own. I need to be able to say I accomplished something on my own." It wasn't the entire truth, but it wasn't false, either, since technically the money from Quamae was for her to do as she pleased.

"Well, if you need anything, just let me know and I got the rest." Blue leaned forward and kissed her forehead. "I'm sorry from the bottom of my heart.

Sasha nodded her head. "Okay."

Not even a minute later Blue's phone alerted him of an incoming call, and in his mind he was hoping it wasn't Emani. After ending their fling so abruptly, he was sure she wouldn't walk away so easily.

Removing the phone from his hip, he peeped it was his mom. "What's up, mother dear?" he said playfully.

"Is Dream your daughter?" she screamed furiously into the speaker.

"What are you talking about?" Blue was dumbfounded and had no idea where that question would come from, so he put her on speaker so Sasha could hear.

"Is she your daughter? 'Cause I was at the hospital, and she is there with my patient's fiancée. I asked him where did he get my granddaughter from, and he said she's his daughter." Darlene was upset as she cried into the phone with zero understanding.

Sasha and Blue stared at each other for what felt like an eternity before he actually spoke. "What's his name, ma?"

"Quamae," she responded.

This was the moment he dreaded the most, having to come clean to his mother about the ordeal. Blue sighed long and hard, trying to put the words together.

"Darian, answer me," she shouted.

"That's her daddy, ma, but we just found out about it a few days ago. I was waiting for the right time to tell you," he answered

177

truthfully.

"So you mean to tell me we've been taking care of somebody else's child all this time? Sasha knew you wasn't the daddy, didn't she? That nasty heffa had us believing that baby was a part of this family, and it's been a lie all this time." Darlene never questioned the paternity of the baby because she solemnly took their word for it.

Blue felt bad for his mom because he knew exactly what she was going through. To say she was devastated was an understatement. Sasha just sat there with no words to say.

"Ma, it's a long story, and I'll tell you about it when you get home. In the meantime, try to calm down and not think about it."

"I'm on my way home now." She paused so she could switch lanes.

Beep! Beep!

"And I want answers when I get there." Darlene was trying to get home as quickly as possible. It hurt knowing the child she had grown to love and nurture didn't belong to her son.

The sound of the horn caught his attention. "Ma!" Blue shouted into the phone. "You need to slow down before you wreck out."

"I'll be there soon." *Click!* And just like that, she was gone.

Blue was confused as to why Dream was in the hospital in the first place. "What's wrong with the baby?"

"She has a fever, so he took her to the emergency room." Sasha got up off the bed and slipped on her slides.

"Where are you going?" he asked.

"To the hospital to check on NJ, 'cause I don't wanna be here when yo' mama get here." The last thing she wanted was a confrontation with Darlene. This felt like a sign that maybe they shouldn't be together and she should find her own place or give Quamae another chance. He made the ultimate sacrifice to change, and he included her during the process. That was very considerate of him, being that he inflicted so much pain on her.

"Yeah, that will give me some time to sit her down and explain everything."

"Aren't you even gonna ask why he's in the hospital?" Sasha was puzzled.

"I'm sorry, with all of this going on I meant to ask. What happened?" He pretended to not know what was going on.

"He was jumped and beaten." She placed her hands on her hips. "Did you have anything to do with that?" Sasha knew he had it out for her son and Nate, but she was praying he didn't because that would cause a major problem between them.

"No. Why would I do something like that and cause problems between me and you?"

"You sneaky, that's why."

"Well, I didn't have nothing to do with that," he lied.

"Okay, I'm gone." Sasha left the room in a hurry to avoid the confrontation she wasn't in the mood for. She wanted peace and dick, and Nate was about to give her both.

***

Emani was sitting down on the floor in her bedroom, bawling her eyes out. Taking the razorblade she held between her fingers, she placed it against her wrist and made a smooth line.

"I loved you, Blue, and you hurt me in return." She placed her wrist to her mouth and sucked the blood. Every time she called Blue her calls went straight to voicemail, therefore she knew he had blocked her calls. He was the reason she didn't go to school and was sitting at home, plotting a way to get him back. He even went so far as to sit far away from her.

"Why would you do this to me?" she sobbed and held her pillow tight while rocking back and forth. "I was everything you wanted me to be."

Scrolling through the gallery in her phone, she reminisced about the good times they shared, and she was desperate to get him back. She just didn't know how. No one knew about their relationship except for one of her close friends, who advised her to leave him alone. Emani needed someone who had been in her shoes before, and she knew just who to call. It had been a long time since the two of them spoke to one another, but it was long overdue, especially since things had officially changed, according to Quamae. She quickly found the number and pressed send.

"Hello," Sasha answered.

"Hey, it's Emani. How are you?" She wiped the tears from her face.

"Hey, I'm good. What's going on?" Sasha was curious as to why she had called all of a sudden.

"I need someone to talk to, and I can't talk to Quamae about this."

Sasha immediately thought the worst. "Oh Lord, don't tell me you pregnant."

Emani shrugged her shoulders. "I don't know. I mean, there's a possibility."

She knew it had to be something to warrant this call. "Girl, you know your brother is gon' kill you."

"Sasha, please don't say anything. But there's more, so can you meet me for lunch?" Emani needed to get out of the house and talk to her face-to-face.

"Sure. Where do you wanna meet?" she asked.

"Finga Licking down here on 7th Ave. Can you meet me now?"

"Yeah, I'll be there in 45 minutes." She was lucky 'cause Sasha had nothing to do at the moment.

"Okay. Thank you."

"No problem."

"Oh, is my niece with you?"

"No, she with your brother."

"Okay, see you soon."

"Okay." Emani jumped up from the floor and got herself together quickly, placing a Band-Aid on her cut. It was time to stop crying and be about that action. After she was ready to go, she grabbed her purse and stormed out the door, locking it behind her.

Finga Licking had a nice little crowd even on a weekday, but that wasn't her main concern. Backing her car in, she left the car running and waited patiently for Sasha to pull in. The radio was starting to get on her nerves, so she popped in a slow jams mixed CD and went to her favorite song, Bryson Tiller's *The Sequence*.

Am I asking for too much?
Say this shit once, say this shit two times.
I won't stop 'til I get back what's mine.
I know I fucked up one too many times.
Is that too much?

By the time Emani listened to that one song on repeat five times, Sasha was finally pulling up. Killing the ignition, she picked up her purse and got out of the car. The girls greeted each other with a hug.

Emani pulled back quickly and touched her stomach. "Excuse me, but what is this?" Emani forced a smile. She already knew the baby didn't belong to Quamae.

"Another baby," Sasha giggled. "That's it after this, though. I just had a damn baby."

"Yeah, you better stop while you ahead." Emani was hurt seeing Sasha happy and pregnant again. She wanted the same thing for herself with Blue.

"And what about you? 'Cause if you are, I'm gon' have to do a lot of talking and persuading to ya' daddy on all the reasons he shouldn't kill you or the one responsible for putting that in there." Sasha poked at Emani's flat stomach.

"Yeah, I thought about that already, so we will find out soon enough." Emani grabbed her hand. "Come on, let's go inside and order."

"Yes, 'cause I'm hungry as a hostage," Sasha added while walking beside her sister. "It's been so long since I've seen you."

"I know, it's just that with everything you and Quamae was going through, I didn't want to get in the middle." Emani paused and looked up at her. "However, I did defend you and told Quamae he was wrong for what he did."

"Thanks, sis, I appreciate that. He's trying real hard to get me back."

Emani opened the door to allow Sasha to walk in first. "So,

are y'all getting back together or what?"

"Honestly, I don't know. I'm in another relationship and I'm pregnant again, so who knows what my crazy-ass future will bring. My boyfriend is trying to get back in my good graces, but I don't know about that, either. I'm just confused. I love them both."

They stood in line to place their orders. "Damn, you having an issue on deciding who you should be with and I'm having a hard time getting through to the one I was with. All of a sudden he's acting funny, and I don't know what to do."

"Did you tell him you might be pregnant?" Sasha gave Emani her undivided attention.

"No. He hasn't been answering my calls. I want him back, but I don't know what to do."

When Emani brought her hand to her face, Sasha caught a glimpse of her arm and grabbed it. "What happened to you?"

"Oh, it's nothing." Emani pulled away from her. "I got cut by accident."

Sasha wasn't buying that for a second. Her brows slanted downward. "What happened to you, and don't lie to me? Did you do that?"

Emani hesitated, but they were interrupted by the cashier. "Next in line."

As soon as they placed their order, she was ready to continue the interrogation. "Did he do something to you?"

"No, Sasha. I promise he is nothing like that, and I didn't do this either. It was an accident."

"Okay." Sasha hugged her. "Don't feel like you have to keep anything from me. No matter what happens between me and your brother, you will always be my little sister."

Being held and comforted was what she needed, but she wanted it from Blue. He was her world, and he didn't even know it, but soon enough he would find out just how serious she was about getting him.

The ladies sat at an outside table and enjoyed their lobster dinner while engaging in more conversation. The sunshine state was breezy all of a sudden, and it felt damn good to get some fresh air, not that humid shit they were used to. Before they knew it, two hours had passed and it was time to wrap things up.

Sasha's phone rang, so she answered it. "Hello."

"Hey, where you at?" Blue was clearly out of breath.

"Finga Licking. What's going on?" She sensed something was wrong.

"I need you to pick me up by Barry University." He tried catching his breath.

"What you doing at Barry University?" she reiterated what she had just heard.

"My homeboy got into it with some niggas, and now they got troll all over this bitch. I ain't trying to go to jail."

"I'm on my way."

"Okay."

Sasha hung up the phone slipped it into her purse. Then she looked up at Emani. "This damn boyfriend of mine is really getting on my last nerve. I gotta pick him up, so I'll catch up with you later."

"It's okay, girl. Go handle yo' business," Emani winked.

"Okay, babes."

"Thank you so much for coming, Sasha. I really needed that talk, and now I know what to do." Emani hugged Sasha once more, then picked up her trash. "I love you."

"You're welcome, pooh, and I love you, too." Sasha rolled her eyes. "Even though you didn't tell me his name."

Emani burst out in laughter. "Absolutely not! I don't need Quamae hunting him down like a rabid dog before I get the chance to work things out."

"You right about that," Sasha agreed. "We will do this again soon so you can give me the update."

"I will."

They both parted ways and went to their cars. Emani got into her car, pulled out her phone, and opened up the navigation app. She then proceeded to type in the address for Barry University and saw it was only five minutes away. That was more than enough time.

Scanning the area, she peeped the Shell gas station across the street from the restaurant, so that's where she went. Emani parked next to the air pump and opened up the glove box. In her hand she held a Smith and Wesson blade. She looked at it and laughed out loud. Emani opened the car door and got out, walking to the rear of the car. Flipping the blade open, she bent down and stabbed a hole in her tire.

Psssh!

Once the tire was completely flat, she got back inside. When she checked the time, seven minutes had passed. Grabbing her phone, she made the call.

"Hey, what's up?" Sasha answered.

"My tire flat, can you come and help me get the spare on, please?" Emani pulled down the sun visor and smiled at herself in the mirror.

"Where are you?" she asked.

"At the Shell gas station across the street from Finga Licking." Emani could hear someone talking in the background, but she couldn't make out what was being said.

"It's my sister. She has a flat tire," Sasha responded to Blue before replying to Emani, "We on our way, so sit tight."

"Okay."

Emani watched the clock in slow motion. What was supposed to be a five minute ride felt like an hour wait in her eyes, putting the time at a standstill. Finally, after a ten minute wait in real time, she saw Sasha appear. The car crept toward her slowly and parked. The lights cut off, and when both doors opened, two bodies emerged and she couldn't believe her eyes. Exiting her own vehicle, she closed the door and eyed Sasha's man up and down.

When they were close enough, Sasha introduced them. "Emani, this is my boyfriend, Blue." She then looked at Blue. "Baby, this is my sister, Emani."

Blue looked at Emani with a straight face. "Nice to meet you."

Emani couldn't believe he was playing it so cool. She expected him to have a heart attack on sight once he saw her face, but he acted as if he didn't know her.

"I'm surprised y'all never saw each other, 'cause y'all both go to the same school."

Blue shook his head and got to the subject at hand. "Pop the trunk so I can get the spare out." All he wanted to do was change her tire and haul ass before anything transpired.

Emani turned around and opened the car door once more and popped the trunk. Sasha was standing at the front of the car, so she went to the trunk with him to get the tools he needed.

"It's a small world," she smirked.

"Emani, don't start that shit. Keep yo' mouth closed so I can change yo' tire and g'on 'bout my business."

Being the devious woman she was, she grabbed his dick. "I wonder how my sister would feel knowing I was fucking and sucking this fat-ass dick."

Blue smacked her hand out of the way. "Stop playin' with me befo' I put yo' ass in this muthafuckin' trunk."

"You ain't gon' do shit." She peeked to see if Sasha was close to them, but she was walking toward the front door of the gas station. "I used to always wonder who had you under lock and key like that, and now it all makes sense 'cause I know how my sister is. Yo' ass whipped," Emani joked 'cause she was about to have fun at his expense.

Blue grabbed the spare and the jack and sat them down by the passenger tire so he could get started. She watched him loosen the nuts and lift the car in the air.

"I missed you so much. Did you miss me?"

Blue was trying his best to ignore her, but she just wouldn't leave him alone.

"So, you mute now? But you wasn't mute when I put this pussy on you."

She was really irritating the hell out of him.

"I think I'm pregnant."

Suddenly he stopped what he was doing and looked up at her in silence.

"I thought that might get your attention. I'll be going to the doctor soon 'cause I missed my period." Emani could see Sasha was heading toward them, so she needed to try her luck. "Meet me at my house after you get your truck."

"You got me fucked up. I ain't coming over there," Blue barked, but she wasn't moved by his tone.

"If you don't want me to tell my sister who I'm pregnant from, then you will be at my house."

"Tell her shit, I don' give a fuck."

"Suit yourself." Sasha was closer now. "Sasha, I need to tell you something. Come here."

"Okay, okay, I'll be there later."

"You promise?"

"Yeah."

"We'll be waiting."

Sasha walked up and looked down at Blue, who was breaking a sweat. "You got my baby out here working in this hot-ass sun."

"I know, right? He's such a gentleman to help his sis-in-law."

Blue couldn't wait to put her in check behind closed doors, 'cause she was pushing her muthafuckin' luck playing with him like that.

"Oh, what you wanna talk to me about?" Sasha placed her hand on Emani's shoulder.

"I wanted to know if you would accompany me to the doctor." She paused for a few seconds. "I don't want to go alone."

"Now, you know I will go with you. Just set the appointment and call me with the details," Sasha smiled.

"Thanks, sis. I love you."

"I love you, too."

When he was finally done, Blue sighed. Never in the history of niggadom had it taken so long to change a damn tire with a psycho hanging over his shoulder. He had never been through no shit like that in his entire life. After he tossed everything back into the trunk, he walked away.

"Come on, bae, let's go." He grabbed Sasha's arm.

"See ya, E. I'll talk to you later," Sasha responded.

"Thanks, y'all. I appreciate it."

"No problem."

Blue let Sasha answer her 'cause he didn't have shit else to say to her. Instead, he kept walking like he didn't hear her.

Destiny

Chapter 18

Blue was enraged when he got to Emani's apartment. With a closed fist, he pounded on the door until it swung open.

"Why you –"

That was all she could manage to get out before Blue pushed her in the chest, causing her to stumble backward. Slamming the door behind him, he walked up to where she was standing in the living room and yelled in her face. "What the fuck is yo' problem? Why you doing all this?"

"I loved you, and you left me." Emani tried her best to muster up some tears in order to put the icing on the cake. "All I wanted was to be with you, and you shitted on me for nothing."

Blue placed both hands on his head and took a deep breath. "Listen, it wasn't like that. I'm going through a lot of shit with my girl right now, and I can't focus on two women at once."

Emani folded her arms across her chest, displaying her attitude. "You mean my sister?"

"Nah, that shit sound funny 'cause I didn't know that, and if I did this would've never happened." Blue dropped his hands, then went over to the couch to sit down. He wondered to himself, *How did I manage to fuck with two sisters?* That was the million dollar question.

Feeling like she had him where she wanted him, Emani knelt down and grabbed his hand. "I don't care if you with my sister. All I want is you."

The first thought that popped into his head was this bitch was really crazy if she thought he would knowingly fuck his woman's sister. What was done was a thing of the past, and he could guarantee it would never happen again. "Now you know I can't do that, and you shouldn't want to. Despite my actions or what she said, I love your sister, and I would never hurt her on purpose. We had issues and I didn't trust her, but we working on that."

"I don't see how, 'cause she still married. He trying to get her back, and she thinking about it." It was a low blow, and she could tell he was caught off guard based on his facial expression, but the heart wanted what it wanted and she didn't care who she had to hurt in order to be happy.

Blue stroked his chin. "Is that right?" He couldn't say he expected her to be one hunnid with him, but he had reason to believe there was some truth to what she was saying. It wasn't like he hadn't accused her of doing that very thing anyway.

"Let's just say we had a very, very long, informative lunch. We got a chance to catch up, and I told her about this guy that got me pregnant and up and left me and didn't bother to answer my calls." Emani looked him up and down with her lips tooted in the air.

"Well, I know you didn't tell her it was me, 'cause that would've played out differently. I'm confused, though. That's your sister and you love her, so why would you want to hurt her like this? She having my baby soon, so how do you think that will make her feel?"

Emani placed her hand close to his face to silence him. "Listen, you wasn't worried about her when you was here laying between my legs, so don't make it seem like I'm the bad person."

"That was before I knew y'all are sisters. I know now, so I'm not crossing that line anymore. Point blank, period." Blue thought for a second. "Y'all must be half-sisters or some shit. What, y'all got the same daddy or some shit?"

"Nope. We don't have the same nothing. She's married to my brother."

And boom, there it was. All this time he had been sleeping with the enemy's little sister. "Get the fuck outta here!" Blue shouted and jumped up from his seat.

"Nope. We have the same mama and daddy. Is that a problem?"

"We had our little run-ins wit' each other." Blue checked the time on his watch. "I gotta go."

"Not until you give me some." Emani licked her lips.

"That ain't gon' happen, and I told you that already." If she was going to tell anything, it wouldn't be after the fact of them being introduced. If anything he could easily confess since he wasn't aware of their relationship in the first place.

"Well, if you won't fuck me, be prepared for me to tell her all about us. And I'm sure she won't take you back." She shrugged her shoulders. "Then she will just get back with my brother."

Blue walked up on her, grabbed her wrist, and squeezed it tightly. He had peeped the Band-Aid, so he was ready to cause pain without hitting her.

"Ouch! Let go of my wrist," she begged.

"I don't know what you think is about to happen, but you not about to pull my strings like I'm yo' fuckin' puppet or some shit. I run this shit, and what I say goes." Blue release his hold on her. "Do you understand that?"

"What's wrong, you don't like being blackmailed?" Emani grabbed her wrist and held it close to her chest. "I don't understand what I've done that was so bad to where you could just up and leave me on a whim. I guess I was only good enough to fuck when you and my sister was having problems or whenever you thought my brother was fucking her. When you wanted to get away for a few days," her voice heightened and now she was yelling, "who did you call? It was me. I was always there for you."

On so many levels she was right, but he had to follow his heart. However, the more he sat with her and listened to her talk made him realize they had more issues than he originally thought. "Emani, stop and listen to me very closely, 'cause after this I will not repeat myself. Then I am going to walk out that door for good." He made direct eye contact so she would know he meant business. "I apologize about the way things went down. I would never hurt you intentionally, but I felt I had to let you go because you became too attached and your feelings were too strong. You are everything a man could want, but I'm not that man for you. I can't give you what you want or need beyond sex or money, and that's not fair to you."

The tears that crept up on Emani were slowly rolling down her cheeks. Yes, she was hurt, but she wasn't crying for herself. She was shedding tears for Sasha because she knew how much pain she was about to inflict on her when she came clean about her relationship with Blue. Standing for a few more seconds, she watched him closely in silence before she finally uttered a word. "Okay, Darian. Or should I call you Blue?"

The sarcasm was strong, but Blue always had a comeback for that sass. He shrugged his shoulders. "It doesn't matter, 'cause you won't be calling me anything after I walk out that door for good."

"Sarcasm won't get you very far, so how about this?" Emani walked toward her door and opened it. "Walk out this door and watch what happens."

"How about I tell her myself? I don't have time to sit around and play muthafuckin' mind games wit' cho ass. She'll either forgive me or she don't. There's plenty more Sashas and Emanis in the sea." Blue rubbed her chin and left her in her thoughts as he walked out the door.

***

Blue stood at the front door of his home, unsure of what the outcome was about to be. True enough he loved Sasha and the ground she walked on, but he couldn't allow Emani to blackmail him for time and dick. That would eventually get old to her, and she would still tell anyway, so he might as well come clean and disarm the strong-arm bandit. The only thing that could save him right then was honesty. The trust had been destroyed, so that was all he had left. Hopefully she could forgive him, then they could move on.

Unlocking the door, he walked inside ready to learn his fate. Thank God his mama wasn't home 'cause she didn't need to witness what was about to happen. The mistake had been made, and there was no way he could undo what had already been done. The walk down the hallway felt like a 5k walk, like he would never get to his destination. The Giuseppe shoes that normally glided his steps were now holding him back like they had cement in them.

The long walk finally came to an end, and he was standing at the bedroom door debating when he should open it.

"Come on, Blue, you can do this." He took slow, quick breaths while pep-talking himself in the hallway. "It's better if she hears it from you."

After standing there for another sixty seconds, he finally placed his hand on the knob and turned it. When the door opened slowly, Sasha had a smile on her face, so that was confirmation Emani hadn't called yet. Seeing her smile was all he ever wanted for her after being in a bad marriage, but now he had also become the villain. That made him no better than Quamae, 'cause he too had slapped her up a few times and cheated on her.

"Did you do what you needed to do?" she asked sweetly.

"Yeah, but I also need to talk to you." Saying those words put the biggest lump in his throat, and he hadn't even confessed yet.

Sasha tilted her head to the side. Based on his demeanor, whatever he had to say couldn't be good. They had been together long enough for her to know something was terribly wrong, and suddenly it clicked. This was the same way he came at her when he slept with Red.

"You cheated, didn't you?" Sasha shook her head, already knowing what was about to roll off his tongue.

Blue walked over to Sasha and stood in front of her, taking her hands into his. He needed her to know he was truly sorry. "What I'm about to confess to you will probably ruin everything we are building, but I have to get this off my chest even if you decide to leave me after you hear this."

"You're scaring me, so just say it."

Taking one last breath, he was ready to put it all out on the table. "Today wasn't my first time meeting Emani. I actually met her when I registered for school."

Sasha was lost. "Okay," she dragged out that word for dear life. "And what does that mean?"

Giving her eye contact had just become harder than Geometry. "I slept with her."

As soon as those words rolled off his tongue, Sasha's eyes shifted and suddenly became filled with water. Everything on her body became limp, and she eased her hands from the palms of his.

This was not the confession she was expecting at all, and out of every female on campus, why did it have to be Emani?

"How many times?" As bad as she hated to hear the truth, she needed to know the facts.

"I don't know," he answered truthfully.

"How long has this been going on?" By the time she hit him with the second question, her tears were falling down.

"Since I first started class." Blue gently wiped her tears. "I'm sorry." He meant it, but it was too late to apologize.

"So you must be the one who broke up with her and won't return any of her calls. Did she tell you she might be pregnant?"

"She's lying. We used condoms." Confession time was harder than he thought, 'cause every time he looked at her it broke his heart to see her crying.

Sasha prepared her heartache and pain for her final question. "When you were gone all those days, is that who you were with?"

That was the one question he wanted to lie about, but he knew it didn't make sense to start lying now. He had gone this far, so he might as well keep going. He nodded his head. "Yeah."

Sasha let out the most horrific, gut-wrenching scream from the pit of her soul. "You lied to me. You told me you stayed at a hotel to get your thoughts together, and all along you been laying up with my sister."

Dream was startled from her sleep and began to cry. Blue quickly rushed to her side and gave her a bottle to get her quiet. Once the noise subsided, he went back to the one who needed him the most.

"Come on, let's go in the living room and finish discussing this so we don't interrupt her." Grabbing her by the arms, he pulled her toward him and escorted her out of the room and down the hallway. When they made it to the living room, Sasha stood in the middle of the floor. "Baby, I'm so sorry. I didn't know that was your sister, but that's why I'm telling you now, 'cause I don't want any secrets."

"All this time you've been accusing me of cheating, it was you all along. The accuser is always the doer," Sasha sobbed loud enough for the neighbors to hear. The newfound weight on her shoulders applied too much pressure to her knees, making them buckle. They felt like spaghetti as they shook uncontrollably. Blue noticed she was shaking and reached for her in the nick of time, right before her body started to collapse.

"I gotchu, baby."

"No, you don't, so let me go," she shouted. "If you had me, you wouldn't have cheated on me. If you had me, my sister wouldn't be claiming to be pregnant from you." Sasha's body slid to the floor, but that didn't stop her from crying and swinging at the father of her unborn child.

"Calm down, please. We can get through this. I promise." No matter how many times she took a swing at him, he was prepared to take them all. He was willing to wear a black eye and busted lip to prove his love.

"No, we can't! Leave me alone," she screamed.

"Sasha, stop. I broke things off with her 'cause I knew it was a mistake and I wanted to make things right with you."

No matter how much he pleaded, she wasn't hearing that shit. "I'm leaving you, so let me go."

Blue grabbed her arms to restrain her and make her calm down. "Sasha, relax before you hurt the baby, please." That wasn't working at all, so he pushed her down to the floor and pinned her. That was the only way he could get her to stop fighting him.

The grip he had on her was tight like grip pliers. "Let me go." Her face was soaking wet, and her eyes had become red from all that crying.

"Not until you calm down. I'm worried about the baby. Just relax." He leaned down and tried to kiss her, but she moved her head.

"Stop. Don't kiss me."

"Baby, I'm sorry, and I want to make this work." Blue planned on begging all night if that was what it was going to take.

"I'm leaving you."

"No, you not, 'cause I'm not letting you go." He refused to loosen his grip on her.

"You gon' lay on me all night? I swear when you let me up, I'm leaving you for good. What you did is unforgiveable."

"Damn, just like that?" Blue couldn't believe what he was hearing. There was no difference in her sleeping with Chauncey, who Quamae saw as a brother, and that was intentional.

Sasha took a few moments to catch her breath before she responded. The tears were still flowing. "I love you, and you know I do, but I will never forgive you for sleeping with her. That was just too close to home, and she's saying she's pregnant. If you are worried about your child, don't be. I would never stand in the way of you being a father, but what we had is over. I will start looking for a place tomorrow."

Blue was lost for words, and he was heartbroken. Maybe they couldn't work it out and stay together, or maybe she was just mad. Whatever the case was, he wasn't giving up on them until he exhausted every option humanly possible. Sasha was his world, and he refused to live without her.

***

One month later

Sasha's life was finally on track as far as being independent, and she couldn't be happier. She had recently opened up her own boutique and moved into her apartment. Things were looking good for her. Now, in the relationship section she was still hurt, but she knew she had to do what was best for her, even if it killed her on a daily basis. She knew walking away wouldn't be easy, but staying was just too hard. If it had been with another female, then maybe she could've forgiven him. The relationship he carried on with Emani was unforgiveable and too damaged beyond repair. There was no coming back from that.

On the other hand, Quamae kept his word and made sure he continued to help with their daughter. That was a huge weight off her shoulders since she was on her own, especially the fact he had a nanny to care for Dream while they were at work. Daycare was out of the question. She didn't trust strangers with her daughter, so if Quamae could trust Ms. Mildred after all this time, then so could she.

Whenever he wasn't at the lounge, he spent all his spare time with Dream. After work he would come by the apartment and check on them. Quamae made it very clear he still had a sense of hope she would come to her senses and have a change of heart. He craved the family life, and he knew it needed to be with him. After all they had said and done to one another, he still didn't want to let her go.

Sasha constantly tried to convince herself things were better off with the two of them apart and she should leave well enough alone, but her conscience wouldn't allow it. The counseling sessions were working miracles and moving mountains, but in the back of her mind, the size of a mustard seed, she was afraid one day he may snap and revert back to his old ways.

Sasha's thoughts were interrupted when the chimes on the door alerted her that someone had entered her store. She stood up to greet her customer.

"Good morning, welcome to Dream's Boutique." She smiled and shook her head when she saw the familiar face.

"Good morning, beautiful! What's all that for?" said Mark.

"Nothing," she replied, wearing the biggest smile on her face.

"So, what's new?" he asked.

"Same shit, different day. Still married, pregnant, and confused." She laughed because it was nothing but the truth.

Mark walked up to the counter and handed her a cup of coffee and a bag.

"Thank you." She blushed. No matter how much she turned him down, Mark wouldn't take no for an answer. He was going to get her, no matter how much she objected. He had a charming smile and pearly white teeth behind a pair of clear braces. She couldn't see them unless she was staring directly into his mouth. He had smooth chocolate skin and a neatly-trimmed goatee. He was an older dude, so that made her a little reluctant to go on a date with him. It was clearly not about his looks, because the man was fine. She thought about giving in to his charming ways, but quickly dismissed the idea. After the mess she had been in, it was hard to trust anybody. "Thanks a lot, Quamae and Blue," she mumbled. Those two were to blame for all the confusion in her mind and heart.

"So, when are you going to take me up on my offer?" he asked seductively. Mark had a way of making everything sound so damn sexy.

Truthfully, she didn't want to be bothered. Too bad her hormones weren't listening to her. She was always horny and ready to hump at any time of the day or night, but she put herself on restriction, and she was doing well. Her main focus was her three kids and grandchild who would be born around the same time she gave birth.

"I don't know," she hesitated.

He laughed. "I'm wearing you down, huh?"

"Why do you say that?" she smirked, knowing damn well what he was talking about.

"At first it was a flat out no because you thought I was shopping for a woman, but that all changed when I came in here with my niece." He was absolutely right. He leaned on the counter and stroked his beard with his forefinger and thumb. "You need a real man in your life." His baritone voice sent chills down her spine. "Stop messing with these young thugs that don't want anything out of life." He pulled a card from his wallet. "Call me when you're ready."

She took the card and sat it on the side of the cash register. "Okay."

He walked away. "Have a good day."

"Thanks, and you do the same."

He pushed the door open, but he turned back to face her. "Sasha, don't miss out on your blessing," and then he walked out.

She couldn't do anything but laugh. Mark had been coming to the store since her grand opening, and he'd been trying to win her over ever since. At first she wouldn't accept his breakfast offers, but he caught her off guard when she was rushing and starving.

Sasha sat back down on the stool and picked up his business card. It read *Mark Walters, District Attorney.* "Hmm. He has a good job." Sasha tucked his number away just in case she wanted a free meal. Women loved free meals, so that wasn't a surprise. And besides, she was eating for two.

The morning crept along pretty slowly, and she had to admit it was kind of depressing. Not having someone to talk to on a personal level could do that to a person. Lelah was still her friend, but she needed someone who knew her better than she knew herself. It hurt because she no longer had that.

It was noon when she checked the clock on the computer screen. "Ooh, it's lunchtime." Sasha snatched up her belongings quickly so she could step out for a few. It was time to pay her friend a visit. It was long overdue.

Sasha pulled up to the cemetery and parked her car. She walked up to India's final resting place, clutching an arrangement of flowers. She took a seat on the bench and the tears began to fall. She hadn't been out to her grave since the funeral. It was too hard. The pain had ridden her for so long, to the point she could never make it out there. She sat the flowers down and began to talk.

"India, I hope you can hear me. I know this visit is well overdue, and that's why I'm here." She wiped her eyes and took a deep breath. "I want you to know I had the baby, and her name is Dream India Joyner." Sasha released a small giggle. "The funny thing is that's Blue's last name, so I have to have it changed to Banks. Quamae and I did a paternity test to ease his mind, and of course it proved what I already knew to be true. I miss you so much. Not a day goes by that I don't think about you."

Sasha's face held a blank stare as she caught flashbacks of their girl talks, arguments, and disagreements. "I hope you are proud of me and the progress I've made so far. The advice you gave me is finally being put to use. I opened up my very own boutique with the one hundred grand Quamae gave me. You would be surprised, but he is a changed man. I'm even going to counseling with him for moral support and to express my own feelings and address my own issues."

Folding her arms across her body, she rocked back and forth slowly. She observed a car posted up by a tree. No one emerged from the vehicle, so she went on about her business. "It's so hard not having anyone to talk to or give me advice. Carmen and I are no longer friends because she tried to fuck Blue. I can't believe she would betray our friendship like that. That was something I never saw coming. I love you so much, India, and I would've said it more had I known our time was cut short. We were supposed to get old together and take senior trips to foreign countries." That made her laugh. Wiping her tears, she sighed. "Life is so not fair, and you didn't deserve that. They still haven't made an arrest yet, but I promise to get on them about that. I will make it my business to speak to the detective and demand answers. I promise."

She stood up to leave. "Before I go, I want you to know I will never stay away from you this long or forget about you. I promise you that. I love you, baby. Sleep in Heaven." Sasha kissed her hand and placed it on the bench.

Making good on her promise, she prepared herself to make the call to the detective who had been working on India's case, hoping for the best.

***

Later on that night, Sasha stood over the stove whipping up a special meal for her guests: lobster tails, shrimp, garlic potatoes, and red lobster biscuits. It had been a while since she cooked a nice meal like this, but she wanted to do something special for NJ. He made a full, yet speedy recovery and stepped away from the dope game for good. After the incident that took place, Sasha and Nate made him promise he was done. There was no way they could sit back and watch him kill himself. Ain't no telling who was watching or planning his demise, but it wasn't going down like that on their watch.

"Ma, I'm hungry. You not finished yet?" NJ shouted from the living room.

Sasha looked over her shoulder and smiled. "No, greedy. Nothing has changed in the ten minutes since you last asked."

NJ was sitting on the floor, rolling a ball to Dream. She was at the stage where she was taking steps and moving quickly out of the way for the new baby. It did help she would be turning one soon. Nate was so into the basketball game that was on that he wasn't paying them any attention.

"I swear it felt like I asked you that an hour ago. Me and my sister about to die from hunger over here, I swear." NJ was dedicated to being a big brother. Doing so would help him be a good father when his own child was born, but with his family in his corner, he knew it would all work itself out.

"You always starving, according to yo' daddy." Sasha added the butter and garlic to the potatoes and proceeded to mash them in the pot. "How are things going between you and Jazz?"

"We working on it." He kept it short and sweet, but he knew she was about to dig for more information. He knew how important it was for her to be a part of the restoration process with the mother of his child.

Sasha stopped whipping the potatoes and turned around to face him. "And what does that mean?"

"It means I took y'all advice and apologized. We both agreed to work on our relationship before the baby gets here. I told her to focus on school, and I will work so I can take care of her and the baby." NJ clapped his hands when Dream stood up on her feet. "Come here, fat girl." Dream walked over and sat on her brother's lap.

"NJ, don't you think you should be focused on school, too? In this society you can't be a high school dropout." Sasha turned the stove off and placed the spoon down before she walked toward the living room. "Nate, do you hear this?"

Nate swiveled his head around. "What happened?"

"You didn't hear what your son's plan is?" She placed her hands on her hip. "He wants to work instead of going to school. Can you mute the TV and put your input in?"

Nate did what she asked and turned to face his son so he could school him. "NJ, graduating is not an option. It's mandatory. There is no place in the world for a black man with no education. You have to exceed all expectations and do better for yourself. If I could go back in time, I would've listened to my mother. She not telling you nothing wrong, son. We want the best for you."

"Well, babies don't eat air pies, and I thought y'all wanted me to be responsible?" Dream pulled on his lip while he was talking.

Sasha walked over to the couch and sat down beside Nate. "We do, but not at the expense of stopping your education. Okay, how about this: you and Jazz focus on school and your father and I will take care of the baby."

"I can't ask y'all to do that. I've been taking care of myself for years, and I don't know how to take someone doing everything for me." NJ had been hustling on the block since he was eleven years old, so it was hard to revert back and be a dependent.

Nate spoke up because he knew exactly what he meant. "I understand that, but we missed out on your entire life, and we owe you that much. Don't worry about nothing. We got this."

"All you have to do is focus on school, and on the weekends and your school off days you can come work with me at the boutique. That will keep you from giving up your independence. How does that sound?" She was praying he was game.

"Okay, we have a deal. I'll focus on school." NJ was happy to finally have a strong support system after all the years of depending on himself alone.

Sasha was relieved. That was the answer she had been hoping for. "Good."

"Now can we eat, please? I am starving, for real this time." NJ rubbed his stomach.

"Yeah, let's eat." They all got up and headed into the kitchen.

Chapter 19

The next morning Sasha pulled up at the shop and Mark was standing out front, waiting on her with breakfast. It was a nice surprise. After trying to push him away for so long, today was going to be his lucky day. She was going to take him up on his offer for conversation and a free dinner. He had been persistent since the day she met him, and he never eased up, not even a little bit. She walked up on him with a smile.

"Good morning, sunshine," he greeted her.

"Good morning to you." She unlocked the door and they walked in.

"It's nice to see that beautiful smile of yours."

"Glad you like it."

"Yeah, I do, since I don't get to see it that often." Mark sat the food down on the counter.

"Well, I'm glad someone likes it." She placed her purse underneath the counter.

"So, how are you doing?"

"I'm good. How about you?"

"I can't complain."

"That's good."

Mark didn't waste any more time and cut straight to the chase. "So, I get to take you out now?"

"Of course. I would like that very much."

He couldn't believe his ears. Every pass he ever threw in her direction was returned to sender. Mark looked around and scanned the room. "Say what now? Am I being punked?"

"No. I think going out would do me some justice." Sasha pulled the stool out and sat on it.

"Dinner tomorrow night at eight?"

"That works for me."

"I'll pick you up at seven."

"Okay," she smiled.

Mark tapped the counter before walking away. "Have a good day."

"You have a good day as well," she replied.

"Oh yeah, text me your address." He felt like he was on top of the world. All his flirting and nice gestures were finally about to pay off.

"Actually, I close the shop tomorrow at 7, so just pick me up from here." She could tell he was a little disappointed when his smile turned upside down, but he was not about to get her address. She didn't know him like that to show him where she laid her head, especially since she lived alone. Quamae taught her better than that.

"Okay, I'll be here." Just before he exited the shop, he turned around. "Enjoy the breakfast."

"I most certainly will."

Once he was gone, Sasha got up to secure herself since it wasn't time to open up shop just yet. As she turned the lock, she glanced outside and saw a familiar car parallel parked across the street. It was an all-black Mercedes Benz with custom rims on it. "I swear that looks just like the car I saw at the cemetery the other day," she mumbled to herself. "I don't know, maybe I'm tripping."

Sasha shook off the thought and dismissed it as she wasn't getting enough sleep at night. Taking advantage of the down time, she decided to do a little paperwork. She pulled out her manila envelope and checked her finances. "Damn, I need an accountant," she huffed.

A few moments later her cell phone was interrupting her work. It was an unknown caller. "Hello." The line was completely silent. "Hello?" she screamed. Someone was definitely breathing into the phone, but they still didn't say a word.

She hung up because that wasn't the first time, and she was getting worried. She had her gun tucked away in her drawer for emergencies, although she was hoping she didn't have to use it. She was trying to convince herself it was nothing and she was getting herself worked up for no reason. Out of curiosity, she went back to the window since her nerves were working overtime. The same black Mercedes with tinted windows was still there.

Sasha was so spooked she had to call someone, so she chose

Lelah. They were still friends after the whole ordeal with Blue.

"Good morning," Lelah sang cheerfully.

"Aren't you happy this morning?" Her voice was dull as could be.

"Yes, I am. It's a beautiful day, why shouldn't I be?"

"I guess."

"Uh-oh, what's wrong now? Is Mark still harassing you?" she asked playfully.

"Yeah, but that's second nature now." She took a deep breath. "I'm used to that by now."

"I don't know why you won't give that fine-ass man a chance since you kicked my brother to the curb."

"That was for good reasons, and I'll give you three reasons why. I'm still married, I just got out of a relationship by force, and I'm pregnant. Is that good enough?" she laughed.

"I hear you, girl," Lelah replied.

"I'm not ready yet, and who knows when I will be ready again. Honestly, I'm not over him, and I don't want to jump into another relationship." She could feel herself tearing up. "Okay, I don't want to talk about this because I'm about to cry." She tried to laugh it off, but the pain was too intense. There was no joking about that. Blue hurt her bad. Real bad. "Well anyway, that's not why I called you. I called you because I keep getting these blocked calls. At first all of the calls were silent, but the last one I got I could hear heavy breathing." She didn't tell her about the strange car she saw parked out front.

"Change your number."

"I really don't want to because some of my clients call me on it." She didn't have any enemies that she knew about, so there was no reason to change the number.

"Well, maybe you're just being paranoid. I mean, like, who really has a reason to play on your phone all of a sudden?"

"Yeah, I guess. Maybe I am being paranoid."

"I would come up and keep you company, but I have so much to do today, and Zoe is gon' drive me up the hill and down a damn cliff if he don't leave me alone. Then I'm going in for overtime."

"Damn, Zoe doing all that?" Sasha asked. "Wait! Who forced you to go in on your off day?"

"Benjamin."

"Who the hell is Benjamin?" She was obviously confused.

"Benjamin Franklin," Lelah cracked up. "You are super slow."

"Girl, it's too early for charades. I'm still sleepy." Sasha yawned and rubbed her eyes.

"Uh-uh. Stop yawning. That shit contagious, and I know Mark brought you some coffee today."

"And you know he did." Sasha took the lid off of the coffee and smelled the inside of the cup.

"I mean, personally, I think you should talk to him. And I bet he's a good man, too. If you say it's really over between you and Blue, then I don't see why you can't move on. But if you're not sure, then I understand that, too."

"You're right," she sighed. "I'll just swear off dating until I have my baby."

"Don't just say it because you think that's what I want to hear. Say it because you mean it."

"I'm serious. I just need a break." Sasha took a sip from her coffee. A beeping sound came through the phone and got Sasha's attention. Realizing it was an important phone call, she needed to hang up quickly. "Lelah, I have an important call coming in. I have to call you back."

"Okay, babes. Talk to you later."

"Okay." Sasha clicked over. "Hello."

"This is Detective Cooper. May I speak to Sasha Banks, please?"

"This is Mrs. Banks."

"I received your message and wanted you to know we did make an arrest in India's murder. We got a full confession from a woman by the name of Janice. Does that name ring a bell to you?"

Sasha thought hard. The name sounded familiar, but she couldn't put her finger on it. "I'm thinking, but I'm drawing a blank right now."

"She's the wife of Steve, which was India's boyfriend at the time of the murder. She indicated she shot and killed her because of an ongoing affair and pregnancy."

A loud howl escaped her mouth as she had the hardest time coming to grasp with what he just revealed. Sliding down to the floor, she cupped her hand over her mouth and cried. It was all their fault. They told her to send him the fake test to get back at them.

"Mrs. Banks, are you okay? Do I need to send over a response team?" He needed to ensure her safety because he normally didn't provide those types of details over the phone like that.

"No, you don't have to do that. I'll be okay." Taking quick, then slow breaths like she did during delivery, she was able to elevate her breathing after a couple of minutes. When she looked toward the door, she saw a figure standing in front talking on the phone. "My husband just got here."

"Again, I'm very sorry for your loss and hope this gives you closure so you can start the healing process. If you ever need anything or any info, please don't hesitate to give me a call."

"Thank you."

"Take care of yourself," he added.

"I will."

"Bye-bye now."

When the call was disconnected, Sasha just sat there in a daze. Seconds later the phone slipped from her hand and onto the floor. Everything had finally come full circle, and she now felt responsible for the death of her best friend. If they would've never suggested she send the fake test, she knew India would still be alive.

That day was so fresh in her memory that it felt like yesterday. She and Carmen went over to console India after she found out Steve was married. It was their bright idea to send a fake pregnancy test and write a letter to Steve's wife indicating she would be seeking child support through her attorney. India agreed because she wanted Janice to hurt just as much as she was hurting, and Steve needed to pay for his mistakes. No one knew the outcome would be so deadly, and now Sasha had to live with that for the rest of her natural life. Something in her wanted to call Carmen and fill her in, but the other part of her said fuck that shit.

The door finally opened. When she looked up, Quamae was finally coming inside.

"What's goin' on, wifey? Why you sittin' on the floor?"

Sasha sat there shaking her head. The words wouldn't come out.

"Are you crying?" He proceeded to walk toward her, kneeling down in front of her and placing his hand on her shoulder. "What happened? Why you crying? If that nigga did something to you, I'll kill his ass." He meant every word he said.

Sasha shook her head no. "He didn't do anything to me. It's. It's India."

That threw him for a loop, and he thought she was losing her everlasting mind. "What do you mean? 'Cause India is dead."

"I know." She proceeded to sniffle. Her shoulders and chest moved up and down. "They made an arrest, and it was her boyfriend's wife that killed her."

"Damn, I'm sorry to hear that." Quamae wrapped his arms around her body and rubbed her back. It was his job to console the woman he loved in everything she faced. He just wished he had done that sooner and none of the chaos in their lives would've happened. If he hadn't been so far gone in the dope game, then he could've paid his wife some attention and she would've never strayed from the jump. Going forward he was prepared to give her one thousand percent in their marriage. He refused to let her go. "I think you need to call it a day and go home to get some rest. You can't work like this." Releasing the hold he had on her, Quamae grabbed her arms and pulled her up on her feet.

"Somebody been playing on my phone. When I answer all I hear is breathing. I don't know what to think." Sasha was so upset she didn't know if she was coming or going.

Quamae stared into her eyes. "I promise I won't let anything happen to you. I'll be around to protect you even when you don't see me."

"Okay," she nodded.

"Come on so I can get you out of here. You can stay with me tonight if that would make you feel safe. You can sleep in the guest room if you want to. It doesn't matter to me. I just want to make sure you okay."

"I would like that." Going home was a little too nerve wracking, so she agreed to spend the night. It ain't like they were having sex. Quamae agreed to take things slow until they figured out what they wanted to do once they reached their therapy goals.

Once Sasha closed up the shop, they headed out the door.

Destiny

Chapter 20

The next day she was feeling a little better thanks to her husband. It was a work night for him at the lounge, so she kept her word on going to dinner that evening. Dream was in the care of Ms. Mildred, so she was baby-free. Sasha and Mark were seated in a dark restaurant enjoying each other's company. Their connection was crazy, and it also helped that he was open to any question she could think of. So, of course, it was a must to find out why he was single. Come to find out his last relationship ended when he caught his best friend and fiancée in bed with one another. Sasha was surprised by what they had in common, 'cause little did he know she was just like his ex.

"Sorry you had to go through that," Sasha said, being empathetic.

"It's cool. I'm just glad I found out before it was too late."

"You're right about that."

As she sipped her wine, the phone began to ring. She reached into her purse and stared at the screen. It was Blue. She silenced the phone and continued her conversation. "So, how long have you been in your line of work?"

"Eight years," he replied.

The phone started to ring again, so she silenced it again and put it on vibrate.

Mark looked at her. "Do you need to get that?"

"Nope, it's nobody important." She was still upset with him for cheating on her with Emani. True enough he didn't know, but it still hurt the same. The constant vibration of the phone was irritating her soul. Mark couldn't hear it because of the soft music the band was playing.

Sasha waited a few minutes before excusing herself to use the restroom. "I'm going to the ladies' room. I'll be right back." Sasha got up and headed toward the back of the restaurant. Once she was safely inside the stall, as if she was hiding from someone, she called him back. He picked up with an attitude.

"Where are you?" he shouted.

"I'm busy, so what do you want?"

"I need to talk to you."

"For what?" she snapped.

"We need to talk."

"Well, I'm not ready to talk to you," she huffed. "When I wanted to talk, you didn't. The sun doesn't rise and set on you."

"Since when?" he said sarcastically.

"Since now."

"Yeah, right."

"Oh no, you had it like that, but you ruined it 'cause you couldn't keep your dick in your pants. Those days are done. I have to go."

She hung up the phone while he was trying to talk. For the first time it felt good to be in control. She turned her phone off completely so there would be no more interruptions.

After dinner they went back to Sasha's shop so she could get her car. She really had a good time with Mark and wasn't quite ready to call it a night since Quamae was still working. All she wanted was a little company, but she was tired and didn't want him to get the wrong idea, because pussy was not on the menu. The way he looked into her eyes and the way he had been a complete gentleman all night long let her know that he was into her. Mark parked the car adjacent to the shop and got up to meet Sasha on the passenger side. When he opened up the door, he grabbed her hand so she could step out.

"Thank you so much, Mark. I had a really good time, and you were the perfect gentleman," she smiled.

"You're quite welcome, and I thank you for the opportunity to show you a good time." Mark kissed her hand before he let it go.

"You're welcome. I needed to get out and clear my head, you know?"

"Yeah, I know. I'm glad I could help with that." His focus was no longer on her because he was too busy surveying the area. And to be honest, that made her a little nervous.

"Well, I'm going to call it a night so I can get on home to my daughter. Thanks again."

Just as she was about to walk off, he stopped her. "Do you mind if I use your bathroom before I go? I have a long ride ahead of me."

Sasha hesitated at first, but she quickly changed her mind. "Sure thing, come on."

Unlocking the door quickly, she pulled the door open and let him walk in first. "Walk straight back through that door and I'll turn on the light so you won't trip and fall. I have Florida No Fault, so you ain't suing me," she said in a joking manner.

"I would never." Mark made his way through the back door and into the bathroom. Sasha followed suit. "I'll make it snappy."

"Thanks, 'cause I'm tired." Sasha sat down in a chair while she waited on him to return.

A few minutes later he walked out drying his hands with a paper towel. He was walking very slowly toward her with a smirk on his face. "You know, I waited a very long time for this day to happen. At first I didn't think you would go out with me, but then I finally got you to accept my dinner date."

"Hey, a girl gotta eat," she giggled. "You kept asking, so I was like, *what the hell*?"

"Yep, and you should've been a little more consistent and stuck to your guns. That was your first mistake."

Now she was scared as hell 'cause she didn't know where his new demeanor came from. All of a sudden he looked possessed. Sasha stood up, but before she could take a step he was standing in her face. She could feel the air coming through his nostrils. "Mark, what's wrong with you?"

"You don't remember me, do you?" He stuck his hand inside of his jacket pocket.

"No, I don't. Should I?" Her voice cracked 'cause she didn't know what to expect and her gun was too far away. In the midst of leaving earlier she had forgotten to put it inside her purse for safe keepings.

"Let me refresh your memory." He handed her the photo he pulled from his pocket. "You certainly remember my father, don't you?"

Sasha held the photo, and when she focused in on the face, she stopped breathing altogether. That was a face she would never forget. It had haunted her for years. "Frank. Frank is your father?" she stuttered. Those words were hard to say, knowing she made the biggest mistake of her life.

"You mean Frank *was* my father, but thanks to you and your punk-ass boyfriend, Nate, he's no longer with me."

"Your father raped me when I was twelve years old. Did you know that? And he continued to do so until I was fifteen. He took away my childhood."

Mark slapped her across the face, but Sasha kept herself together and stood toe-to-toe with him. She couldn't let him see her become weak.

"You stop lying on my father. He would've never did no shit like that when he had my mother at home." He let that sink in for a few seconds. "Your mother told me you would lie about what happened." He had every intention of breaking her heart before he killed her.

"My mother?" she asked with the screwed-up face.

"Yes, your mother. She told me everything that happened because she wanted me to get closure. She even gave me this in case you don't believe me." Mark handed Sasha the picture of herself, the same one Carol had given to Quamae.

Sasha's legs became weak underneath her because she couldn't fathom the reason her mother would put her in harm's way like that, but then again, who was she fooling? This was the same woman who allowed Frank to rape her in the first place, so yeah, it was natural for her to put her in danger.

Unable to stand any longer, Sasha tried to sit down before she fell, but Mark lunged toward her and knocked her to the floor. Sasha landed on her back, and she could feel the pain settling in quickly. On instinct she cradled her belly.

Mark stood over her and straddled her lap. "I am going to kill you for killing my daddy. Do you know what type of fucked-up life I had after you killed him? You and that hoodlum of yours."

Mark placed both hands on her throat. "Of course you don't, and that's why I'm going to kill you."

Sasha was trying her best to get him off of her, but he was too strong. She dug her nails deeply through his arms, breaking the skin. "Mark, stop! Please don't do this," she pleaded.

"Did you let my father live after he begged for his life?" Spit flew from his mouth while he shouted in her face.

She didn't answer the question, knowing it wouldn't make it better. Mark tightened the grip around her throat and pressed down hard on it. Her mind was racing as her life flashed before her eyes, but she continued to kick, scream, and claw away at him in hopes he would give up.

Out of every scenario she had been through, she always managed to escape and live through the pain, but this time it was finally over for her. In a matter of minutes her life was going to come to an end, and at the hands of a monster. She would no longer see NJ and Dream's faces, and she would never meet her unborn child or grandchild. Every obstacle she conquered had been for nothing because her life was being taken away. Sasha gave up and stopped fighting. This was a fight she would never win. It was over. Closing her eyes, she said a prayer and made peace with God in hopes he would forgive her for all of her sins and allow her to walk through those pearly gates. A single tear escaped her eyes as she mouthed the word *Amen!*

Pow!

The sound of an explosive made Sasha open her eyes and scream from the depth of her soul. When she looked up, Mark had a hole in his head with blood gushing out. He fell sideways in slow motion until his body hit the floor with a loud smack. She was so lost at what was going on. Effortlessly, she managed to push his legs off of her. When she finally looked up, she saw her savior.

"Are you okay?" Quamae asked while walking over to where she was lying.

He picked her up from the floor, and she hugged him for dear life. "Quamae, you saved my life. I thought I was about to die," she rambled. "He was about to kill me. How did you know I was here?"

Quamae placed both hands on her shoulders and walked her to her desk. "I need you to calm down so you can tell me what happened. Take a few deep breaths and count to one hundred."

Sasha did as she was told. Never taking her eyes off of him, she watched him pull some black gloves out of his pocket and slip them both onto his hands. Quamae walked over to Mark's body and rolled him onto his back. That was when he checked his pockets and pulled out his wallet. He quickly recognized his face as one of her clients. The first question that popped into his mind was why they were together in the first place, and at this hour. Now wasn't the time or place for that discussion, so he would save that question for another day. True enough he was a changed man, but he still wasn't soft, a sucker, or a damn fool.

While digging through his wallet, he stumbled across what appeared to be a receipt. He then sat the wallet on the floor and opened up the paper to see what was on it. To his surprise he saw his home address scribbled down on it. Quamae stood up and walked toward Sasha. "What is he doing with my address in his wallet?" He was heated as he held it up between his fingers.

"Let me see." She held out her hand and he dropped it in her palm. "I never told you this before, but remember the guy Frank who raped me when I was twelve, and Carol allowed it to happen?"

"Yeah," he replied.

Reliving that was not what she wanted to do, but she needed to clear things up for Quamae's sake and her own. "Well, he's the son of Frank. He came back to kill me because I shot and killed his father."

"But why does he have my address?" He wasn't upset with her, just at the fact his personal info was in the pocket of a man he just killed.

"That was Carol's work. She told him I killed his daddy, and I bet that's how he got it."

Quamae scratched his temple. "It's time I pay her a little visit. I'm going to take you home in the morning, 'cause I don't know how far this info went. The shop will be closed tomorrow until I get this body from out of here, and when I am done I will pick you up, or you can meet me."

"Okay."

"Do you wanna go to the hospital?" He extended his hand so she could grab it.

"No, 'cause I don't want to get the police involved." Sasha forced herself out of the seat. She was a little sore, but she was ready to go to sleep.

"You need to check on the baby, even though it ain't mine."

She caught his snide remark, but let it slide. "I'll go to my doctor tomorrow and tell her I fell."

"Okay, let's go."

***

When they walked through the front door of Quamae's house, the nanny was walking down the steps.

"Hey, Ms. Mildred, sorry I'm late. I had a little business to handle before coming in." Quamae locked the door and turned to face her.

"You know that's not a problem. I love spending time with that little angel of yours." She looked Sasha up and down and knew something was wrong. "Are you okay, Sasha?"

"Yeah, I'm just tired." She had her hand on her stomach, feeling for the kicks of the baby.

"She fell and doesn't want to go to the hospital, so what should I do for her?" As soon as he blurted that out, Sasha cut her eyes at him. "What?" he asked.

"Well, is the baby at least moving, since you don't wanna go?" Ms. Mildred sweetly asked.

"As we speak," she answered. "I told him I was going to my doctor tomorrow."

"Okay, well, take a nice warm bath and let this husband of yours rub you down." Ms. Mildred patted him on the arm and smiled.

Destiny

"I can do that," Quamae smiled. "Is she asleep?"

"I just put her in the bed a few minutes ago. She tried her best to wait on y'all, but it was getting too late for her, so I told her a bedtime story and rocked her to sleep."

"Well, I guess I'll go up and say goodnight, anyway." Quamae grabbed Sasha's hand and pulled her toward the stairs. "Come on."

"Okay. I'll be on my way, since you're home now." Ms. Mildred removed her apron.

Quamae stopped and turned back to Ms. Mildred. "That won't be necessary. Sleep in the guest room, because it's too late for you to be driving alone."

"I'll be okay, and I don't want to impose." Walking over to the door, she grabbed her keys.

"Do I have to come and take your keys? You might as well go up and go to sleep. Stop being so stubborn. It's too late for you to be alone, seriously. I'll kill somebody if something happened." Quamae wouldn't feel right if she didn't make it home. Things weren't the same with all the craziness in the world.

She thought for a few seconds and hung her keys back up. "Okay, since you put it that way, I'll stay."

"Thank you. That's all I ask." Quamae and Sasha proceeded up the steps.

Quamae went inside the bathroom to run her a bubble bath. That was the least he could do since she rejected going to the hospital. He figured a nice, hot bath would get her prepared for a good night's sleep, just as Ms. Mildred suggested.

Looking inside the cabinet, he saw he didn't have any type of feminine body wash in there. All he had was Disney Princess bubble bath he bought for Dream. He picked up the bottle and walked over to the tub.

"I guess this gon' have to do." Quamae sat on the side of the tub and put the stopper in before turning on the water and adding the soap.

Moments later, Sasha emerged from the bedroom to join him. "Are you ready for me?" she asked softly.

"Yeah, come on." He stood up so he could get out of the way.

218

"I need help taking off my clothes."

"I gotchu." He walked up and grabbed the bottom of her shirt. "Hold your arms up." Quamae pulled the shirt over her head, followed by the rest of her clothing. There was no shame in his game as he zoomed in closely on her naked body. Just seeing her in that state made him realize he missed out on a beautiful pregnancy with his princess. Quamae vowed that when they got back together, they were going to make another child. A second chance was what he needed to fill in the absence from the first time.

Quamae did the honors of bathing Sasha, then carrying her into the bedroom and giving her a full body massage, feet included. Before he finished, Sasha was calling the hogs all the way home. He stared at her smooth chocolate skin for a few seconds before he covered her up with a blanket. As bad as he wanted to slide up in her, he couldn't do it. That would violate everything they were building and standing on, so he decided to wait it out just a little bit longer. Instead he climbed into bed with her and went to sleep.

Destiny

Chapter 21

After her visit with the doctor, Sasha learned the baby appeared to be okay. She needed to pay close attention to the movements, not let long periods of time go without feeling a thing, and look out for spotting. That would be a bad sign. Since the boutique was closed, she stayed at home and binge-watched *Empire*. It had been a while since she sat around and watched TV.

Suddenly there was a knock on the door. *Boom! Boom!*

"Who is it?" she shouted while getting up to answer the door.

"It's me," a man responded.

Standing on her tippy toes, she looked through the peephole and saw Blue. "He think he so slick," she said to herself. Sasha had called him and told him about the fall, so of course he was worried and decided to do a pop-up visit. Removing the locks, she opened the door and let him in. "What you doing here?" she asked while stepping back so he could come in.

"I came to check on you and that baby. That is why you called me, right?" Blue walked past her and went to the couch and sat down. Sasha did the same.

"Yeah, I thought you needed to know what happened to us."

"Well, that's why I'm here."

"Okay, just asking." Grabbing the remote, she started the next episode.

There was no conversation between them for at least fifteen minutes before Blue finally looked over at her. "Sasha?"

"Yeah?" she answered, but she never took her eyes off the show.

"I want my family back," he admitted.

That caught her attention, so she turned to face him.

"I'm tired of living apart, and it's time we get back together. It's been too long. I just want to be in the house with my son."

"Your son. That's the only person you're worried about?" She paused the TV.

"Dream has a father, but nevertheless I still love her, and that will never change. But I'm talking about my son right now, so don't try to turn this into something that it ain't, 'cause you know how I feel about her."

"I never said you didn't love her." In her defense, he didn't need to separate the two when it came to trying to get back with her.

"What's the problem then?" Blue sat up and lifted his dreads from behind him. "I'm starting to think you don't want me to fix this, and if that's the case, then you need to let me know so I can stop wasting me and your time."

"You already know how I feel about this, and that is why I moved out in the first place." She exhaled slowly. "I cannot get over the fact you had a full-blown relationship with her, countless times of sexual favors, and a possible pregnancy. That was more than sex, and she is a sister to me."

"We don't know if that girl pregnant or if she just lying. I haven't talked to that girl." This was not what he was hoping for on this surprise visit. He sighed 'cause he knew this wasn't going anywhere with her. "You act like I knew she was your sister."

"It doesn't matter. We were supposed to be in a committed relationship, and you ruined that. It ain't like you slept with her once. You did it repeatedly and stayed with her when we were going through it. If I would've did that to you, it would be over between us for good without a second thought."

"You don't know that," he rebutted.

"Oh, I do. But anyway, let's call her and see what she says. You claim y'all used condoms, but now you lying and saying you don't know if she pregnant or not. You need to make up your mind. I tell you what, though. We gon' call, 'cause I wanna know." Sasha's phone was beside her, so she picked it up and scrolled through her list of contacts until she reached Emani's number. Sasha put in on speakerphone so he could hear.

The phone rang several times before she picked up. "Hello," she answered.

"Emani, this is Sasha. I need to talk to you." Sasha paused and waited on a response from her.

"Sasha, I'm so happy you called. I've been trying to reach out to you, but you wouldn't take any of my calls. There's so much I need to say." Her words tumbled out as she quickly tried to get her point across.

"I wasn't ready to talk you, so that's why you haven't heard from me. How are you?" Sasha did miss Emani, and maybe it was time to forgive her since she and Blue were no longer together.

"I could be better, but I made this bed, and now I must lay in it." Emani exhaled into the phone. "Sasha, I'm sorry for everything. I didn't know you and Blue were together. If I did, none of this would've ever happened. Please forgive me."

Sasha looked at Blue, and he was just sitting there nodding his head. Listening to Emani acting innocent and putting on this show was getting on his nerves. That same day she found out, she was trying to fuck. All he wanted to hear was that she wasn't pregnant.

"In due time, this will all be water underneath the bridge. But as of right now I have an important question to ask you." Her real anger was solely at Blue since he was the one who cheated. She was mad at Emani for not saying anything to her when they shared a bond as sisters.

"Anything," Emani replied.

"Are you pregnant?"

The phone fell silent for a while, so Sasha looked at her screen to see if she had hung up. She was still there.

"Hello?"

"I'm here."

"Okay, so are you pregnant or not?" Sasha repeated.

"Yes."

Sasha was taken by surprise since he denied having unprotected sex with her.

Blue's eyes were stretched to capacity, and the pace of his heartbeat increased. His biggest fear had just been confirmed. During his three-day break away from Sasha they weren't using condoms, relying on the pull-out method only.

"What the fuck you mean, you pregnant?" Blue shouted.

Sasha had the meanest look on her face. "You need to calm down, 'cause she didn't make this baby on her own. You helped with that." From experience she knew what Emani was going through, and it didn't feel good to deal with a pregnancy all alone The love she had for Emani was still there. The closeness was what was absent.

"Blue, you know damn well we didn't use condoms all the time, so you can stop puttin' on." Emani was tired of being quiet about the truth. "When you came here for those three days we fucked all day and night, so I don't see why you questioning how this happened in the first place."

"Okay, stop, 'cause I heard enough." Sasha didn't need to hear all the details while he was cheating on her. "Have y'all spoken since then?"

Emani didn't hesitate to speak up. "He blocked my number, so I have no way of getting in contact with him."

Sasha looked at Blue and shook her head. "Unblock her number. I don't know why you doing all that now. You have to deal with this."

"It's okay, Sasha, he doesn't have to. On Friday all of this will be over, after I get the abortion, so I'll be out of the way for good." Emani rubbed her stomach and let the tears fall. It hurt to be rejected by the man who got her pregnant.

"Well, I'll make sure he brings you the money to pay for it," Sasha promised.

"I don't want anything from him. I already got more than what I bargained for, so I'm good. Anyway, I hope in due time we can work on our relationship. I know we won't be as close as we were before, but I would like to be on speaking terms. Oh, and another thing, please don't tell Quamae. I told him about the situation, but I didn't mention the pregnancy."

"Okay, I won't say anything. Well, one day we'll get together and hash things out. I can't promise when, but it's in our future." She did look forward to working things out with her for the sake of Quamae.

"Hopefully it's before I leave and go to Michigan."

"Oh wow, when are you leaving?" Sasha was confused 'cause he never mentioned that to her.

"After I take my final exams, I'm transferring to the University of Michigan."

"Okay."

"Well, I have to go so I can finish studying for my exams. I'll be in touch with you before I leave."

"Talk to you soon."

"Bye."

Sasha closed her eyes, ended the call, and sat it down in her lap. The news she received was not what she wanted to hear. True enough she and Blue were over, but it still hurt nonetheless. Raising her head slowly, she finally made eye contact with Blue. "Condoms, huh? See how you lied to me?"

"I didn't. The shit had to bust. The whole time I was there I was drunk, thinkin' 'bout you." He didn't care what Emani said, he was not admitting to that.

"So, while you was dickin' down another female, you was thinkin' about me, huh? Get the fuck outta here with that bullshit, Blue. What you take me for? A dummy?" Sasha rolled her eyes, then turned her head. The sight of him was pissing her off.

"We can get through this. I promise I won't do it again. Just give me one more chance, please. I want us to raise our son together," Blue begged.

"Do you know how stupid that sound when you have a whole baby developing over there? You have the mother blocked so she can't call you. That's not right."

"That girl ain't pregnant. That's why she said she gettin' an abortion. But you don't believe me, though. It's cool."

"You damn right! I don't trust you anymore. You lied to my face about everything." Their conversation quickly turned into a yelling match.

Just then her phone started to vibrate on the cushion in between them. When he looked down, he was furious. Blue looked up at Sasha. "What the fuck he calling you for?"

She rolled her eyes because she was a single, yet married woman who could do as she pleased. "He does have a daughter that lives here, or did you forget that? Maybe you should call and check on your baby mama."

"Whateva!" Blue hated Quamae with a passion, and he didn't want her to answer the phone.

"Blue, just stop."

The phone was silent for a moment, but it started right back up. Sasha knew she had to answer it. If not, Quamae would be there in a few minutes to make sure she was okay.

"Back-to-back calls, huh? He looking for something, and it ain't his daughter." Blue got up and walked into the kitchen.

"Hello."

"How you doing over there?" Quamae asked.

"I'm good. The doctor said the baby seems okay and I need to monitor the movement."

"Good. Well, I have something special planned for you, so I'll be over there around nine to pick y'all up."

"Sounds good."

"A'ight. I'll see y'all later, and kiss my baby for me."

"Okay, I will. Thanks."

Blue was standing at the foyer, leaning against the wall with his arms folded when she hung up the phone. He had a look of disdain on his face. "Now it all makes sense to me."

"What are you talking about?" She placed the phone beside her.

"That's the reason we can't move forward, because you still stuck on that nigga. I guess that's why you never got a divorce in the first place." Of course he was being selfish, but he was a typical man. It was to be expected.

Sasha rolled her eyes because she had enough of his selfish ways. All of a sudden she was to blame when he was the one cheating on her. "Tuh." She rolled her eyes. "Meanwhile, you was fuckin' his sister."

"Would you let that go already? Stop acting like I knew she was his sister," he became defensive. "Just tell me one thing." It was the one question that ate his soul alive. He had to ask the question, but he was too afraid of the answer, so he took a deep breath and let it out. "Did you start back fuckin' him?"

"No, I did not," she shouted. "Damn, that's all you think I wanna do, fuck all the time? That's why I'm caught up in this bullshit now, but all of that has changed. I'm not fucking you, him, or anybody else." That was an honest answer coming from her that time around. Her main focus was to figure out what she wanted to do, and sex would only cloud her judgment. For the first time in her life, she held out on giving up the goods so she could make the best decision for her and her children. Sex and her infidelities put her in the position she was in, and she was finally ready for a change. She hadn't slept with Nate, either. "You know, Blue, I still love you. The sad part is I left him on the pretense things would be better with you, but in the end you proved me wrong. You hurt me just as bad, mentally and physically. I don't doubt your love for me, but you not ready to be in a committed relationship. You hate to communicate, and you run to another woman when things get bad. I just don't see a future for us anymore, and that hurts."

Blue heard more than enough, so he eased himself off the wall and headed toward the door. "I appreciate you telling me how you really feel, so with that being said, I'm going to step out of the way and let you be free. I made my bed, so I guess it's time to lie in it. I wish you nothing but the best, and remember I will always love you, and I never meant to hurt you the way I did."

Blue walked out the door and didn't look back. He ruined the one thing that meant so much to him.

***

At 9:00 p.m. on the dot, Quamae pulled up to Sasha's apartment complex and parked in front of her building. The time had finally presented itself, and he was ready to address his wife once and for all. There were so many things that needed to be said and done. Hitting the ignition switch, he turned off the engine and got out of the car. This was going to be a night she would never forget.

Quamae jogged up the two flights of stairs and knocked on the door. Seconds later, Sasha opened the door with Dream attached to her leg.

"Hey," she smiled. "This little girl is so aggy right now. If this wasn't an overnight thing, I swear she would be sleeping right now."

"I see. So, I guess that means y'all ready to go?"

"Yes."

He bent down and picked up his daughter. "Hey, princess."

Dream took her hand and slapped Quamae's lips repeatedly. "Da-da."

"You ain't seen me all day, and the first thing you wanna do is fight? I missed you." Quamae kissed her on the cheek. "Did you miss me?" She nodded her head up and down. "Come on, and let's go. We on a timed schedule."

Sasha snatched up her and Dream's bag, then they walked outside together. Once she locked the door, they were finally on their way down the stairs.

"So, where are we going?" Sasha asked.

"It's a surprise," he replied.

"But." Sasha stopped dead in her tracks when she hit the bottom step. "This can't be. Maybe I'm tripping," she whispered to herself.

Quamae didn't notice she'd stopped. He opened up the car door and strapped the baby into her car seat. When he was done, he looked back at Sasha and waved his hand. "Come on, let's go."

Sasha found the strength to move her feet and walk toward the car. When she got inside the car, Quamae started it and pulled off.

"Who's car?" Sasha asked while looking around at the nice, black leather interior.

"Mine. Do you like it?"

"Yeah, it's very nice. I didn't know you got a new car." If her memory served her correctly, she'd seen this vehicle before.

"Yeah, I just got it not too long ago." Quamae got onto I-95N and hit the gas. If he wanted to be on schedule, he had to be there in the next 20 minutes. It was all mapped out.

"Oh, okay." Sasha sat back and tried to ease her mind, but she needed music to assist her wild thoughts. "Can you turn on some music, please?"

"Yeah, just give me one minute to make this call." Quamae picked up a phone from the console and placed a call.

"What it do?" Amp answered.

"Is everything ready for me? Me and the wife headed there right now," he coolly asked, then glanced over at Sasha.

"Yep. Everything set up and ready to go. Oh yeah, instead of the blocks I got a tire rim. That muthafucka heavy as hell. It's guaranteed to sink some shit."

"That's what I'm talkin' 'bout. I know she gon' love this shit," Quamae laughed.

"No doubt, big bruh."

"A'ight, I'll be there in ten."

"Cool."

He then hung up the phone and put it in the side of the door. As promised, he put on some music for Sasha. Quamae took it back to the good days and put on Jon B.'s *They Don't Know*. Fifteen minutes later he got off on State Road 84 and went east toward the beach. He was excited, and Sasha was anxious and nervous at the same time. Finally they arrived at the port in Ft. Lauderdale.

"Is this where we going?" she asked calmly.

"You'll see in less than five minutes." Quamae parked the car inside the garage and they got out. The lot was well lit, and she got a better view of the car in the light. At that moment she knew her mind wasn't paying tricks on her. Whenever they got to where they were going, she would ask him.

After walking for what seemed like an eternity, they were on some sort of dock. "How much further do we have to walk?" Sasha was notorious for whining.

Quamae just laughed at her and the fact she was still impatient. It wasn't like she was carrying the baby. "Right up the dock. We're seconds away."

As promised, their walk came to an end in seconds. "You can stop now."

Amp was sitting on a fold-up chair. When he saw them, he

stood up and walked over to Quamae and dapped him up. "What's happening, King David?" Amp joked.

"Shit! Ready to slay this bitch named Goliath."

Sasha just stood there with no clue as to what the hell they were talking about.

Amp looked at Dream and smiled, grabbing her tiny hand. "What's up, princess?"

She pulled her hand back. "No."

"Damn, she still don't like me wit' her li'l mean ass."

"That's right, stay away from hood niggas," Quamae laughed and kissed her head.

"What's up, sis? How you doin'?" He looked in the direction where she was standing.

"I'm good, and you?"

"I'm good." Amp grabbed his chair and folded it up. "I won't hold y'all up, so be easy. Hit me up when you get back." Amp handed Quamae the burner phone they had been talking on.

He put it into his pocket. "A'ight, bruh." Quamae turned to Sasha. "Let's ride."

"You want me to ride on a boat with you? Hell no. I'm scared." She folded her arms.

"Baby, this is not a boat." He pointed toward the water. "It's a yacht. Come check it out."

They walked up to where a jet-black yacht was posted. It was definitely worth some money. As soon as she saw what they were riding in, she got excited. Jumping up and down and shit. In beautiful silver letters, the stern read *Princess Dream*. "Quamae is this yours?" she screeched in excitement.

"It's ours. The three of us." He knew she would love it. "It's the Sunseeker Predator."

"It's beautiful. Is this the surprise?" She couldn't hide her happiness even if she tried. The nervousness she had in her stomach during the car ride was long gone and replaced with butterflies. This was the Quamae she fell in love with.

"It's one of them. Come on, let's go inside." He thought back to what he told Christine, and he was right that getting her back

230

would dent the pockets. However, it was worth it.

Quamae escorted them on board and gave her a quick tour of it. Sasha was so impressed with the layout, the beautiful rooms, lounge, kitchen, and bathroom. And the best of them all, beside the stainless steel appliances, was the garage with an abundance of water toys. "Damn, this is really nice. Makes me wanna give up my apartment and move in. How the hell they put a garage on this thang?"

"Sounds like you ready to take me back?" he smirked.

Sasha leaned in and placed her lips on his. "You awfully close."

Quamae slipped her some tongue. He had been waiting to that and more for a long time. With the baby in one of his arms, he used the other to palm her ass, giving it a little squeeze. He could feel his shit getting ready to rock up, so he pulled back. "Let me put her in this crib so she can go to sleep. Fix her a bottle."

Sasha walked away and did as she was told while Quamae slipped his baby girl into some pajamas. When he was done, he put her inside the crib and turned on the musical mobile. Sasha returned quickly with the bottle and gave it to him.

They stood there for a few moments and she was out like a light.

"Come on, let's go," he whispered.

"We leaving her in here?" She was a little skeptical, like she would crawl out of it and jump overboard.

"She ain't going nowhere." He walked over to the dresser and picked up a baby monitor. "We have this and a monitor by the captain's station."

"Okay. Just make sure you close the door."

"Let's go." He placed his hand on the small of her back and pushed her toward the door.

Quamae fixed two drinks and handed one to Sasha. "Wine for you and liquor for me. A two-glass maximum for you."

"Thanks." They walked to the captain's station and sat down. "You know how to drive this?"

Quamae licked his lips and put his hand between her legs.

"Just as well as I know how to drive this."

Sasha didn't push his hand away that time. She was ready to open up shop for him. "You so nasty."

"You like it, though."

Quamae started up the engine and pulled off slowly. Trusting he knew what he was doing. Sasha leaned back and enjoyed the ride.

Chapter 22

The boat ride was smooth as hell. Quamae handled that boat like a pro. Sasha felt a tingling sensation inside thinking back to what he said about handling her va-jay-jay, but he ain't never lied about that. In her mind she couldn't wait for the boat to stop so he could fuck her good for old time's sake. Shaking her legs back and forth, she tried her best to keep from creaming right there on the spot.

Staring up through the sunroof, the moon was full and bright enough to put a huge spotlight on the water. The stars were even twinkling. This was like a dream come true, and she didn't want to wake up from it. "It's so beautiful and peaceful out here."

"Yep. No interruptions, and no one to get in the way." Quamae brought the boat to a stop.

"I know, right?" This was the moment she was waiting for.

He turned to face her. "Let me ask you a question, and I want an honest answer from you."

"Okay."

"What was Blue doing at your place tonight?" Taking a sip of his drink, he waited on her answer.

"He came by to check on me and the baby. He was worried when I told him about the fall." Sasha paused and tilted her head to the side. "Wait, how did you know he was at my place?"

"I told you I would be watching you, even if you didn't see me." He proceeded to take another sip. "Is he trying to get back with you or some shit?"

"He asked me if I wanted to work things out with him, but I told him there was no way I could do that after he slept with your sister."

Quamae bit down on his lip. Just hearing that Blue was fucking his sister made him want to kill him even more. When Emani first mentioned it he wanted to choke her out for dealing with a nigga like that in the first place. "Okay, and what about Mark? What were you doing with him at that time of night outside of the shop?"

Sasha was really thrown off because he was calling her out on everything. "You had to work that night, and I wasn't ready to go home yet. So, to kill time, he asked if I wanted to go and get something to eat, so I said yes." Sasha scratched her head. This shit wasn't adding up. He knew her every move. "Well, let me ask you a question. Have you been following me in that black car? Because I have seen it parked in front of the boutique a lot, and I saw it at the cemetery."

Quamae brought his hand close to his mouth and rubbed his lips and chin. "I'm guilty of that, but for good reason."

"And what is that?"

"I saved your life, didn't I?" He sat his drink down on the floor.

"Yes, you did, and I'm grateful for that."

"Sasha, do you really love me?" he asked with a straight face.

She had seen that face on several occasions, and he normally looked that way before he kicked her ass. "Yes, I do. Why do you think I'm here right now? You saw I answered the phone when you called me in front of him earlier. What we had is over. I just want to work on my marriage."

"It's you and me forever?" he confirmed.

"Yes," she nodded her head.

"Okay." Quamae stood up and pulled out a gun. "Stand up, and let's take a walk."

"Quamae, what are you doing?"

He could hear the nervousness in her voice and the chatter of her teeth. "I'm about to show you."

Quamae escorted Sasha to the bottom of the boat. She was scared shitless. They were in the middle of the ocean, and no one would know where to look for her. The way her heart was beating out of her chest, the coast guard could hear it. Her thoughts were everywhere. *Was this all a part of his sick and twisted plan? Lure me in, kill me, and raise my child without me?*

"Watch your step," he instructed.

When she looked down, she saw rope and the floor covered in plastic. She panicked. "Quamae, please don't kill me. I love you, and I'm sorry for everything I did. If I could take it all back, I

234

would. But I can't, so you have to forgive me the same way I forgave you for pistol-whipping me."

That surprised the hell out of him. Last time he checked, she had memory loss. "What was that?"

Sasha had tears in her eyes when she turned around to face him. "I remember everything about that day. You called me over to confront me about the video. When I tried to leave you, you shot at me, but you missed on purpose. After that you hit me with the gun, and everything went black after that. When I woke up, I was in the hospital. I was in a coma for a month."

Hearing her recall every detail hurt him to the core. The reason behind him buying her all those things was because he felt like he owed it to her after the horrible way he treated her. Quamae stared into her eyes as he teared up himself. "Damn, that just fucked me up. But I didn't bring you out here to kill you. I already did that to you mentally. We're here because I want us to start over and forget about the past. I bought you all those things and gave you all that money because you deserve that and so much more. I was a horrible husband, and I want to spend the rest of my days making it up to you. Sasha, I'm truly sorry you remember that day. I prayed so hard it would never surface, but I'm willing to do any and everything to make that pain go away."

Sasha took a step toward him and grabbed his hand. "Quamae, I've already forgiven you, and you need to do the same. We've changed for the better, and we can do this together because I wasn't the perfect wife either, and that's why I agreed to go to counseling with you. You have already shown me you were willing to change for me, and that meant the world to me. It wasn't about the money you gave me, but the love you have for our daughter and the lengths you went to make sure I gave you that paternity test. I know you put those results in my car, and I know you wanted to make sure he found out about it."

Quamae's brow creased in confusion, wondering how she knew all of that.

"Yes, I know. I've been with you for years, and I know how you operate. I just didn't confront you about it because I wanted to

235

see how far you would go for your family."

He was truly surprised she was able to pinpoint all of that. All he could do was laugh. "Damn, I'm busted."

"It's okay, but what I need to know is why you have that gun out like you about to shoot me."

"Stand right here and I'll show you." Quamae walked over to the closet and opened up the door.

When he bent down, Sasha watched him grab something, but she couldn't see what it was. When he backed up, she saw him pull out a body. "Quamae, who the hell is that?" She backed up.

He then stepped around so she could get a good look. "Say hello to your mommy dearest." He snatched the tape off of Carol's mouth, then kicked her. That ass was bound. She yelped in pain. "Say hey to your daughter," he laughed.

Carol looked up at Quamae with an evil stare. Her eyes were piercing his soul. "I thought you were divorcing her trifling ass."

He kicked her again. "Shut the fuck up, junky-ass ho."

Sasha couldn't believe he kidnapped Carol. She just stood there, staring at her.

"Come on, Sasha, let's get this over with. Ask her why she did it." He dragged her to the middle of the floor.

Following her husband's command, she walked up on Carol. "Why would you give Mark my address? You allowed that man to rape me when I was only a child. That was all your fault."

Carol was a little dazed and high off anything she could get her hands on, and that made it easier for Amp to kidnap her. "Listen here, you ungrateful bitch. My mama did the same to me, and you don't see me around here crying and whining about it. I sucked that shit up and kept it pushing. You should do the same."

Sasha was slowly getting over her past thanks to those sessions with Christine. Going to counseling was the best thing Quamae ever did for her. The therapist said she needed to confront her problems head-on, and that's exactly what she was doing. "What kind of woman allows a grown-ass man to molest her child for drugs? You were supposed to love and protect me, but you cared more about your glass dick than you did me."

"Don't act like you were this angel when you were running with Nate, getting pregnant and shit. You were fifteen years old, fucking that grown-ass nigga."

"Say what you want about Nate, but he loved and protected me when the trifling bitch that gave birth to me didn't. He was the best thing that happened to me back then. The only reason you wanted me to stay was so you could continue to live off the government."

"Yeah, yeah, whateva! I don't care about none of that shit, and I don't care about you, either. You chose dick over me and sent me to prison, so fuck you."

"I don't give a fuck about you, either. I wish you would've died slow in prison, but since that didn't happen, you had to show up and try to ruin my life once again, telling my husband all types of lies about me. What you should've told him was how you and your friend took me from my bed when I was asleep and aborted my first child with a fucking hanger, you evil-ass bitch."

Thinking back to that horrific day sent a pain through her vagina, and she could feel that cold metal hanger all over again. Tears were pouring down her face profusely as she went back in time.

Quamae could no longer take the way Carol was breaking her down even in that moment. Discussing her childhood was painful, and he realized he should've never left her after hearing the lies she told him. Quamae walked over to Sasha and put his arms around her tightly. She gripped the back of his shirt tightly and buried her head deep into his chest.

"It's okay, baby. You don't have to cry anymore. This shit about to be over in a few minutes. I'm about to put his bitch out of her misery."

"Okay," she sobbed.

Quamae let her go and walked back over to Carol with his pistol in his hand. She was lying on her side, so he kicked her hard in the stomach. "Roll over, bitch. I wanna see your eyes roll to the back of yo' head when you die."

When she turned over, he aimed the gun in her face.

"Wait!" Sasha shouted.

"What's wrong?" he asked.

"Let me do it. She sent Mark to kill me and my unborn child. I owe it to myself to pull the trigger."

Sasha walked over to Quamae and he handed her the gun. She aimed it at Carol and froze. "What if the bullet puts a hole in the boat?"

"It's bulletproof. Kill that bitch so we can carry on with our night." Quamae leaned against the wall, cool and calm, waiting on her to pull the trigger.

"I hope killing me makes you feel better. My job here is done." Carol closed her eyes and waited on her flesh and blood to take her out.

With no hesitation, she pulled the trigger. *Pew!*

Those were her final words before Sasha put a hole between her eyes, splitting her melon to the white meat. She handed the gun back to Quamae.

"We have one more thing to do. Grab that rope off the floor while I carry her up to the deck." Quamae pulled the plastic together, making sure no blood leaked out. Snatching it up and tossing it over his shoulder like a bag, he felt like old Saint Nick on Christmas. "Turn right and go to the back."

Quamae stood at the back of the Yacht and tied the tire rim to a chain, then he wrapped Carol's body with the remaining piece of chain, making sure he left enough to toss her over. When it was nice and tight, he picked up the tire rim and tossed it over. Carol followed behind it, making a large splash when she hit the water. They stood there to make sure she sank right along with it. When the bubbles subsided, they knew she would never be found.

"It's finally over." Quamae wiped the remaining tears from her face. "I told you I wouldn't let anybody hurt you."

"Thank you for protecting me."

"You really thought I was gon' kill you?" He put his arms around her waist.

"Hell yeah. You had me scared as fuck," she smiled.

"I would never hurt you again, and that's a promise. We have

238

some miles to go before the final surprise."

"Okay."

They held hands and walked back to the captain's station. Quamae sat down and started up the engine.

Sasha walked over and stood in front of him. "Before we go, I want to do this right here and right now."

He watched in silence as she pulled her dress over her head and tossed it to the floor. It didn't make sense to sit back and watch 'cause he'd been ready. Quamae unbuckled his belt and pants, then pulled them down to his ankles. His soldier had been on standby, so he was already at attention.

Sasha straddled his lap and eased down onto his dick slowly. She wanted him to fill her up inch-by-inch. "Mm," she moaned as the thickness of his dick penetrated her opening. It had been so long since she was intimate with him, but she never forgot how it felt. Rocking back and forth, she got into her groove before she started grinding on him aggressively.

Quamae placed both hands on the back of her neck and pulled her close to him. Covering her mouth with his, he tongued her down sloppily. The intensity drove them wild, and their chemistry was still crazy. Not much had changed in that long period of time.

Sasha started to bounce up and down on it, but he wasn't ready to come just yet, so he pulled her down it to slow her down.

"Shit!" Quamae mumbled.

Sasha tossed her head back and continued to grind on him. Quamae gripped one of her breasts gently and played with the nipple before he popped it into his mouth like it was a bottle and sucked on it. Sasha held his head tight and whispered in his ear, "I can feel it coming."

"Go 'head, 'cause I feel cheated. We gotta take this to the bed."

"Okay," she gasped. "I can feel it. It's coming."

Quamae rocked with her.

"No, be still. Let me get mine."

He followed her orders and let her get off first. Sasha was concentrating on getting that nut. Her eyes were closed so tight.

He knew she was there 'cause she rocked just a little bit harder than before and her body had the shakes. It lasted for about two minutes, then she slowed down and came to a complete stop.

"Whew!" she exhaled. "That was long overdue."

"I'm tryna tell ya. Just wait until it's my turn, though. I got somethin' for that ass."

"Well, let's go, 'cause I'm backed up." When she eased up slowly, his limp dick fell to the side.

"We have about a forty-minute ride before we get to our destination, and I'm all yours. But if we don't leave now, we gon' be stuck."

"Okay. I can hold out until then." Sasha slipped her dress back on and sat down in her seat. "Let's ride," she smiled.

Quamae looked at her with dreamy eyes. "I love you so much."

"I love you, too."

"Would you marry me again?"

"Yes. Of course I will."

Quamae put the yacht in drive and cruised the Atlantic Ocean. Out of all the bullshit he'd been through, he finally got his wife back, and nothing else in the world could make him a happier man. Nothing else mattered in his eyes besides his family. Picking up his diamond-cut cross with his right hand, he brought it to his mouth, kissed it, and raised it toward the ceiling. He made God a promise that if he brought his wife back to him, he would *never* lay hands on her again.

It took a special kind a woman to put up with a man like Quamae, and vice versa. They inflicted so much pain on one another, but they were able to get back on track and raise their baby girl together.

In the end, everyone discovers who's real, who's fake, and who will risk it all just for them.

Epilogue

Sasha opened her eyes, blinking several times to clear up her vision. The sound of the alarm pulled her from a peaceful sleep. Quamae was out of bed, and Dream was no longer in her crib. Climbing from the bed, she wiped her eyes and yawned. "Well, did they leave me?" she asked herself. Taking zombie steps, she made her way to the bathroom to pee, brush her teeth, and wash her face. Once she was done, she made her way out to see where they went. "They probably in the kitchen."

When she walked in, they weren't there either, but she saw a beautiful flower arrangement and a card. She picked it up and read it out loud. "Good morning, sleepy head. Hopefully you woke up in time to meet me at noon. Go inside the closet and put on the dress I picked out for you. It's picture day, so get beautiful for me and meet us at the Oceanfront Gazebo. See you soon."

Sasha looked at the clock and saw it was 11:15 a.m. She must've slept through the first alarm.

Rushing back to the room, she pulled out the dress. It was an all-white linen dress with lace. "This is beautiful." She smiled and laid it across the bed. "Let me hurry up."

In exactly 45 minutes she was completely dressed and ready to go. She rushed out to the deck in search of the gazebo. Sasha had no clue where she was going, so she stopped to ask for help.

"Excuse me, can you tell me where the Oceanfront Gazebo is?"

The man working at the bar smiled. "It's right that way, beautiful. Where the white fence is."

"Thank you so much." Sasha didn't want to run because she didn't want to be all sweaty and she was pregnant, so she took her time since she didn't have far to go.

Quamae had surprised her with a trip to Sandals in the Bahamas. A weekend getaway was what she really needed. Having her life flash before her eyes had that effect on her.

When she made it to the gazebo, Quamae was standing there holding Dream and talking to two men, who she assumed were the photographers. When he turned around, his eyes lit up. The dress he picked out was beautiful.

As soon as she begin to walk down the aisle, music started playing.

Butterflies is what I feel inside,
And every time it's like my first time, ooh wee.
And I can never find the words to say
You're the perfect girl,
You're made for me.
It's so easy to love you, baby.
We're compatible, incredible, and natural, we are.
And girl, I've never felt this way before,
From the bottom of my heart.
Baby girl, I just wanna tell you that you are
The reason I love,
The reason I trust.
God sent me an angel.
You are the best in the world,
A wonderful girl.
Knowing you're by my side
Brings tears to my eyes.

As Sasha walked down the aisle at a slow pace, she knew what was going on, and the tears fell instantly. Quamae couldn't contain his emotions, either, as he watched the love of his life walk down the aisle for the second time. Tears began to stream down his face as he waited on her to get to him. When she finally made it, he reached out for her hand.

"Quamae, why didn't you tell me?" she cried.

"I did in so many words last night, but this is the other surprise. I brought you here to renew our vows. Are you having second thoughts?" He had to ask, although he was confident in her answer.

"Of course not. There isn't anyone else I would rather spend my life with."

Quamae turned to the man standing beside him holding a bible. "We're ready, Reverend."

The Reverend signaled for the music to stop, then cleared his throat. "Dearly beloved, we are gathered here today in the sight of God and a witness to join this man and this woman in holy matrimony for the second time. In this holy agreement, these two persons come together once again to be reconnected. Marriage is a sacred union between husband and wife and shall remain unbroken. It is the basis of a stable and loving relationship and is a joining of two hearts, bodies, and souls. The husband and wife are there to support one another and provide love and care in times of joy and times of adversity. We are here today to witness the joining in wedded bliss of Quamae Banks and Sasha Banks. Through God, you are joined together in the most holy of bonds."

Quamae pulled a ring from his pocket and nodded toward the Reverend.

"Sasha Banks, do you take Quamae Banks to be your lawfully-wedded husband once again?"

"I do." Her response was quick.

"And Quamae Banks, do you take Sasha Banks be your lawfully-wedded wife once more?"

"I do."

"I now pronounce you man and wife again. You may now kiss your bride."

The End

Submission Guideline.

Submit the first three chapters of your completed manuscript to ldpsubmissions@gmail.com, subject line: Your book's title. The manuscript must be in a .doc file and sent as an attachment. Document should be in Times New Roman, double spaced and in size 12 font. Also, provide your synopsis and full contact information. If sending multiple submissions, they must each be in a separate email.

Have a story but no way to send it electronically? You can still submit to LDP/Ca$h Presents. Send in the first three chapters, written or typed, of your completed manuscript to:

LDP: Submissions Dept
Po Box 870494
Mesquite, Tx 75187

DO NOT send original manuscript. Must be a duplicate.

Provide your synopsis and a cover letter containing your full contact information.

Thanks for considering LDP and Ca$h Presents.

Coming Soon from Lock Down Publications/Ca$h Presents

BOW DOWN TO MY GANGSTA

By **Ca$h**

TORN BETWEEN TWO

By **Coffee**

BLOOD STAINS OF A SHOTTA **III**

By **Jamaica**

WHEN THE STREETS CLAP BACK **II**

By **Jibril Williams**

STEADY MOBBIN

By **Marcellus Allen**

BLOOD OF A BOSS **V**

By **Askari**

WHEN A GOOD GIRL GOES BAD **II**

By **Adrienne**

THE HEART OF A GANGSTA **III**

By **Jerry Jackson**

LOYAL TO THE GAME **IV**

By **T.J. & Jelissa**

A DOPEBOY'S PRAYER **II**

By **Eddie "Wolf" Lee**

IF LOVING YOU IS WRONG… **III**

LOVE ME EVEN WHEN IT HURTS

By **Jelissa**

DAUGHTERS SAVAGE

Destiny

By **Chris Green**

BLOODY COMMAS **III**

SKI MASK CARTEL II

By **T.J. Edwards**

TRAPHOUSE KING

By **Hood Rich**

BLAST FOR ME **II**

RAISED AS A GOON V

BRED BY THE SLUMS

By **Ghost**

A DISTINGUISHED THUG STOLE MY HEART **III**

By **Meesha**

ADDICTIED TO THE DRAMA **II**

By **Jamila Mathis**

LIPSTICK KILLAH II

By **Mimi**

THE BOSSMAN'S DAUGHTERS 4

WHAT BAD BITCHES DO

By **Aryanna**

<u>**Available Now**</u>

<u>RESTRAINING ORDER **I & II**</u>

By **CA$H & Coffee**

<u>LOVE KNOWS NO BOUNDARIES **I II & III**</u>

By **Coffee**

<u>RAISED AS A GOON I, II, III & IV</u>

By **Ghost**

LAY IT DOWN **I & II**
LAST OF A DYING BREED
BLOOD STAINS OF A SHOTTA I & II
By **Jamaica**
LOYAL TO THE GAME
LOYAL TO THE GAME II
LOYAL TO THE GAME III
By **TJ & Jelissa**
BLOODY COMMAS I & II
SKI MASK CARTEL
By **T.J. Edwards**
IF LOVING HIM IS WRONG…I & II
By **Jelissa**
WHEN THE STREETS CLAP BACK
By **Jibril Williams**
A DISTINGUISHED THUG STOLE MY HEART I & II
By **Meesha**
PUSH IT TO THE LIMIT
By **Bre' Hayes**
BLOOD OF A BOSS **I, II, III & IV**
By **Askari**
THE STREETS BLEED MURDER **I, II & III**
THE HEART OF A GANGSTA I & II
By **Jerry Jackson**
CUM FOR ME
CUM FOR ME 2
CUM FOR ME 3

Destiny

248

Bride of a Hustla 3

By **Nikki Tee**

GANGSTA SHYT **I II &III**

By **CATO**

THE ULTIMATE BETRAYAL

By **Phoenix**

BOSS'N UP **I , II & III**

By **Royal Nicole**

I LOVE YOU TO DEATH

By Destiny J

I RIDE FOR MY HITTA

I STILL RIDE FOR MY HITTA

By **Misty Holt**

LOVE & CHASIN' PAPER

By **Qay Crockett**

TO DIE IN VAIN

By **ASAD**

BROOKLYN HUSTLAZ

By **Boogsy Morina**

BROOKLYN ON LOCK I & II

By **Sonovia**

GANGSTA CITY

By **Teddy Duke**

A DRUG KING AND HIS DIAMOND

A DOPEMAN'S RICHES

By Nicole Goosby

Destiny

BOOKS BY LDP'S CEO, CA$H

TRUST IN NO MAN

TRUST IN NO MAN 2

TRUST IN NO MAN 3

BONDED BY BLOOD

SHORTY GOT A THUG

THUGS CRY

THUGS CRY 2

THUGS CRY 3

TRUST NO BITCH

TRUST NO BITCH 2

TRUST NO BITCH 3

TIL MY CASKET DROPS

RESTRAINING ORDER

RESTRAINING ORDER 2

IN LOVE WITH A CONVICT

Coming Soon

BONDED BY BLOOD 2

BOW DOWN TO MY GANGSTA

Bride of a Hustla 3

CPSIA information can be obtained
at www.ICGtesting.com
Printed in the USA
LVHW021925030921
696898LV00011B/313
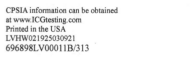

9 781987 767308